Tom Nash was brought up in East Bergholt, Suffolk, where John Constable grew up. He worked as a rural architect and an artist, and has taught drawing courses at Flatford Mill. He has written five novels, four plays, all performed, and numerous short stories. He has an MA in Fine Art and lives in a small South Norfolk village.

THE TRIPTYCH

T P NASH

Matador
9 Priory Business Park,
Wistow Road, Kibworth Beauchamp,
Leicestershire. LE8 0RX
Tel: 0116 279 2299
Email: books@troubador.co.uk
Web: www.troubador.co.uk/matador
Twitter: @matadorbooks

ISBN 978 1800462 885

British Library Cataloguing in Publication Data.
A catalogue record for this book is available from the British Library.

Printed and bound in Great Britain by 4edge Limited
Typeset in 10pt Minion Pro by Troubador Publishing Ltd, Leicester, UK

Matador is an imprint of Troubador Publishing Ltd

For Roger

How did John Constable evade nineteenth century family responsibilities to become the artist we recognise today?

DISCLAIMER

The Constable family, the family business, John Dunthorne, Mr. Crush, *The Telegraph*, Mr. Rhudde and Maria all existed, but this is a novel, and their characters and actions, and all the other persons, are entirely fictional. I have made the date of Constable's friendship with Maria Bicknell much earlier than reported.

The buildings and constructions at East Bergholt and Flatford all exist, or existed; the lock has been rebuilt in a new position and Bergholt House, completed 1774, was demolished in Victorian Times (c.1840?). Some latitude must be allowed concerning the descriptions of fields, and the size of John's studio.

John Constable was born in 1776, and went up to the Royal Academy Schools of Art in February 1799. In the village, he was known as "the handsome miller" and was, presumably, expected to follow his father into the business.

Tom Nash, 2020

1

OCTOBER 1791 SUNDAY

A skiff comes round the bend. A light shell of a boat, it swings on the current, swerves and leaps with a nervous energy. In it a young man, smart hat and coat, oars skimming the water; he glances over his shoulder and tugs on an oar; again, harder.

The flood sweeps towards the bank, boiling and rolling. The skiff rides high as though to escape, but it lifts and swings sideways to be flipped over against a dam of debris on the roots of a willow.

He is gazing upwards, up to the thin skeins of cloud stretched over miles of sky. They must be ice, he thinks, so transparent; the sun would evaporate water vapour… it does when I'm mending leadwork, crouched on the slope of a morning roof. But ice sticks; even thin skins to trick and deceive boots. I've known men, those with a lifetime of experience, go arsey versey, and whistle towards a fall… What winds are blowing up there to stretch them as tight as muslin on a line?

'Oh Bull! Would you leave me 'ere?' A whimper.

He drops his gaze and is blinded, the sun reflecting off the standing water, and looks away. The meadow stretches green to the distance, stands of winter trees casting thin shadows. He would like to stride the length of it as far as Dedham to see the swollen river, the broken trees and those things that have survived the storm, cattle and birds. It would feel good to stretch on his only free day of the week. He asks himself now, have I made a mistake bringing Emily Jane down here on the river meadows? Her dress; look at the state of her… if only she had turned out in smock and boots. A practical girl like that, one with a bit of common, what's she moaning for on a day like this? Good grief! For a moment only he wonders what she thinks of him now.

It was a big storm last night and he wants to see the devastation caused by wind and water, and to see the river. In the village, there have been a few trees down, chimneys toppled, the roads carpeted with twigs and leaves. A window has been blown out in the Church, a large north aisle window; perhaps he will see the repairs when it comes into the yard. He has heard of no deaths but a few roofs were badly damaged, a skirl of thatch blown overhead. And down here, there are branches and a tideline of straw, twigs, leaves and small dead animals. The water is receding leaving clear pools; water as innocent as a baby's smile. He scoops up a handful allowing it to run through his fingers, sparkling teardrops. Harmless; but what power. It could be useful, or it could destroy. He looks at the river, hearing the roar that tells of damage and danger, and shivers.

'What if the ice were to fall on us? An ice shower?' he asks.

She stares at him. Perhaps she would rather be elsewhere.

He had forgotten his promise to her, to walk her out this Sunday forenoon. He knows that Emily Jane is keen to catch him. Perhaps he is a good prospect, a man who can read and write – and there are plenty in the village who can do neither – and a good worker, one who may go far. He doesn't care; what would he want to get married for, harnessed with a wife and, no doubt, a young'un to care for? He's only looking for some fun, an innocent walking out with a village girl.

'Come back now, Bull. How can I walk here? What are we doing here, in this mud an' all?'

He laughs, an open burst. 'Look at the day, girl. Isn't it good?'

It's a day to be alive, a day of sun and fresh thinking, not moaning about a bit of mud. God's sakes, can't she see the sun and… all? What sort of girl, or anybody for that matter, could not taste the day and with it the new beginning that always comes after a storm? What does she feel or think? I don't understand her, I really don't.

A gull flies overhead and dives to the surface of the river. How easy, how effortless to wheel and soar a few inches above the current with a tilt of wings, scouting for alien fish, then flaring up to climb over the willows and away into the sun. To see as the gull, to feel the lift and hover…

He gazes up again into the heavens. It must be cold up there; he has read that it gets colder as you climb mountains, as you go higher.

'What a lot of fiddle faddle, Bull. It's closer to the sun. When are you going to take me back to the village, away from all this water?'

She does not look happy; a frown dents her pretty face. She is dragging her feet slowly through the mud.

He turns away from her. He wishes they didn't call him Bull; he knows he is not small but they will call him Bull. It was fine when he was young, a year or so ago, but he can do without it now. He knows he has a broad head, barrel chest, long arms, huge hands and short curly hair like a Hereford bull. That was what got him his name, not that there were many Herefords around; plenty of Friesians and other dairy cattle, along with Red Polls and beef breeds. He has a good name, Dunthorne. That is how he should be known or by his first name but Dunthorne carries more weight. And men don't forget it.

She is frowning again with a silly pout. Looking away, he picks her up, swinging her in his arms over a trickle; she wriggles and giggles, kicks her feet in the air. She's in no hurry to be put down, it seems, but she's no small weight either. Is he going to carry her or buy her a new pair of shoes? Is this what young missies want? He is not going to get caught on that one and drops her on a patch of grass with a squelch, wondering aloud whether the storm has made the world turn faster.

'Don't be daft, Bull. What will you think of next?' Softer. 'Oh Bull, sometimes you say the silliest things. You make my world turn faster you do. Why don't you come here…'

She dressed for a suitor, didn't she? A dimity bonnet with ribbons, a long over-dress trimmed with velvet, slight pumps, lemon yellow; all the latest fashions and covered with mud. She has given up complaining; he laughed at her. She half turns and looks at him over her shoulder, tossing her hair, and wonders for the first time only, was it a big mistake teasing him into walking her out? He hadn't paid me much attention before but it wasn't too hard as I recalls it. And there he is, starin' away at something, back turned to me. Oh blast it! It ain't right. I have never ever had some lad treat me like this, dumping me in the mud. What if some ol' biddy saw me in this state? Cloak, pumps, stockings… all ruined… it would be round the village in a trice; Jenny would give me no peace. Oh darn, I don't understand him; when he was so keen to see me, ask me out to walk with him…why and I thought he was the serious sort, you know, a bit more than a lad, a man… he's a good man, that's what they said in the shop. Mind you, Jenny did say she did, I should look out… Bull wasn't no pushover, no easy conquest like… well, like some I could name… but I says to her, just watch me, my girl; I'm goin' to haul 'im in… all the girls said what a catch he'd be, a cut above the rest; go on, girl… an' I wouldn't be no labourer's wife nor no aproner, I'd have the living of a master tradesman… it earned respect, didn't it? Hah, look where it got me. What will Mother say? And now he's not even looking at me.

She moans quietly, her feet squelching in her shoes.

He is looking away towards Dedham. The ground stretches as flat as a lead casting bed, level and smooth grazed by the cattle that he can see at a distance. A panorama, a wide perspective before him; like a painting, framed by the sides of the valley and banks of trees. He knows about perspective. Miss Hambleton taught him a long time ago. And showed him pictures, how it worked. And now he would like to make it work for him, to tell him useful things like how far away the cattle are. Perhaps one can buy a telescope that shows distances. That would be something. It's rare this stretch of flat land. Elsewhere, the horizon is no more than a few miles, often less and not flat. You can't see the land as it fades into the distance as it does here, a blue haze. Why is it always blue, a blue haze, not yellow or red? Though sometimes the sunset and the sunrise, a shepherd's warning…

On the other side of the river, the meadow is flooded. When it gets cold in two or three months, there will be skating. The village girls turn out, pretty bonnets, hanging on the arms of fathers or some young man, slipping and sliding as the few who can skate weave lines around them, and swoop at speed through the tangle of bodies and chairs and cloaks. Would Emily Jane be there, hanging on his arm? No, she would rather be buying ribbons or perambulating the lanes, I dare say, a tangle of gossipy girls. Reckon she can't skate. She wouldn't be there to see the disasters; when somebody has gone too far and ends up soaked, standing up to their waist in freezing water. Then there is a hurry to bundle them against the cold and beg a horse for a swift ride to a warm hearth. Nobody has ever drowned, thank God, only an old dog; he was scrabbling away for purchase, disappeared beneath the ice. Nobody could get near. Poor old thing.

The river is high, higher and faster than he has ever seen it. The water moves with an awesome solidity as though carved from marble. It barrels against the bends, an ominous roar as it passes, sometimes with a gulp of earth. In places, it has brought down the bank, coming upon the meadow. It is grey and black and brown and green with its load. Boughs roll lazily in the stream; occasionally the sodden back of some animal, large or small. Branches, twigs, leaves, turves appear like a scum rising on a stockpot.

He wonders at the waste of force, the energy flowing away in front of him. The river could be put to work, not only for mills but to serve a multitude of machines, maybe even provide heating. There are so many tools that could be driven to save manpower and horse power: to grind, hammer, cut, saw, pump. The list goes on and on. Why, if they had a table saw at the boat yard powered from the river right there to plank the butts, wouldn't they save a load of work in the pit, get the job done faster? He dreams of the future, new machines, improvements, the changes that he reads and hears people talk of and he wants to be there, part of the new age…

Something catches his eye; a boat rising like a perch as it leaps from the jaws of a pike. And flips over. Arms are flung up, a young man who disappears with a cry, desolate in the bright morning. The oars drift away.

The boat lodges upside down. Water piles against it, washes over it; it can't hold long. Dunthorne runs to the bank, and peers into the maelstrom. Downstream, there is no break in the solid surface.

'Did you see? Where is he? For God's sakes, where is he?'

He can't decide what to do. There's nobody in the water… I can't see him, anyway… what shall I do? Nobody can last long in this flood, they'll… has Emily Jane seen anything? No… oh God… where can he be? What shall I do? In the river, I… can't even swim…

A hand appears, grabs the keel, then an arm, two arms, a bedraggled head and shoulders. Thank God, he hasn't drowned; yet. He pushes Emily Jane away and steps into the water, seizes the boat. The current roars around his legs, tugs at his boots; he feels himself slide on the muddy bottom, losing balance. Digging his heels in, he pulls the skiff towards him, foot by foot, back onto the bank and keeping his eyes on the figure at the stern.

'Here.' He throws the painter to Emily Jane and steps back into the water to grab the young man. Turns out he is no weight and Dunthorne has him on the bank in a moment; he is only a young lad after all.

The boy bends over; the water pours from his mouth, his clothes, his hair. He looks as if he will never be dry again. He is a slender lad and, judging by his clothes, a gentleman. And he is shaking, teeth chattering as though they would fall out.

'Here.' Dunthorne takes off his coat and wraps it around him; Emily Jane offers her shawl, but takes it back before he can reach for it. She's standing on the rope as though her knot might give, her arms hugged tight around herself, looking away towards home. A tear runs down her nose. He pulls the skiff high on the bank, reties the painter to a branch and turns to the boy.

'No... no... I have to...' The lad makes to return to the river. 'I have to...' He sinks to his knees.

Time to move.

'You come along with me. The boat, it's all right. I'll send someone down for it. It's not going anywhere now.' He helps the boy to his feet and with a nod to Emily Jane sets off along the bank.

The morning has disappeared, replaced with a short time to get this lad to shelter, to warm him. Before it's too late; lives are lost like that... he wonders who he is.

'But... but...' The boy pulls back.

'He'll be all right, Bull,' says Emily Jane. 'Why don't you leave him be? I could do with some help, all this mud an' all.' She gives a smirk. 'He's old enough to get hisself home. What do yer think I'm a'doin' down 'ere, dawdlin' on a flooded field watching my shoes ruin?'

He gives her a look; for goodness sake, hasn't she got any common sense? They set off along the bank. She follows, but dawdles further and further behind.

The boy has ceased to struggle; he seems weak, close to collapse.

'I've... I've lost my... lost my... hat, my new hat... and my, my boots. Mother will... will not be p... pleased.'

Dunthorne smiles, briefly. 'Let's get you home.'

'It's... it's...'

'In the village would that be?'

'Yes... yes, the... Constable house.'

'You must be Master John, then.'

'It looked so... so good, river running... been with Father... see the mill... Dedham... make sure... sluices were open.'

John's mind is a muddle of thoughts; that he capsized on a river he knows so well... and came so far without mishap... only to be caught by the corner… how did that happen… knew that corner… that he was rescued when he should have been lost… and by a man he doesn't know… what will Mother say… and the girls… oh… what should he do about the skiff? Where is… what do… He shivers, unable to hold a further thought, gives himself up to the strange man, and struggles to keep going when he would like to curl up in a ball and wish the world away.

They cross the meadow; Emily Jane jumps the runnels of standing water. She does not want to be left behind after all.

'The miller… he's new. I told Father that I would walk… walk home. It's such a… a beautiful morning. The colours, the light… I happened upon this skiff… the miller told me… Oh, the skiff. What shall I do?'

When they get to Flatford Bridge, the water roars against the piers, a hollow awful sound. A tree trunk has lodged against the posts, a large oak butt felled ready for planking and swept away in the night. It's huge, a mature tree; Dunthorne reckons it must weigh maybe a couple of tons or more and the battering it is giving the bridge will destroy it. As they walk onto the bridge, he feels it move beneath his feet with a groan. Emily Jane has caught up with them; she gives a shriek and runs ahead onto the road.

John stares at the river; it has become a stranger. For years he has walked by it, rowed on it, swum in it, played by it, but he has never known it dangerous and malevolent and he shivers without control.

Dunthorne pauses on the crown of the bridge, looking down at the posts. He would give a hand to do something about that; he doesn't know how long they can hold. He thinks of the weight of the trunk; the bridge could be carried away and charge the lockgates or ram the mill sluice. Wouldn't do much good to the mill business or the river trade. As he listens to the bridge, he looks at the boy beside him. Shivering, his knees are knocking and his face is white, a small pool of water at his feet.

He does not feel happy about leaving the bridge. He is sure that there are no men around on this Sunday morning who can tackle such a job, and he knows what to do. Where to start and how to make all safe. And it needs doing soon.

But John is turning blue, coughing.

2

SUNDAY

Dunthorne walked on, forcing the boy to walk fast. A face appeared at the window of Bridge Cottage; Dunthorne pointed back and shouted a warning.

Emily Jane called out, whining. She was back at the bridge, standing in the roadway. What does she want, he thought. There's nothing amiss with her; can't she see I have to get moving? He shook his head at her and she came trotting up to them. And he took her arm in his, hauling her along, her feet tripping without mercy as they climbed Tunnel Lane back up to the village. It had to be done; return the soaked boy to his home.

The lane, deep ruts set beneath high banks on either side, was full of twigs and branches. A man from the mill was sweeping; they exchanged a few words but didn't stop. It seemed endless, this mile uphill to the village so familiar and now laced with worry. Emily Jane was panting and Dunthorne reckoned he was near carrying John. The road flattened out by degree rolling up and down until they came out onto the open top, looking over the valley towards Dedham and Mistley glowing in the sunshine. The river wound silver below them. A pigeon took off, a loud clatter as it flew away towards the Hall.

John hung back, pointed towards Dedham and started to speak but Dunthorne pulled him on. Emily Jane was silent, her bonnet fallen back, her face a mask of misery. In the Street, he glanced at the Church, remembering the window but he couldn't see it. By the time they had reached East Bergholt House, John had revived a little. Dunthorne dropped Emily Jane's arm. She stared at him, her face twisted in a frown.

'Here Bull, aren't you going to see me home? And after you take me through that mud an' all when you were walking out with me? What am I to say to Mother?'

He shook his head. 'Best be getting the lad indoors.'

'I'll be waiting for you.'

'I'll be awhile.'

'All the same, I'll be awaitin'.'

'Now Emily Jane, don't you be awaitin'. I'll have to explain it all and then get down to the bridge afore it goes. You'd best be getting off home now.'

He turned towards the house, following John around the side.

She stamped her foot and growled. 'Oy, you…'

But he was gone.

It don't look good, she thought, not good at all. What did he want to take me down on the meadows for? What a way to treat a girl… I'll tell 'em, don't be messin' with Bull… Won't be telling Jenny an' all; she would just snort like she do, and laugh. You've got your head in the clouds, girl, she'd say… And my Ma and Pa they was so hopeful; do I tell 'em that there'll be no weddin' this year?… He'll pay for a new pair of pumps, that's for sure.

She stamped her foot again and turned up the Street.

He followed John around the back of the House; John needed to be cared for without delay and there would be questions, what he had been doing, how come he ended up in the river, how he was pulled out so quick… not his business what the lad was doing on the river on such a day, but all the same he'd better be there… apart from that, he was curious about the house; it was new and he wondered whether new thinking had been built into it.

In the kitchen, John shivered and dripped onto the clean flags. The cook and two maids stood at one end, exchanging whispers, while his sisters hustled around him, firing questions, all busy and useless. He stood dumb, head down. They wanted to know how John could have ended up in the river when he had been walking home… why hadn't he come back in the trap with Father… anyway, he knew the river well didn't he, knew its moods, should know when it was dangerous… Didn't he? What was he thinking of?… And look at his clothes; Mother will not be pleased.

John wondered what he would say to Father; he had left him in the mill, telling him he was walking back to Flatford across the meadows. And then he had seen the skiff… I shouldn't have been tempted but it looked so good. My God, it was quick, shooting Fen Bridge, down the straights and through the bends… faster than I'd ever been before. It was glorious, skimming under the willow branches, keeping to clear water… it'll be something to tell the men… and my school fellows… That damned corner. I've known it for ever, that twist in the current there. He groaned to himself.

His mother appeared; sisters were dismissed on errands, maids instructed, water put on to heat and John sent to find dry clothing. In the bustle, Dunthorne stood to one side, ignored until the cook came to him and his coat was hung up to dry over the range.

He looked around; the house was well designed, that was clear. A large efficient range with the baking oven built in, sinks against the outer wall, and… could it be? Yes, taps over the sinks. So the water was drawn from a tank above somewhere, pumped up daily from the well no doubt… I would have a steam pump to do the work like in the Cornish mines I have read of… I wonder; could I persuade them to put in a copper? It would save the servants and give hot water at a tap. An adjustment to the flue, maybe… He thinks like me, I reckon; he has taken trouble to look at things afresh, how things are done, how the house works… And blast, it do make life easier… And give time for other things.

He was pressed to sit near the range and dry himself; his boots were leaking water. John reappeared, a shy smile.

'Sir, I wanted to thank you…' But was swept away by his sisters, his mother taking up the rear. She had glanced at Dunthorne, at his working breeches, soaked from the ducking, at a shirt that was none too clean, at his old socks, and turned away. Dunthorne sipped a glass of small beer, warm and spiced, and watched the servants. Cook pressed him with a fresh roll, crisp from the oven. He knew her; she was a village girl, grown now and married to the blacksmith. He wondered what she would say about Mrs. Constable behind her back.

One sister remained, standing clear of the pools on the floor. She asked him about his family.

'We live up the street near the Lambe School, Miss.'

'Do you have any brothers or sisters? I don't know your—'

'My mother, she died young.'

'Are you an only child? It must be strange; I have sisters and brothers around me all the time.'

He looked at her. A pretty young woman, about his own age. There was a lively curiosity in her eyes. He had heard the mother call her Patty and wondered how she spent her days: perhaps helping her father, or more likely obliged to stay at home attending to her mother. He had heard that the oldest sister, Nancy, kept animals, rode to the hounds and liked to be outside. But he knew nothing of the other sisters.

'I'm sorry,' she said. 'Will you have another roll? Sarah, please—'

'No, no, that's fine, Miss Patty. I have enough.'

'Where do you work? I haven't seen you… oh, I'm sorry, that's very rude.'

She sat down at the table opposite him, no sign of embarrassment. She was nice.

'I'm up at Wheelers, you know, the builders.'

'That's interesting… is it interesting?'

'Depends on what is interesting. I guess. I'm training to be a master plumber.'

'I don't know, what is a master plumber? I mean… a plumber does pipework and things, doesn't he, but if you are a master… master of what?'

He was surprised; he didn't know any young women who were interested in his work. For the most part, they were interested in trying to have and hold him; they were always after him, the village girls. Miss Patty was different.

'Well, Miss, it's like this. A plumber works with lead and he does roofwork and pipework and windows. And a master is skilled in all these things.'

'Windows? I thought…' Her gaze turned to the kitchen window, a double casement, leaded lights in a timber frame.

'Oh, you mean—' she said, pointing.

'And big windows, like the ones in the Church.'

'Father says there's a window blown out in St. Marys. I went to see it this morning. The Rector was there; he looked worried. How do you mend a big window like that?'

He sipped his beer; where does one start, he wondered.

Why does she want to know? She should be working with her father, a mind like that. She would be good, clever at figures and the such, and I don't reckon any men would want to cross her. What a waste.

'My father built this house, Wheelers, you know,' she said. 'My father says they are the best around, particularly for joinery.'

'My Dad worked on it, he told me.'

'Is he a master plumber?'

'He remembers the year it were built. I were only little, I don't remember it going up. '74, wasn't it?'

There were a number of large houses in the village. East Bergholt House was not as large as some but well proportioned, a fine brick front, rubbed brick arches, quality work. A stable yard and outhouses. Still new. His father had been proud of it, pleased to have been part of the team that built it. Still talked about it. He said he took his young son down the road most evenings to point out the progress, the work that he had done. Dunthorne had little memory of it; he had only been four. He remembered riding his father's shoulders, stopping always before this house as it rose from the ground, windows filling holes, roofs topping walls.

'How do you make a window?'

A pause. Did she really want to know? She looked back at him, open curiosity, a hint of warmth. She blushed suddenly, looking down at the table.

After a minute she looked up and said, 'I suppose it must be very difficult.'

He gazed at her, wondering what was difficult. 'My Dad, he's a carpenter. Been with Wheelers all his life. He says.'

'But you didn't become a carpenter?'

'I guess I wanted something harder; you know, more learning.'

He wished that it had been Miss Patty who had been with him on the river meadows, instead of Emily Jane, not that he would waste any more time with her. Miss Patty would not have minded the floods, the mud and the walk; she would have worn sensible clothes and been interested in the clouds and the river, talked about things that mattered. And then they would have stopped somewhere where they could have had a drink and a bite and more talk. And he would have looked at her hands, the way she turned to him, that look in her eyes and…

'Did you hear me?' She had a slight frown; he wondered what she would look like if she were angry or excited…

'Oh… I'm sorry, I was… I was just thinking. Of the Church window; it's big, isn't it?'

And now she was grinning; it was impossible. He didn't know where to look.

'Do you… do you, er, like this house?'

She burst out laughing. 'I haven't seen you in the village. Where do you work?'

'Here and there; depends…'

'Depends?' Their eyes were locked; they were unaware of the cook's stare and the maid's giggles, stifled in a tea towel.

'Where… where… we go… what do you do all day, Miss Patty?'

She looked down at last, and then back into his gaze. 'I read and help my mother and run errands and… oh, I don't know.'

'Do you not help your father? At the mill?'

'Oh no, I couldn't do that, it wouldn't be right.'

'It could be and you would be good at it, I'm sure…'

She had blushed again, looking into his eyes.

'I don't understand it,' he said. 'There are many women I know could run a good business and they are wasted… I'm sorry, I didn't mean…' He grinned.

'I could run a business? Would I not want a man by my side, one who could guide me, give me the law of the land, and so forth? And what business would that be?'

'If I were to say, to choose, I…' He thought of being the man by her side, of discussing work, and at the end of the day…

There were footsteps in the hall.

'I was just asking; how do you train to be a master plumber?'

'It was Miss Hambleton.'

'Miss Hambleton? I don't think I know that name.'

'She was… well, she is…'

A man came into the kitchen. Dunthorne recognised him, leapt to his feet. Here was a man who carried himself with confidence, a bit heavy but moving with lightness. Mr. Golding Constable was not tall but stood straight looking directly at him, stern eyes that twinkled easily. A kind man by appearances; bacon-faced you might say, well lived in but nobody's fool; a fair employer and a man who cared for those he employed. That's what they said in the village. And there weren't many like that, they said. Dunthorne knew he was a landowner, mill owner and trader, but he had never met him before, nor seen him in the alehouse.

His shoes were good, better than could have been made in the village. Probably bought in Ipswich or Colchester. Or even London. His hands were broad, not soft- or smooth-looking. Working man's hands. Dunthorne warmed to him. He wondered how he had started, who gave him the chance to own such a business, whether it was true that he knew how to run a windmill and a watermill and to construct a lighter. He knew his boatyard down at Flatford with a clever dry dock that drained through a lead pipe to the ditches in the meadows below the river on the other side. As a boy he used to pester the shipwrights, ask questions, play with the special tools and earn pennies picking oakum. When he was older, he was allowed to use the mallets and bolsters to drive it into the joints; the men were happy to take a break, stand with their pipes while they criticised his work, grinning. He didn't care for that; he would try to do a good workmanlike job, a job that would not need to be picked out and started again. When they left his work with a word of praise, he felt a flush of pride and they talked of bringing him into the yard, making him a boatbuilder.

'Ah, there you are. Have they looked after you? Patty, have you looked after this man? He has just done us a considerable favour; rescued John from the river.'

'Yes, Father. He was telling me about his work.'

'Well, I'm sure that he has better things to do than chat with young women.' And to Dunthorne. 'Come into my study; I'd like a word, if you please.'

Dunthorne looked round; Miss Patty was standing, her shoulders hunched. He would have liked to spend more time with her. They gazed at each other, an appraising look. And then she smiled and was gone.

Dunthorne had tugged off his boots and drained them into a sink. Wouldn't do to be making a mess here, he thought. He looked down at his socks; pity about the holes. He peeled them off too and hung them over the rail on the range. Cook gave him a look; he grinned and followed the master from the kitchen through a thick six-panelled door into the hall. A black and white paved floor, walls decorated with pictures and hangings, an elegant staircase curving upwards, turned mahogany balusters, good skirtings and architraves, doors a dark wood, perhaps cherry. A high moulded ceiling with a hanging oil lamp. A large bowl of flowers on a side table. All quiet. He had seen these things before in the larger houses where he worked but they always brought him to a stop. To take it all in and have time to wonder and learn, and at the same time, to recognise the solid signs of money and power, and proceed with caution. Into the study, a book-lined room, a good rug, solid furniture. Mr. Constable closed the door behind them and turned to him.

3

SUNDAY

'I am indebted to you, sir. That you took the trouble to immerse yourself and rescue both the boy and his craft. As I understand it. I don't know what he was thinking; he's been on the river ever since he was young. He should know better; I confess I am confused. How was it that you were so close?'

Dunthorne looked at him, unable to answer; how could he explain about the river, the force and potential, the ice clouds and the effects of the storm? He was not going to mention Emily Jane. Was it that Mr. Constable could not understand why any man should be beside the river on such a morning? 'I was inspecting the river, Mr. Constable. The storm, I was worried… the water… it was a sight…'

Golding looked at the young man before him; how old was he, he wondered, twenty or so? Perhaps older, but much the same age as my Patty. Can't say that I have ever seen him in the village… There is something different about him, though; something that sets him apart from many of the men that I employ. For a start, he holds himself better than most of them.

'Believe me, I am grateful. But how did it come about?'

The young man was silent; he looked uncomfortable, standing just inside the door like a farmer waiting for his grain payment. I should like to know more of this young man, thought Golding.

'Sit yourself down; make yourself comfortable. I'll be back in a moment.'

Golding gave a sweeping gesture towards the room and went out. Having made a brief enquiry into John's health and had a word with Cook, he returned.

Dunthorne was on the other side of the room, a large book in his hands, turning the pages with obvious interest. So he could read; that was a start. He went over to him; it was a book on building.

'Are you interested? Yes, have a look; an English book, nothing mysterious about it but an interesting architect. William Paine, isn't it? One who likes to introduce convenience into living, hot water, flushing water closets, sufficient daylight and fresh air. Perhaps you would like to keep it. Of course, there's always something heavier, Robert Adam, a great architect, and others—'

'I'd wondered if such things were possible, sir. I mean, the conveniences. I have seen the *Builders Magazine*, an old copy at Wheelers.'

'They are coming, I'm sure of it. You haven't seen any changes yet? From the good old days?'

Dunthorne wondered whether he was joking, the 'good old days'. Surely, things were much better now. He looked at the shelves of books, at the book in his hands, and thought of the thousands of ideas locked up in them, ideas that should make life better. He was silent.

'Please forgive me, I forget myself. Golding Constable,' Golding said, offering his hand.

Dunthorne hesitated looking at the hand, rubbed his own on his shirt, and offered it. Golding laughed and gripped it, looking into his eyes. Yes, there was something more valuable than he was accustomed to seeing. He was used to assessing men; he employed a large number and did all the employing himself. It wasn't often that he was wrong about a man, particularly a working man. He noticed the bare feet, toes splayed over his rich Persian rug, and smiled. Taking the book from him, he pressed him to sit down. A maid brought in a jug of hot chocolate, and started when she recognised the visitor; Dunthorne gave a shy grin.

'I am not offended by a little honest dirt. But whom do I have the pleasure of meeting?'

'My name is Dunthorne, John Dunthorne, but most people call me Dunthorne, though if I'm with my father they call me—'

Golding laughed. 'We needn't go into that. Well, Dunthorne, tell me about young John and his ducking. Though whether I should call it an accident I can hardly say.'

'Well, sir, I was, that is to say, we was walking down on the river meadows. There was a fearful storm last night—'

'Walking on the meadows? Surely, it must have been hard going; were they not flooded?'

'A little, sir, some debris, branches and stuff, but the river… the river was a marvellous sight. I have never seen it so strong. That was some storm.'

'I've seen the damage here in the village. But heard no report of trouble down at Flatford.'

'The bridge, sir, there is a tree against it. I'm not sure it will hold.'

'Is that so? I'm grateful for your advice, but I'm sure my yardmen will see to it. But John?'

'Well sir, we were walking and it happened that I saw something on the river. And there was a boat capsized against the bank but there were no sign of anybody until this lad, I beg your pardon, sir, I mean this young gentleman came up at the far end. So I pulled him out.'

'Pulled him out? I imagine that it must have more than that. Why, your boots are soaked and more than that, I'll be sure.'

Dunthorne was embarrassed. He wondered if the chair he was sitting on would be ruined.

'From what you tell me and what John has told me, it might have been much worse; it is most fortunate that you were there at that time. Is there anything I can do for you? Please, I am indebted to you and if there is anything that I can do, please say it.'

Golding noticed Dunthorne surveying the room, the fireplace, furniture, books, curtains, joinery, even the floor. He watched curiosity overcoming him, his head on one side as he read the titles of books, his eyes narrowing as he assessed the furniture.

'You look as if you are no stranger to either books or good furniture. What work do you do?'

'I'm apprenticed to Wheelers, sir. To be a master plumber.'

'A good firm by all accounts. I use them myself; in fact, they built this house, a few years ago. I expect you were too young to remember that.'

'My father worked on it, sir.'

'Really? Well, they did a very good job. What work do you enjoy the most?'

'Well sir, it isn't that I have a choice. But I do like a good bit of lead roofing and lead glazing.'

'Where do you get good timber? For the roofs? I'm bringing in some pine from the Baltic, amazing stuff, long lengths. Used mostly for ships' masts, I understand. But it would last well in roofs.'

'We mostly use local oak; the yard saws and dries it. Of

course, the churches get the best. When they get round to repairs.'

'And where do you get the lead from? It's a devil of a job getting good lead; the merchants seem to sell all the dross, full of rubbish. I've even seen bits of brick crushed into it.'

'The yard casts its own, sir. Then we can turn out the weights we want.'

'I'll remember that. Wheelers have never sold me lead; what I need I have always bought in London. I ask the captain of my ship to pick up a load when he is in the Port. He says it's cheaper that way.'

Dunthorne gradually slid back into his chair as he relaxed. His wet breeches clung to his legs.

'Did you know about *The Telegraph*? She is only a brig but I use her to carry goods into London. Would you like to see the City? I'm sure that I could arrange it and you would be able to sleep aboard.'

'Well, that's good of you sir. But I have never been on water, except on the work barge down at Flatford.'

'Oh, you know my yard?'

'Well, sir, when I were a lad, I used to pick oakum and when I were older they let me caulk the joints.'

'I never heard it.' Golding laughed. 'It was good work experience, I'm sure. Did you ever think of working in the yard?'

'No sir. My father is a carpenter with Wheelers and I was always going to follow him into the business.'

'But you can read and no doubt write?'

'I was brought up different. From the other lads I knew.'

'How so?'

'Well sir, it's a bit of a story, I wouldn't want to—'

'No, don't you worry about that. Tell me, do.' And he poured more chocolate.

And Dunthorne told him about his mother dying young and of Miss Hambleton, a neighbour and a teacher, who taught him to read and write and do his figures. Which was more than his father could do. And how she wouldn't let him off when his friends were running off to the river or the woods or chasing girls, but kept him at work, a bit of English history, kings and queens, great houses, furniture, paintings and geography, a map of the world.

Golding listening closely, asking a question now and then while never stopping the flow. This young man seemed to know more of the practical world than many a young gentleman he had met and had a natural confidence. He would be an asset to any business.

'Did you see the taps in the kitchen?' he said.

'Oh sir, they are a wonder. But you don't have them on the copper yet?'

The copper, eh? That was an idea. He must think about it; perhaps this was the man to put it in. The conversation ranged widely, from house construction to new inventions, from boat-building to harvesting and milling. Golding probed Dunthorne's knowledge and his attitudes. He didn't know anyone apart from the surveyor in the yard with whom he could talk of such things, and was surprised at the extent of Dunthorne's knowledge, interested in so many fields.

'I expect you know,' said Golding, 'I own the mills at Flatford and Dedham and a couple of windmills. Have you ever wondered what the life of a miller is like? I wonder sometimes… John will make a good miller. He is interested, observant of the weather…' He gazed out of the window.

Dunthorne felt his feet sinking into the carpet and worried about the wet chair. He looked at Mr. Golding; he had not expected such a conversation, and with a gentleman: building rather than architecture, lighters instead of carriages, books and not pictures. Practical matters. He wondered what Mr. Constable was thinking about and how he worked. He had never seen such books. Of course, he had been in great houses for work; but there, all the furniture and books were old. Dark leather tomes, classics and history, he had been told. But here were books on things which were important: construction of mills, patterns of weather, the growing of wheat, trade with France and Holland, the construction of locks, use of timber, tax laws, decorations, even house construction. An unusual gentleman. And he was the father of Miss Patty; she must have something of his nature, his abilities. He wished he could spend more time with her. But it could never be; could it?

So Mr. Golding was running a substantial business and must have many men. What was it like to employ men? Dunthorne was an employed man but he did not feel that he could take on a man himself; he saw the waste of time and materials at Wheelers every day; he didn't know how the bosses could afford it or whether they were aware of it. Couldn't stomach it myself, he thought, employing men and knowing that the profits would be wasted. It makes my blood boil, sometimes, the careless waste and casual pilfering; but how could I snitch on my fellow workers? Reckon I'd be out of a job as quick as greased lightning. Perhaps Mr. Golding has a way of avoiding waste and conflict. He would be an unusual employer, a man to be looked up to.

It came back to the hands. How often does he use them, rather than sitting in his office, doing bookwork? He must use them sometimes. Perhaps everyday. Perhaps that was how he earned the respect of the men and knew all the details of the working in yard and mill.

'What is London like, sir? We hear so many tales; it must be a wonderful place.'

‘Well, in part, in part. But you know, it’s really like a collection of villages, each with its own character, people and trade. Of course, there are the rich areas in the west. But I have been there a few times only and I have never visited the theatres or Vauxhall Gardens, or other such pleasures… oh, Vauxhall Gardens. They say they are not really gardens, more a sort of outside theatre; I have heard some strange things but theatre is not really my taste.

‘No, I travel there for business, trading and buying in. Though Suffolk farmers are more canny than any traders that I have met there, far harder to drive a contract on wheat here than in London. There, they seem happy enough to believe in dreams rather than harsh reality. Did you ever hear of the South Sea Bubble? Scandalous, making profit out of dreams until it all went bust. Thousands lost. Extraordinary. A bit like the Hollander bulb craze… more madness. Though at least they had goods to trade on. And now I find the Dutch merchants to be the hardest to strike a bargain with.

‘Not my style, Dunthorne. All this trading on nonsense. But I would be happy to arrange a journey there if you would care for it. Time off from Wheelers, all arranged.’

‘That’s very good of you, sir. I don’t know… it’s like going overseas, really. I always thought I would be going to Holland before London.’

‘Well, I suppose I could arrange that if you wished.’

‘No, no sir, you are too good.’

Golding wondered whether Dunthorne was a local boy who could never conceive of a different world over the horizon. Perhaps he was afraid of losing his job, a common enough thing. Business could be better and there were men laid off in the towns and in the villages, though not in this one. And yet, for a local boy, he talked with knowledge of the new inventions…

'Tell me, have you thought about your work? Where you would like to be after your apprenticeship? You will be a valuable man, a good trade, always wanted.'

Dunthorne was silent. He had ideas, plans, but he never talked to anyone about them. They remained close to his chest, unseen and private. He didn't want to upset his father who could barely read and who would work at Wheelers until he had to give up. His father's life; a hard grind, the loss of his wife, work without change over thirty years or more, the bitter sweet reward of Miss Hambleton who gave company and food and took his son away from him into a life with expectations for something better. Where would I go, he thought, if I had as much money as Mr. Constable? The Colonies or America?

Around him, the house was quiet, close. There was no sound though he knew that it was not empty; it must be well built, solid. The door was six panelled, three inches thick; a beautiful piece of joinery, close fitting, well hung, two pairs of four-inch brass butts. The floor eight-inch oak boards, butt-jointed, close fitting. The window: double hung sash, slim glazing bars, the latest brass furniture. He looked at the rug, his toes sinking into the Indian pattern, deep and soft. The desk was mahogany with papers, a pen tray, an inkwell, an oil lamp, all well made.

A pony passed on the street and a bird landed on a bush outside the window.

Golding, sitting the other side of the desk, was watching him, a slight smile. Dunthorne laughed, a brief shout.

'I'm sorry, sir. Nobody ask me that one before. I've never said… no, I've never told anyone. But I have thought about it.'

'You have thought about it?'

'Well, I have another year apprenticed to Wheelers. And then I have five years that I have to spend with them because they funded my apprenticeship and pay me. And after that… well, that's a little way off, sir.'

Dunthorne had thought ahead, what he might do after his contract with Wheelers; five years was not for ever. He thought of setting up by himself; he reckoned he could make it work with a bit of help with the books. But he did not want to talk about it, just yet. It was his own plan and he didn't want help with the thinking of it.

'You must be skilled now. A plumber, and what else do you do?'

'Lead glazing, sir. All sorts though I've not been given the chance of a big window yet.'

'But you know what to do? You would be able to do a large window?'

'I think so, sir. I have worked on them with the glazier. But only as an assistant.'

'How would you like to repair the window in the Church? I have been to see it. Blown out last night.'

'I don't reckon Wheelers would put me onto that one; Church might even get another firm in. I hear the Rector's particular about repairs.'

'I could have a word, if you like. And square it with Wheelers.'

'That would be good, sir.' He smiled, a tight smile; for a moment, an image of mending a large window warmed his thoughts. But then, Mr. Constable may be an important man but the Rector has a reputation for going his own way and I can't see that Wheelers would risk their reputation putting an apprentice on to a large Church window. No, it's not going to happen. I reckon Mr. Constable has met his match. Pity. But it was a kind thought. I'll be getting back to my everyday life, small lead repairs and small windows.

4

SUNDAY AND MONDAY

Golding showed Dunthorne to the door, the front door, shook his hand, repeated his thanks and appreciation and closed the door as quietly as possible, retreating into his study before he could be waylaid by family. He did not notice Patty on the stairs watching Dunthorne's departure. Sitting at his desk he stared at the list of duties that he had laid out in front of him, constantly updated and religiously followed, but saw nothing. He sat back with a sigh.

What astonishing luck, that Dunthorne was by the river and his good sense to restore the boy home as fast as possible. He offered a brief prayer of thanks that his son was restored to him. And wondered for a moment what Dunthorne was doing on a flooded meadow after a storm; it would not be the first place that he would have walked…

John! What was he thinking of? Going on sixteen years old, almost a man and getting into trouble like that. Was he a dreamer? No, surely more practical than that… always interested in the mills, though never in the office, the figures and the accounting… and here I am, going on fifty-two, and would have expected to have a son working beside me, to succeed to the business, to build on it as I have; a son to take some of the load off my old shoulders.

Young Golding; the eldest, apart from the girls; no chance there. His mother's darling… but, as she says, he is not capable, so she fashions him after a country gentleman, huntin', shootin', fishin', but it's only the shootin' that interests him. It won't be the eldest gets the lion's share of the inheritance, I shall have to give them all an equal share. The girls… I hope they find husbands. Nancy's a hard one. It would take a tough man to rein her, she would need a hard bitt and a farthingale… but Patty, a chance there. Young Dunthorne seemed to find her interesting; what a pity… Mary and Abram, still in the nursery.

I shall bring John into the business when he leaves school… and if he has trouble with the figures, I'll find a bailiff to straighten his columns, check his addition… Mrs. Constable talks of a respectable profession, the law or the Church; it's not his nature, it's nonsense… he would never take to those but he loves his life here and he has a better grasp of milling than many millers.

He pushed back his chair, and went into the parlour. His wife and daughters were sitting there, Patty buried in some novel called *Cecilia*, romance no doubt. The others were attending to their sewing and perusing *The Lady's Magazine*. There was a busy hum of chatter, of dresses, horses, houses and other young people. Nancy looked up and laid her work aside.

'Father, do you have the time now to consider the horse that I have seen? It would make a good purchase, improve my position in the field at the next hunt.'

'Nancy, my dear, I will consider the matter, but not this week.'

'And not this month either, Father? Oh, I know—'

'Now child. You must know, have seen, that the harvest this year has not been good. There is the war, a tax upon us, and the harvests have been poor, again. And you know that means less milling for us, less trade on the river. And less money in the village. How do you think the men would feel if I'm laying off labour and you ride out on a new horse? I've heard that it is bad elsewhere.'

Nancy dropped back into her chair, took up her sewing and ignored any word from the others. Patty set her book aside.

'Father, the man who rescued John, who is he? He seemed a... very capable man.'

'His name is Dunthorne. You are perceptive; he has an unusual grasp of things. He would be an asset to any business, I believe.'

'Shall he... will you see him again?'

'Perhaps. He—'

Mrs. Constable gave a little cough; Golding looked at her. He sensed an issue that she needed to air.

'My dear?' He leant towards her.

'Well, I was wondering.'

'Is there anything that I can do for you?'

'I know you will not appreciate it. But it is a matter of form, Mr. Constable.'

'Of form? Is it about Golding?' Again, he thought. There had been a number of incidents and small sums had been paid out on a frequent basis. Only the last week, he had had to settle with a cottager who was distressed at the loss of his prize cockerel. He gave a small sigh.

'Not at all, my dear. You were very generous, the new gaming piece. I believe he is well thought of and that is a matter close to my heart, as you well know.'

Nancy raised her head from her work. 'And is he still shooting the chickens around the village, Father?'

'Hush, my child.' Ann was not as severe as she might have been. 'He is bored, that is all; needs to spend time with the young men around. But they are so busy, he doesn't see them much.'

Nancy laughed, a coarse bark. 'You mean they don't wish to see him.' The oldest child, she felt no hesitation in criticising her brother, even if he was the eldest son.

'Nancy, do you wish to retire and prepare for Evensong?' Her mother was sharp.

The girls rose and left the room, Nancy ahead, Patty and Mary exchanging glances. A whoop of giggles from the hall. Golding sighed, settled into his chair, and wondered whether a dish of tea might arrive before long.

'My dear, there is a small matter to which I must draw your attention,' said Mrs. Constable.

'Pray, continue.'

'The young man who visited. Was he known to you?'

'What a Godsend he was. It was really very fortunate.'

'I am sure that John cannot have been in great danger. Why, he has been upon the river for many years without our guiding arms. Would he not have swum to the side? He is very capable.'

'Now, my dear. I doubt whether you have ever seen the river in full spate. It is an awful sight; everything is carried before it. Trees, animals, the very banks of the river. It is a considerable force and dangerous for any man to be on it or in it. I do wonder at John's folly.'

'Oh tush. He is not so young. I believe you deceive me—'

'Indeed I do not. Now, my dear, I shall not accompany you to Evensong today; I have matters to attend to. Shall we sup after Church?'

'I am sad that you will not accompany us. Of course we shall dine late.'

Golding made to rise.

'The young man; was he known to you?' She was busy with her embroidery, avoiding his eye as she questioned him.

'He works for Wheelers. A very capable young man, I don't doubt. Educated to an unusual degree, I gathered. Have you met Miss Hambleton?'

'Have I seen her at Church? She may be… But it raises my concerns.'

'I really cannot see why, my dear. Particularly as the young man, whose name is John Dunthorne, rescued our son from a certain death. We should be eternally grateful to him.'

'I am sure that he is a very fine young man. But, my dear, do you not see? It is really not right to show a tradesman out of the front door. What would the village say? Were any of the gentry passing? What would they think?'

'My dear, I am a tradesman. And I would not hesitate to give the highest recognition to some person who has just rescued my son from a watery grave.'

'But, all the same—'

'Mrs. Constable, I hope you recall the timely arrival of Mr. Dunthorne and John's salvation at Church this evening.' He rose and left the room, closing the door behind him and calling for tea.

Sitting at his desk, he took up a pen, made notes, and paused to think. He looked around the room and lit on the book that Dunthorne had been reading. An involuntary smile, the memory of the conversation, the young man's bare feet, his firm handshake. And now, nothing to be lost except time. Pausing often to think, he prepared drafts, scribbling amendments. Eventually, he wrote a clean copy to the Rector. It could not do harm, a charitable intrusion. It wouldn't be cheap, he was sure, but would be a suitable homage to the rescue of his oldest son; no, he must not think like that, but in every respect except one, John was the oldest son.

He heard the womenfolk departing for Church; they did not enter.

The following day, he was out early. High clouds, a chill in the air, but early sunshine promised. No wind; a quiet after the storm of the weekend. The lad had put the horse up to the trap and stood holding the bridle, his mouth gaping in yawns. Golding asked after his mother; had she got over her sickness and did it spread to any of his brothers and sisters? How many were there? He couldn't remember but recalled that there were too many of them, and a father whom he employed around the mills. Not a good worker. It seemed to happen too often that the larger families had the poorer fathers. 'What jobs do you have?' he asked. 'Don't forget to work for the gardeners as well as tending to the stables. And make sure there is enough hay in the loft.' He left him, still yawning, to close the side gate.

As he trotted down the lane to Flatford, he had to stop the mare and descend to clear debris from time to time. The storm had left a spread of branches and leaves over the road and once he had to move a bough, torn away from a chestnut. Away over the valley, the sun was shining on Dedham Church tower, standing out among the trees. The fields were bare, many under stubble, but the day was becoming warm, autumn with a breath of lingering summer. As always, he blessed the opportunity that had led his life to this place, the inheritance from an uncle, and considered the manner in which he had increased the value and extent of his business: the mill at Dedham, the extra windmill, the lighterage business on the river almost a monopoly, the family moved from the mill house to a new house in the village. And now all I need, he thought, is a son to step into my shoes. Well, at least one of my shoes. Perhaps I ought to consider a partner, a junior partner, to relieve me of some of the load; I hate the idea, some other family involved in our family affairs. It is not right.

Down by the river, he handed the reins to a man arriving for work and walked over the bridge; the river was in spate, roaring about the posts. A cable held the bridge against the current, fastened to a tree, and upstream, a huge oak trunk was made fast against the bank. Someone has been resourceful, he thought. A trunk that size could have carried away the bridge with ease, and done much damage. My God, it would have ruined business for a good while; I would have been laying off men, moving the milling elsewhere and rebuilding the lockgates. The river would have been scarcely navigable and there would have been a storm of trouble with the merchants and owners. It was a good piece of work and it has saved me a great deal of trouble. I wonder which of my men was responsible? I should reward him.

Recrossing the bridge, he walked along the bank past Bridge Cottage and into the boatyard. It was early and two men only were there, sorting timber for a lighter repair. He asked if they knew anything of the bridge repair but they knew nothing and ran off to look. Past the granary and into the back of the mill. And still he did not meet anyone who had been down at Flatford on the Sunday.

5

SUNDAY AND THE FOLLOWING SUNDAY

Dunthorne left the Constable house, pulling on his cap, and looked up; the sky was clear, afternoon beginning to fade towards evening; there would be a frost tonight, he thought, and a roof to repair tomorrow. Home for a bite. Wouldn't want to be on the leads too early. And then he remembered and set off for Flatford, settling into a stride, easy and fast. His damp breeches clung to his legs and his boots squelched.

What a good time. He thought of his interview with Mr. Constable, and the study, the books, the desk and the rug. It lit up his thinking; it confirmed all that he had read about new inventions. Would he be able to talk to him again? The copper; that might be a start; maybe he would ask him to work on it… the Church window. Well, no doubt kindly meant, but it is not likely, is it? An apprentice leading on a major window repair? Why, I can just see old Mr. Wheeler going along with it; he would cough, look into the distance and come up with some reason why only the best glazier in the firm could take charge. Of course, young Dunthorne could assist him as long as he didn't get in the way. No, it's not likely, is it?

On Flatford bridge, there was a gaggle of men, arguing as they tailed a rope in the stream, cursing with the odd laugh. He watched them for a while. A light breeze had arisen; the sun was low, deep shadows on the water that roared and rolled as violently as before, blustering and threatening.

'Hey Bull, you come to put in your pennysworth? We're just getting it fixed.'

'Do we need a Bull?' A laugh and a few backs turned against him.

There was a groan from the bridge; the roadway cracked.

The men deserted, rushing down in a jostling crowd to stand outside the Cottage, arguing and cursing. Dunthorne walked past them up to the crown of the bridge, had a quick look over the rail, stepped down to the men, nodded to a few, and sent a couple of boys for a hand winch and cable from the yard.

'Now, who will drop me over the side?'

They stared at him; more laughs and looks exchanged.

'Now why would we want to drop you over the side, Bull?'

'Yeah,' said one small man. 'He's going to put it under his arm, and take it home for the fire.' A weak chuckle; many were silent. The boys returned with the gear, panting and keen to please.

He had thought about it since crossing that morning with John. It was not difficult, an exercise in simple mechanics. He picked out two men who he could trust, persuaded them to come onto the bridge, and fixed a loop of rope around his waist. Climbing over the rails, he stepped down onto the trunk below; the men on the bridge took up the slack on his rope and dropped the tails of two other ropes down, shouting over the roar of the river, fearful.

The trunk was heaving like a bull in a crush; it was hard to get a firm foothold and occasionally he would lose his grip, swinging out from the bridge on the end of his tether. The men above called to him to come back; couldn't he see it was no use, too late and too dangerous. For God's sake, it wasn't worth it and the old bridge could always be rebuilt.

The river split around the bridge posts with a sound that chilled, like water being sucked down a gigantic drain. The current roared at his feet, occasionally coming over the tree trunk, plucking at his legs. Straining against the flow, he found his feet. With a sling in the end of one rope, he swung it out to catch the end of the trunk; it snagged but pulled free. Two or three times more, his legs shaking with the effort, the sling came free but eventually, as he gasped for energy, it caught. He called on the men to pull it tight. Then he stooped, clutching a post, and tied the other cable around it, high up beneath the roadway.

He signalled to the men who hauled him up, helping him over the rail; he collapsed on the ground, his legs shaking, and sat for a time while his head cleared.

The ropes had been passed to a group of men standing on the bank; they had fallen silent, perhaps embarrassed at their own failure but relieved at someone taking charge. Someone they could blame if all failed.

The men on the bridge helped him up. 'That's a neat job, Bull. What to do now?' They stayed with him, self-appointed foremen, keen to be associated with success.

The cable from the post was taken upstream and lashed to a tree, a task performed by an excess of men, all free to act, all knowing best; Dunthorne checked that it was taut. The bridge should hold now, not carry away he reckoned, but it was still necessary to remove the hammering from the trunk. The rope from the sling was taken upstream, where the winch was anchored to an oak, a long way above the bridge. Feeding in the rope from the sling, he called for help to wind in the slack. The men joined him, pushing each other, competing to take turns on the handles.

As the rope became taut, the trunk was pulled clear of the bridge post, lying head to the stream. Water piled against the end of it; it swung to and fro like a young bullock on a halter. For a moment, Dunthorne feared that the rope would fail or that the sling would slip and the trunk would sail free, heading for the mill. It held.

Foot by foot, it was hauled clear of the bridge and came alongside the bank where it was lashed and made fast. When the river dropped, it would be floated down to the yard, rolled out, dried and planked; it would make good boat-building timber. Nobody asked why a mature oak butt could have ended up in the river or where it came from. The cable holding the bridge was left in place, insurance until the stream should have dropped and the bridge could be inspected.

The men gathered outside the Cottage, clapping each other on the back, making forays onto the bridge to look down at the cable and the posts, laughing, relieved, and went away in a happy crowd up the hill to the alehouse. A few nodded at Dunthorne, his two helpers shook his hand and they all left him watching the cables take the strain against the wild current.

He could have sworn that the bridge shook itself, the crack closing.

A week passed. Work continued as usual, some roof repairs to a large house, lead glazing in a new casement window for a shopkeeper, a few minor plumbing repairs. He heard no more from Mr. Golding Constable and put it from his mind, the long conversation about new building and the Church window. His work filled his days and in the evening he read a little in the company of his father or went down to the alehouse. In the Red

Lion, he was bought a few pints, given a clap on the back for saving the bridge, until the acclaim died down and he could have a quiet drink as usual in the corner of the settle, rather than in a crowd around the bar listening to Jem's tall tales.

He thought back to the rescue of Master Constable and the strengthening of the bridge; it had been dangerous but had to be done. He took a deep pull on his mug and gazed into the fire. The familiar smell of wood smoke, the clanking of mugs, and the buzz of conversation came back to him. He went to join a few friends around the bar.

Walking down the Street on a Sunday afternoon, a week later, he heard someone running up behind him. There was a gasp; he turned; young John Constable, panting, hair flopping in his eyes.

'Why, there you are now. Have you recovered from your ducking, Master John?'

'Oh please, please don't call me "Master"; John is my name. I'm well, thank you, Mr. Dunthorne. And I have to thank you for saving me. I don't like to think what would have happened if I had ended up under the bridge, with the tree trunks and the current so strong—'

'There now. And don't you go calling me "Mister"; you can call me what most people call me, just Dunthorne. And you could hardly call me John; where would we be, John this and John that?'

'I have heard that they call you Bull.'

'I don't care for that, thank you, Master John.'

'Oh, I'm sorry… I didn't know. It came from—'

'Never you mind.'

'I have something for you, a letter from my father. He tells everyone, he thinks highly of you—'

'Come now. He has only met me the one time.'

'Ah, well, I think he has asked some people, you know, and… I'm sorry, that is indelicate of me… to suggest that…'

'Don't you worry yourself. That's what makes the world go round, finding out about men and their affairs. Now, how old are you? I was just stepping into the Red Lion for a pint. Would you like to come in with me?'

He looks down at him and suspects that he is about eight years younger than himself, a youth but old enough to accompany him into the tavern.

'I… well, my mother… you see… I've never been in there. Do I have to drink beer?'

'I don't want to be getting you into trouble. But no, you don't have to drink beer; there's—'

'Oh, that would be all right. Thank you.'

They sat near the fire, side by side on the settle, a glass in front of John, a mug for Dunthorne. John came in for some teasing from the good old boys round the bar; he sat silent, looking around, smiling at the quips and ignoring the comments about his father or family. He had been brought up here, knew the men by name and which ones worked for his father. And which ones had worked for his father but had been found wanting. But he had never been in the tavern before; he looked round, innocent and open, watching the men chatting, the ease with which they abused friends and joked with the man behind the bar. He had never seen village men so free; it was like a club to which he had just gained membership. But I must not remind them of who I am, he thought… though they all know me, have known me since I was knee-high in britches… maybe they can separate me from my father. I guess it's a kind of trust, expecting me to be someone else in here. He sat back, at ease.

Dunthorne watched him looking at the men with their buzz of conversation, their joking and drinking.

'Now John, you don't want to be believing anything you hear in here; this is off duty, a safe place for man and dog. Nothing goes out of here that ought not.'

John looked at him, eyes wide, silent. A quick nod.

'I believe you mentioned a letter.'

'Ah yes, I had quite forgotten it. Here, I have it in my pocket. And there is something else.' He opened his bag, rummaged around and pulled out a large book. A book on modern English building.

'My father, he said that this is yours. But you forgot to take it or he forgot to give to you, I wasn't really clear, and—'

'I hope you'll thank him for me. It's generous of him.' Dunthorne gazed at the book in his hands; he had never owned nor expected to own such a volume. He laid it carefully on the bench beside him, rubbing his hands on his coat.

The letter; thick crisp paper. Dunthorne glanced at John; he was gazing into the fire, sipping occasionally at his burdock and picking up the odd newspaper and tract… he looks relaxed, he thought, comfortable with the men and their talk… I suppose they'll know him; I'm hoping they won't be offended, me bringing the young master in here. He broke the seal and sat back in the corner.

To John Dunthorne.

Sir. I am writing to express our Sincere & Deep Gratitude for the rescue of my son John from the river. He was being foolish. He knows the river well & had set aside Knowledge & Common Sense. If it were not for your Fortuitous Presence your Quickness

> of Mind & your Practicality I doubt whether he could have survived the passage of the river its force & unpredictable behaviour. He was in great Danger from which you Plucked him. And further having set him on his feet you hastened him Home ensuring his Warmth & Health. I regret he is not a hardy soul; indeed when born he was not expected to live. You prevented a Fever or worse. I am always in your Debt. I fear that your boots will have suffered from their immersion; allow me at least to reimburse you the cost of another pair. Note enclosed; this is not in any way a Full Measure of my Gratitude.

'That is handsome of him,' Dunthorne said to John. 'But my boots are fine, they were well greased, and you must return this to him.'

He had only seen a ten pound note once before; a King's ransom, it was thought. Why, that would be half a year's wages for a labourer. A large sum for a pair of boots; is this what Golding pays for his boots? Or is there some intrigue in this? Dunthorne was keen not to be beholden to anyone apart from his father, Miss Hambleton and Wheelers. John looked with curiosity; he had not seen the letter, it seemed, and wondered at the ten pound note.

Dunthorne returned to the letter.

> In respect of the Church window the Aisle window blown out in the Great Storm you will recall my promise to speak on your Behalf. Wheelers have assured me that considering your Abilities & Skill you would certainly be able to make a fair Job of the Window in their

> workshop. That is to say that you would repair it in as good a fashion as may be expected from any Glazier. I was pleased to hear of it & addressed Canon Rhudde on the matter. I regret to say that his Response was not at first Promising. However when I reported the High Degree of your Skills your Abilities & Character he has stated that he is prepared for you to Undertake the Repair so long as it is under the Instruction of Wheeler's Foreman Glazier. I assured him that it would be so. The Foreman is to make a Full Report to the Rector; this seems to me only proper & fitting. It will be a Confirmation of your Skills.

Dunthorne stared into the fire. A whole aisle window for him. That was a big step up from the pantry windows that he had been working on though he had assisted on church lead glazing. In his mind, he ran over the procedure: the scaffolding to be instructed, recording the pattern of the glazing, the type of saddle bars and the depth of putty and noting the state of the stonework. Instruction of stonemasons if necessary. Then I would take the window to pieces, making a record drawing of each panel with a note of the lead cames. Carting it all back to the yard; a good layer of straw in the bed of the cart, I'll make sure of that. Protection of the window opening by the carpenters; we can't have birds or burglars climbing in. And I would need a good workshop space with light and materials. Wheelers will have to buy in; I shall be glad of the foreman, his authority. And I can write the Report. Seen them often enough.

A whole window, that was something. His heart sang; he felt a respect that he had not looked to receive for many a long year.

'That's handsome of your father. Very handsome. I hadn't thought…'

Dunthorne thought back to his conversation with Golding, a week before; Golding had more power than he realised, the power to persuade and achieve what he wanted. He could even persuade the Rector, it seemed. Dunthorne had liked him, felt an immediate respect. He would be a powerful man to have on one's side, and a dangerous man to be against.

The letter was not finished. A final paragraph.

> I remember our discussion about your Future. (I don't remember a discussion, thought Dunthorne. Indeed, I thought I'd said that I hadn't decided anything.) I noted your interest & knowledge of Business & Industry. I also took note of your Apprenticeship & the time that you must remain at Wheelers. This last seems to be a Waste of a young Talent that should be Encouraged & allowed to Flower. I hear many Good Things of you of your Knowledge Strength Abilities & Character. Also I am Mindful of the Timely Repair to the Bridge, Work which has Saved a Great Deal of Trouble & Expense.
>
> Therefore, it is with Great Willingness that I should like to offer you the position as my Foreman my right-hand Man to act on my Behalf & in my Absence to see my Instructions carried out. There will always be some Leadwork & Glazing to complete though it might be best to hire an Apprentice for you. You would be required to be away from the Village occasionally, possibly on the Continent. Your Remuneration would be sufficient dare I say more than you could earn as a Leadworker & we shall find you a House suitable to the Employment.
>
> I understand that you will wish to complete your Apprenticeship. I propose that I Purchase the Contract

from Wheelers for the Five Year Employment keeping my offer of Employment open until that time next year.

I understand that you may need to consider the proposal. You may have plans to leave the area or take up with another Builder. However I should consider it a great Benefit to both of us if you will accept my Offer.

Your Servant,

Golding Constable

6

SUNDAY

Dunthorne sat back. His mind reeled from the opportunities that could arise; he saw himself stepping out from a new cottage, bidding farewell to a pretty wife, and striding down to Flatford. Perhaps I would be riding a pony or sitting in my own trap. And I would get down to a day's work, overseeing at watermill and windmill; materials to be ordered, checking the quality, always the best. Walking along to the boatyard to see the completion of a new lighter. Have an easy chat with the men, many of whom have known me since I plucked oakum for them, but always ensuring that work is maintained. A quick word with my plumbing apprentice, putting him in the right way of things. Then preparations for a voyage from Mistley overseas to Holland for the master, or into the Port of London. Why, that could be a fine life, almost my own master. I'd need a new coat, new boots. It could be a wonderful life, rich and full. How would Mr. Constable deal with me? Would it be like Wheelers, simple instructions without any explanation, or would he leave me to run my side of things? He turned to John.

John was wondering what was in the letter; his father had only reminded him to express his gratitude for being rescued. He had said that Dunthorne seemed to be a sound fellow. John looked at Dunthorne; he didn't seem like the men who worked for Father. There is a difference but I can't make it out… look at him, working clothes, tough, brown and well-worn; doesn't look as if he has been to Church… not a church-goer; lucky man… perhaps Chapel; I've never been to a Chapel Service. Mother says that it's not a place to be seen. I went with the parents and sisters to Church this morning and sat through a sermon so boring that I had to start imagining landscapes in the cobwebs on the walls… and then Patty nudged me when everyone was standing for the Creed… a severe look from Mother… I wonder where he lives; Patty said that she spoke to him, but she didn't tell me anything… well, I didn't hear what she said; the girls are always chattering…what on earth do they find to talk about all the time? Why did Dunthorne have a ten-pound note? Surely it's too much for a whole suit of clothes, and he wants me to give it back? He looked awfully serious for a moment… perhaps he'll tell me. I hope Father wasn't distant; he can be, sometimes, and I don't think he means it… oh dear.

John sipped his drink. 'It was good of you, Mr.… er… Dunthorne, buying me a drink; I should be buying you a drink, what with –'

Dunthorne placed a large hand on John's arm. 'Here, give me that note. I have to talk to your father myself.'

John frowned. 'Is everything all right? He hasn't said anything that… you know… well, that he might not have said…'

'No, John, it's not like that. It's fine. Now tell me, what are you getting up to, these days?'

John slid back in the settle, smiled at the fire, and sipped his drink.

'You know, Dunthorne, they keep asking me what I'm going to do, in life. I go over to Dedham, the school you know, but I don't know for how much longer. I won't go up to Cambridge or anything like that; the teachers say my Latin is not strong enough and… Oh, I don't know. My father says that I would make a good miller because I'm interested in natural things and watching the weather. It's important, you know, to watch the weather, especially for the windmill. Though even with the water mills you have to watch the rainfall… and I do know the clouds, a messenger, you know, the ones that come first, often low. That's how you tell when a squall is coming in. My numbers are not good but I can get by; Father has had me working in the counting-house. I didn't like it, being shut up all day in front of numbers, they're so boring, I wanted to get out—'

'You have a good business to step into there.'

'And my mother thinks I should be in a profession, more like a gentleman. She doesn't like the idea of me being a tradesman, or working with my hands. She thinks we should be… no, I must not speak of it, it's wrong… But I don't know. What do you think, Dunthorne?'

'I thought business was all numbers.'

'Numbers… I've never been much good at numbers. Not sums, but you know, working out money and percentages and things like that. At school they tease me, ask me if I am in my studio when they catch me looking at the world outside. It seems such a waste, you know, to sit in a classroom all day learning French or Latin or some other useless subject. Though my father did say that if I had French it would serve the business well. When the war is over.

'I like to go out sketching, drawing the landscape and farming and ploughing and harvesting—'

'Do you like machines, then?'

'I love to see machines working, even simple cogs. The working of the sluices and the mill machinery. It has a wonder for me, the rationality of it. And I love old timbers, waterlogged lock gates, rusting iron—'

'I wish I could draw. I have drawn up schemes, window leading, pipe runs, that sort of thing. And I never think that I could draw a view or a piece of machinery.'

'But, Dunthorne, do you think you would like to walk with me? You can draw, or simply watch, or I can show you the things that attract, that form a good scene. I would not wish to impose on you, not wish to waste your time, it is only if you would care to spend the odd evening, nearby in this valley close to home.'

Dunthorne sipped his beer. He wondered what people would say if he walked with this lad. I suppose that his parents would not be concerned… he seems an open sort of lad and, even if he is gentry, there are probably many things that interest us both… I'm not concerned at what people think, just amused at the stories that drift around the village, idle gossip. Going out drawing! That's a new one; could come in for a mite of teasing… could do with a bit of company that I can talk to… maybe give me a chance to meet Miss Patty again.

'I should be honoured, Master Constable. I may pick up a few tricks.'

John looked hurt. 'Tricks? Tricks? There is no trickery, I assure you. In fact, it is more a matter of truth, the respect of reality. You will see, if I may show you.'

'Well, it sounds attractive. But this drawing business, you can't be thinking to make a living from it?'

'No… no… well, I don't know. I have seen some marvellous paintings in the houses near here, and stayed in London with my mother's family; they showed me things that were strange, marvellous… though not much like the things that I like. Not many windmills and lock gates, and things like that.'

'I guess your Father will be wanting a son in the business.'

John sighed. 'I guess so too. Poor Golding, that's my elder brother; he can't work, you know. Once when my father asked him to organise the unloading of some grain down at the mill, Golding sent the men into the coverts to put up game for him. He forgot about the grain. And then there is me...' He fell silent, a haunted look on his face.

'So your father is looking for a partner?'

'No, he'll never take a partner. Once said that a partner would see him to a grave before time. He would spend his time wondering what a partner was doing and thinking that a partner would be watching over him all the time. If it's in the family, he will be happy; there's a respect. And a son would take over from him and that is me...'

'You're young yet, John. You may change your mind, come to see the good of it.' He looked at the men around, who were chatting easily, dropping the odd look at the Constable son who might, one day, be the master.

The door swung open, a surge in the crowd around the bar. He heard a voice raised, a few laughs. An older man came through the crowd, and stopped in front of him, hands on his hips, feet astride, glaring. Dunthorne sat up, glanced over at the bar; they were all staring, silent.

'They told me you was 'ere.'

Dunthorne made no reply. He knew him, the shopkeeper.

'I wanted a word with you.' The man looked at John.

John stood up.

'Oh John, you wouldn't be leaving just yet? We were talking of work and things. I'm sure this man can say what he has to say in front of you.' He stood up; a head taller than the older man who took a step back, clearing his throat.

'Well, it's about my daughter.'

'Your daughter?'

'Don't you be a'messin' with me. You know who I'm talkin' about.'

'How do ye do. How is Emily Jane? Will you sit?'

'I haven't come here to pass the time of day with you, Dunthorne. Now look 'ere—'

'Jem,' Dunthorne called to the bar. 'A couple of pints, if you please.'

The man shuffled his feet, coughed, scratched his head.

'It's like this. My missus and me don't look on it too kindly. It ain't right.'

'Come to think of it, John here was with me last week. We came up the hill together. Here, sit down. You must tell me what you are talking about.'

John edged away; Dunthorne sighed.

'I'm sorry we were interrupted, John. I hope we meet soon; you must tell me when you are next out.' And he walked him to the door. When he returned, the older man had sat in John's place and was pulling on his pint. Dunthorne sat down, lifting his mug.

'It's not right, I say. My missus, she's not happy, not happy at all.'

Dunthorne looked at him. He wondered what storm the young missies of Bergholt were stirring up; a squall that could breed a gale.

'Our Emily is a good girl; somewhat headstrong, I dare say, but a good girl.'

Dunthorne made no reply.

'And she come back last Sunday in a right mess. Shoes ruined, all mud and—'

'We were beside the river.'

'Now… now, isn't that a rough place to be taking a girl? After a storm? And she dressed for walking out, a little company? You ought to be ashamed of yourself.'

'I didn't think; I'm sorry. It is fortunate that we were there; pulled young John Constable from the water.'

'But that's not all to it, not at all.' The man took a long draught of beer, drew the back of his hand across his mouth. Here was the story, the storm.

'Now, I know that you haven't spoken to me, the proper way, but—'

'Now why should I do that?'

'Well... well... my missus...' He stopped, staring into the fire. Lost.

Dunthorne sighed. 'I'd better be getting along. I'm sorry about her shoes; I'll see what I can do. Good day.' He rose, stretching. What was the story? Would this provoke it?

'Now, now then. Hold on a minute. It's like this. Emily Jane says that you had an understanding, a promise, that you were... were... getting hitched.' It came out in a rush, apologetic.

Dunthorne looked down at him. So this was how the girls of Bergholt spent their time, weaving tales bred out of false hopes to catch innocent men. Blast me, he thought, but it's a dangerous business walking out a girl in this village, isn't it? One moment it's having a little innocent fun at a folly and the next they would be wrapping you up as tight as a bug in a rug and walking you up the aisle. There have been one or two caught this way; they seemed happy, grinning all the way to the altar, not so happy a few years on, weighed down with a young family. I'm not in such a hurry, only twenty-one. I'll take my own time choosing a wife. Why, she might even come from another village, not out of this coven.

The man was talking again.

'So, I thought we better have a word. About you.'

'There's no understanding, no promise. There never was and there won't be.' Dunthorne's words rebounded off the older man like stones; he saw him flinch, rally, and stand up.

'Now, that's not the way Emily Jane has it. And my missus won't have no bad words said…'

Dunthorne had turned and was leaving. A few men stared at him as he went but he avoided their eyes, didn't even bid Jem a farewell. A muttering was breaking out; who did he think he was, treating a village girl like that? He'd better watch hisself; s'all very well, saving bridges an' all but you don't go messin' with our girls.

7

MAY 1796

The dawn chorus, a bubbling rippling chattering swelled by the call of church bells, rolled up from the valley to drown sleep. Across the road, the sun struck the front of West Lodge and slid down to crawl across the wide roadway. A man stood there, still on the rutted chalk earth.

John counted off the peals, five, looking down from East Bergholt House. The man on the road was a working man; you could tell that by his clothes and his hands, broad and scarred rolling a pencil between fingertips, to and fro, to and fro, as he watched the sunlight approaching. Dawn coming across the ground. A cat rubbed itself against his legs and ran as he brushed it away.

John gave a brief sob, deep in his throat, a confusion of guilt and doubt. Standing at the window, he felt overcome. My father is not happy; I have heard him sighing when I sit gazing at endless columns of figures… not so bad when I spend a few hours in Pitts, teaching the millers to see the clouds… but it is not enough work for him… I do help when I can; but I am twenty years old, I must follow what is important to me… I am grateful, God knows, I am grateful for my home and where I live.

The seed of doubt faded as the brightness beckoned and he turned to be with his friend, tip-toeing down through the silent house; not even his father had stirred. Out of the back door and round the house, dog at heel. Caught the side gate as it swung to behind him with a slight bang.

'Heel, Bold.' Down to the road.

Dunthorne smiled, shrugged, pocketing his pencil. 'I was early—'

'As usual. Hush, my sisters. And my mother.'

They walked away from the centre of the village. The Church stood stark against the brilliant morning sky, the stub of the unfinished tower rough against the crisp stonework of the nave. Leaving it on their left, they bore away down the Flatford Lane.

John relaxed; the thick cloak of home, duty and work slid off him.

'Well Dunthorne, how goes it? How come you can leave your work to waste a day with me? On a day as beautiful as this, why should anyone be tied to a dull job?' A stab of guilt; he frowned. 'I know… I know… work must be done, a living must be earned. I should be with my father in the counting-house…' He gazed away over the valley.

Dedham Church tower glowed in the early sunshine, rising above the trees and roofs of the town. The river wound silver below them, an early lighter making slow progress upstream. Cattle grazed in the river meadows and a parcel of rooks rose from the trees. The young wheat was a dark green, stirring in waves with the morning breeze. A blackbird shouted an alarm.

Dunthorne laughed. 'I'm not wedded to my work like you John. There are things to do, always things to do, but they'll wait a beautiful day. How is Mrs. Roberts? I have seen no signs of life at West Lodge.'

'She is away. Brighthelmstone, I believe, carried off by her daughters; you know what they will want, shops and shoes, dresses and magazines. They came on Thursday, three of them, such a carrying-on, hats and bags. My sisters saw them only briefly, took tea with them. I don't think that she will enjoy the pleasures offered there, but the daughters—'

'It will do her good to be with her family. And they should be grateful for her attention.' He paused. 'Why, you look as young and robust as ever. City life has not aged you. Where are we going today?'

John had told him about his visits to London. Staying with the Allens at Edmonton, relations of his mother's. And meeting Antiquity Smith, a drawing master, who had invited him to his house, encouraged him to draw and read; such books as the *Treatise on Painting* by Leonardo da Vinci.

Dunthorne had never been to London. He didn't think that there would be anything of interest in a big city; too many buildings and too many people. Ipswich was bad enough. Why would I want to go, he asked himself, except maybe to see a bit of stained glass in Westminster Abbey and the leadwork on St. Paul's dome? If I want to see something special, I only have to go over to Ely to see the lantern. There's no better place than this village and I do wonder why young John wants to be wasting his time in London; it will only give him ideas that won't do no good. He'd be better off staying here, tending to his father and walking with me. Sketching and such like. He always gets a good bit of painting done. Even if it don't look like anything; well, nothing I could put a name to. He grunted, and walked on.

A moist freshness; the air built into a light breeze rising up the valley from the sea. The tops of the oaks stirred and a pair of pigeons took off, clapping through the leaves. A rabbit bolted for its earth; Bold chased it for a while, tail like a flag. John surveyed the fields, smelling the new day.

'Barley's not fit yet. See how the shadows are green but paler than the wheat. River's running fast; they must have the sluices up at Flatford. Some hay still standing in stooks; it'll be wet. Nancy going on about riding, when would the fields be stubble. She wants to try out her new mare and run with her hounds, and—'

'And make sure that you run around keeping her informed. I don't know, John, you'll have to escape your sisters sometime. Get yourself a good woman, like me.'

John looked at him; what was it like to have a 'good woman' at home? Endless conversations about… nothing, like his sisters… and yet, I don't know, I feel alone often at home, surrounded by family… warmth and food, and always work there in the business if I want it, and many out of work… I should be ashamed… sometimes, it is as though I don't belong, or ought not to belong… Annie, she looks after me. He hadn't told Dunthorne about Annie.

He had been exploring the country to the north, only a few weeks back; heavy oaks, narrow lanes, all a long way it seemed from the village. As he walked, he had noticed a girl walking the field beyond the bank, keeping pace with him, drawing close. At a gateway, he halted and she drew near him.

'Ah,' she said, 'warm day! I was out looking for one of our lurchers, you haven't seen one have you, in your travels?'

He had blinked surprise at her approach. She was a little taller than himself; he did not know her and wondered at her forwardness.

She smiled. 'I know you. You're John Constable; often seen you walking the lanes and fields hereabouts. What are you doing?'

'Oh, it's only sketching; you know. Just fields and trees and things.' He was embarrassed, not used to being asked.

'Would you like to come in for a glass of milk? It's cold,' she said.

'I don't know your farm,' he said. 'Are you near here?'

She laughed. 'My father does business with your father, don't you know that? Sells him grain every year. I'm Annie Walters.'

He bowed. 'John Constable at your service.'

She laughed. 'I'm not looking for service, but why don't you come on in? It's just back there, a field or two.'

As they walked, John asked about the farm, crops and animals, casual questions. She noticed his interest. And how he walked easily, his boots and smock like their shepherds, not smart like she might expect from a Constable. He looked at her, a sideways glance taking in much: golden hair, broad shoulders, a ruddy complexion and eyes that danced. Working hands and brown arms, tough clothes, a practical girl, one to be admired.

At the farm, he was introduced to mother, father being out. A large low kitchen, a cool dairy to one side where running water could be heard. Annie disappeared and returned with a beaker, brimming with cold milk, and an invitation to sit down. Mother asked what he was doing their way and heard about the sketching, the interest in farming, and answered more questions, about fowl and cattle and haywains. She was surprised, didn't expect so much from a gentleman. When he left, Annie asked him if he was going to be that way again.

John went away in a strange frame of mind; it was as though he had an opening through his gentleman's life into that of the farmer and the working family, a view that he had not expected. And Annie; there was someone of interest. Someone he thought he could talk to, who liked to walk the fields and understood his interest in cattle and crops. How old was she? About his age, he thought, though maybe a year or two younger. He wondered how she spent her time, now she'd finished her schooling, what she did in the evenings. He couldn't see her fitting in with his home life, only trouble arising with his mother.

'No,' he said to Dunthorne, at last. 'I don't have time for women. I must study art and history. And work in the mill; my father needs me. Perhaps Abram will take my part one day; he is a young businessman at heart, though he is only thirteen.'

They walked past the grounds of Old Hall, and turned down Fen Lane, into the shade of oaks and chestnuts. Dunthorne strode on, ignoring John's pleas to stop and sketch.

'It seems years ago,' said John, 'that I came this way to school. Poor Grimwood, he never gave up trying to drum sums and Latin into me. And he never told on me when I didn't turn up. It wasn't often, I think.'

'You think? I wonder. My father gave me the strap when I played truant.'

'It is a good school. Much better than my earlier schools, with their heartless ragging so far from home. I hated them and time dragged, you know; you wouldn't believe how cruel teachers can be, and their servants. One would imagine that one's parents were in accord with them, sending us away to be bullied and…'

John groaned quietly, remembering the school sergeant who beat them often for no ill… violence breeding violence, times that should be forgotten but somehow lodged in the memory… uncouth boys revelling in fighting; bruises, cuts and broken bones were common. He had taken the safer path each time but was it right avoiding trouble? Poor Skinner, beaten to a pulp, was how the big bullies called it; once he looked to John for help. I just shouted Stop Stop… and the bullies laughed. Don't I know already the hardship of having an older brother who cannot bear to see me favoured, a bully who will curb any pleasure with a harsh word and often enough a blow?

'And your parents came to hear of it and rescued you,' said Dunthorne. 'I am glad they saw reason though how they heard of the bad conditions… And placed you in a good school where you could play truant. What do you think it was like here in the village school? Plenty of bullying and truanting. Why, we used to get away to the river, fishing or cadging rides on the lighters; they weren't going to give us away. And some of the boys, they were needed on the land. Families couldn't spare a good pair of hands at harvest, or—'

'There's always things to do on the land. You know it well. Harvest; the men weren't going to give me away when I was an extra pair of hands and good with a pitchfork. And when the river flooded, the waterman needed help clearing the timber and debris coming downstream. And the sawmill and the boatyard have both known me—'

Dunthorne laughed. 'I do wonder, you know. I do wonder that you don't want to stay here, take the bailiff's job to keep out of the counting-house.'

'I wonder myself sometimes. But my mother wishes that I were a respectable young lawyer, or land agent, or—'

'Enough. I'm here to enjoy myself. I shall buy us a bite at the Sun. And you can show me how to deal with these shadows; I can't get the way of them.'

They had settled in a meadow, high on the hill looking over the valley, a patchwork of green meadows by the river and a couple of miles away, the far side rising into the distance. John was quiet, chewing on a grass, gazing from side to side. Below them, cattle grazed, moving slowly, tails swishing from side to side. Bold tired and settled in the grass, licking his front paws and dropped his head to sleep. John sighed.

'I wish… I wish it were possible to capture this very moment in which we sit, where we belong. The spread of land from the blue haze downriver at Manningtree up to the bluffs of Stratford.' He swung his arms, a broad sweep from left to right as though he could hold it all in one grasp.

'Can you not feel it all? I mean, really all? The wheat, the smell of morning dew on the grass, leaves in the breeze, that blackbird calling its stupid alarm and the pigeons away over by West Lodge. Smoke rising from the cottage by Fen Bridge. Could one capture it in a picture, do you think? A wide sweep to encompass all, wider than one can see at one time?'

'And you ask me?' Dunthorne frowned.

'I've seen something like it in London; a painter called Robert Barker is showing his views of Edinburgh on a cylindrical surface. He calls it "The Panorama". I believe he is constructing a special building in Leicester Square to show it.'

'The view like travelling on a ship, do you mean, the land unfolding in front of you? Not that I have ever been on a ship. And the coach to Colchester isn't the same thing, I'm sure. The turnpike is not so bad, a great improvement, but the other roads are so rough, you don't want to be having too much breakfast before you—'

'It's grand on *The Telegraph*, apart from the movement, and the sailors' comments, and the business of sailing the ship going on all the time; so many distractions. But yes, there is always a huge view all around, much more than on land. Here, even on what we call flat land, the horizon is barely three miles; at sea we're looking at some twenty miles, further if you are up the mast.' A pause. 'I tried that once, climbing to the masthead. You talk of breakfast; I was sick as a dog. Tickled all the men, the owner's son throwing up like a dog and they tried to—'

'But what about the view, John? What was your impression of that?'

'Ah, the view. One of the strangest things, Dunthorne, is that it is difficult to get an impression of how far off things are. You might see a brig, Dutch or North Country, a collier or a… anyway, then you see a ship of the line, a three-master, but it might appear smaller; the distance you know, it throws your conception of things. And sometimes a buoy will be further than you had imagined and then you think you are running aground at Harwich but you are a good two miles offshore. The captain used to laugh at me for my doubts. But it's all experience, you know; he could tell, always knew where we were. Though we never sailed much at night-time.'

'What does the coast look like? There's your "panorama", surely. The towns and fields, beaches and harbours.'

'You would think so. But it all looks remarkably flat as though the sea could roll over it. When there is a sea running, it disappears altogether. And harbours, rivers, any sort of inlet, they are hard to see, as one side of an opening slides over the other like a sack laid over another so that one cannot make out the opening. Of course, there are the buoys near the coast but most of the navigation is done by experience. Captain calls out when to change course, reduce sail, come about. His word is law.'

'Why, John, you're sounding quite the sailor.'

They were sitting now in one of his favourite places, in a bank halfway down the hill, with good views both ways. His nest had room for one only, but he had kicked out a space for Dunthorne, close by so that he could see him drawing, and make suggestions.

John worked at a sketch of Dedham Church, set beyond the meadows that he had known all his life; walked across to school, returning sometimes in a lighter coming downstream. The river appeared in a bend, sun shining off the water. A mass of rounded shapes: river, willow trees, oaks, cattle, against the underlying framework of fields, tracks and dykes. A backdrop of the far valley side, rising as though a rug had been lifted, to roll over the horizon three or four miles distant. He balanced the distant darks against the near shadows and studied the clouds, now rolling up from the south-west, warm puffy signs of good weather; a few brushmarks of colour, brief, confident, a quick summary of observations.

Another sketch looking down the valley, the land and sky blending into a warm haze, Prussian blue and umber, hints of yellow ochre, a little madder and green earth, promises of distance and the unknown. And then a harder view, more indeterminate, shapes shifting in the rising morning heat, suggestions of valley floor, estuary and hillside.

Away down there in the haze was the brig *Telegraph*, moored at Mistley Quay unless she had already sailed on the tide. He imagined the voyage; down the shallow Stour to Harwich, a sharp turn out to sea to follow the channel between sandbanks and shallows, before turning south and skirting the Essex coast, inside or outside the wrecking grounds of the sands, past fleets of fishermen, colliers, coastal brigs, barges bearing straw and hay down to the City, and occasional Dutchmen coming into Harwich or Colchester, Maldon or the Blackwater. Down, down to the London River where the ship would be one among many: trading ships from the East Coast and overseas, warships of the line out of the Medway, peter boats, ferries, galleons, yaghts, botters, a surging mass of humanity and trade serving the great City that would grow on the horizon, cloaked in smoke, St. Paul's rising above all.

He looked at Dunthorne and wondered if he would ever see it.

Time passed as he dreamt. Of painting great paintings that would be unlike any seen before, to carry one into the landscape and feel the breeze and the cool of the dark green shade of an oak and smell the moisture on wheat and grass... I would travel up and down the valley, a simple farmer's cart in which to sleep and work... what would I take? Apart from the necessities of living? Watercolours, pigments, perhaps oils, paper, a frame to support it, a simple seat or two; it's enough and return home only now and then to family, sisters, Mother and Golding... and Annie would come with me, cook simple meals, meat and eggs from farms, bread from a good housewife... and we would be close, bundled together at night... ah, Annie, what could I tell Mother, or say to her parents? Mother would say not good enough for you for goodness' sake why do you think we took you to dancing lessons introduce you into houses... and still she has been good to me, close... perhaps, one day... what freedom.

It was a week or ten days when he had next walked north; he had been spending more time with his father in the mill, not so much with the figures, but talking to the miller at Pitts, and helping at Flatford. But on a Saturday evening he was up there in the deep dark lanes and wondering what Annie was doing and how close to the farm he would go. When there was a bright halloo and she came down next to him, no shyness or reserve on her part as though she was in her own home, not a public lane and alone with a man who she did not know. Not hardly at all.

'Warm evening,' she said, smiling at him. She laughed at his shyness and became the village girl, teasing and flirting; John was not used to such familiarity, but not averse.

'Show me what you do,' she said.

They had sat, comfortable in a deep bank, side by side, and John brought out his sketchbook, saying look, look at the oaks down the lane and the shadows beneath. Do you see how the lane disappears down and away; isn't that wonderful?

She looked at him, not comprehending. It's where she has been all her life; what is so special about it? And she gazed at him, noticing the turn of his eye, and the way that his hair curled over his ear, and his cheek sucked in concentration, lips full and soft; she thinks, what is it like to kiss him, how would he be? He talks some more and she sees a picture appear; perhaps he would draw her beneath the oaks.

A man had come down the lane. John saw him late, stood to greet him, turned to Annie who still sat, introduced her, and fell into conversation with the man, going off with him towards the village, a brief farewell only to Annie, though he gazed at her, looked over his shoulder as they parted.

Bold wandered, put up a partridge and chased it briefly, returned to his master, throwing himself on the ground, head on paws. John looked down at his drawing; he hadn't done much. Ah, Annie. When would he tell Dunthorne, and what would he say? Probably laugh at him, and say get in there, bor. If only life was that simple.

A cloud shaded them. Dunthorne was asleep, an arm thrown across his eyes, sketchbook set aside. John remembered the day that Dunthorne rescued him from the river and met his father; it seemed a lifetime ago. He is like a brother, he thought, six years older, but never judgemental or a bully like brother Golding. But why did he set up by himself? He might have had an easier life, better off, more comfortable, if he had remained an employed man. Didn't he tell me once that Father had offered him a job but he said he must be his own boss, can't be beholden to others for instruction? Why did he marry? I couldn't, not now.

The young men that I know, not that I spend much time in their company, they all seem to have moved on: the Army or Church, business or farming. Some are married; I remember the last at Bergholt, poor Maxwell being carried off by some great girl. God's teeth, that's not for me, though Annie might want... no, I must pursue my art and help Father and walk out with Dunthorne... he won't give up his village life for that of an industrial town; I don't think he has any idea of what it's like in a busy city... if only I could persuade him to travel to London with me, it might open his eyes. He could see the great ocean-going ships from halfway round the world, masts rising high above the warehouses, and hear the talk of steam engines working in the docks, for unloading tea and coal...

And he might see some of the horrors too: starving women and cripples, the maddened, smoke and dirt and gin and the fights, great meaningless brawls in the Docks, sailors and stevedores, Lascars, Chinamen, Irish, all nations mixed in a great stew... I shouldn't take him there; life is better here.

'I'm hungry,' he said to the air. 'What is the hour? Hungry hour, I'll bet. What would the Sun do for us today, I wonder? Bread, cheese, perhaps a plate of ham, some pickles, a pint of—'

'I hear you, I hear you.' Dunthorne rolled over and sat up, rubbing his eyes and yawning, stretching hugely. 'It was an early start, even for me.'

They brushed grass and hay from their britches and strode down the hill to Fen Bridge. The cottage there was small, colour washed, the garden tidy, neat with an almost obsessive care. They paused, looking at the vegetables in straight lines, the fruit trees, chickens fenced in a corner. A woman came out of the cottage, threw scraps to the chickens and chatted with Dunthorne. John stepped back, occupied himself pulling twigs from Bold's coat. Dunthorne turned and introduced him; she smiled, a quick nod, almost a curtsy. John was embarrassed. She disappeared into the cottage.

'It's not fair, you know,' he said. 'I am not of the company of the people here, on account of my family, my education, my clothes, my speech… oh, goodness, all the things that make one what one is, I suppose. And I would be easy with everyone, as I am with those that know me; the yard men, millers and mill men. But when it comes to the cottagers or the men that work in the fields, it is harder. They don't know me. And I would that it was so.'

He looked at Dunthorne, easy with the local people, many who have known him all his life, and also with those who employ him. No doubt, it did make a difference being your own master. Maybe, if they all knew about Annie, it would change things. Except his mother would never countenance it.

'Come on,' said Dunthorne. 'Let's be getting on. I could do with a bite myself.'

8

LATER

It was a short walk into Dedham, scarcely twenty minutes across the meadows. The river was high; there was interest in watching its course, the level of the water and what it carried. It would be a hard day for any lighters coming upstream. They saw a couple running down, swinging from side to side on the bends as the helmsman hauled on the tiller, the crew fending off from the bank with a pole. Shouted greetings to familiar faces, sometimes some friendly abuse.

Cattle huddled around the gate to the meadow, tails swishing in the shadows. They dodged the cowpats, John slapping the cattle on the rump to move them, and walked on into the main street. Dunthorne remarked on the houses; signs of greater wealth than Bergholt. He pointed out crisp rubbed brickwork, elegant sashes, wrought-iron railings rising to grand front doors. And standing over all a large parish Church, dark shadowed side to the road. There was more traffic, farm carts and gigs, curricles and beer drays, the townspeople busy shopping, promenading, stopping to exchange views and news, and the old boys sitting against the churchyard wall watching the comings and the goings.

John went to look at his old school, the Grammar School, looking out for the schoolmaster. Boys appeared at the windows;

grinning faces, pointing until they were swept out of sight. Eventually Mr. Grimwood came to the door in his long black gown and spectacles.

'John Constable? Have you come to visit us? It is good to see you, but I wonder.'

'Sir?'

'You are not gainfully employed, it seems.'

'Oh no, sir, that is not the case. My friend Dunthorne and I are painting today, sketching the valley. We are—'

'How do you do.' A brief bow to Dunthorne. 'So you are employed then, John?'

'My father, the counting-house, figures, sums…' He faded away; why did it always come back to the sums? Why can it not be respectable to be a painter, an honest recorder of the land?

'Not your great strength, I recall, Master Constable.'

'No sir. My father is very patient.'

'I wonder… I wonder now. Do you think? Would you like to talk to the boys about drawing? There is so little time, to give them a grounding in the Classics and sums and essays, but you may widen their knowledge a little, I believe. A scandalous lot at present. I had to send a boy away recently for… But no, I will not burden you with the ills of a schoolmaster.'

'Sir, you do me an honour.'

John wondered how he would manage in front of an unruly gang of boys only a few years younger than himself; they would ignore his pleas for quiet, and resort to fighting and gaming. Dammit, mayhem would ensue and I would be obliged to flee, calling for help. Oh damnation, shades of past school life. I suppose even Mr. Grimwood might be pressed to restore order. And how would I look then? He swallowed; Dunthorne grinned openly.

‘I would be delighted, sir, though I believe it might be wise to have the school sergeant present. Please to let me know when it would suit you for me to attend.’

Mr. Grimwood made his farewells, bowed and withdrew, the door closing firmly behind him, cutting off a howl of cries; we want to see Constable, let us Sir, oh please Sir.

They walked on up the street, dodging the carts and pedestrians; Dunthorne nodded to a few and John recognised several acquaintances of his parents. Out of the dusty roadway and into the Sun.

They stopped within the doorway.

There was a large crowd of young men, dressed in the latest fashions, drinking with gusto, shouting and jostling and handling the barmaid. She didn’t look too concerned, brushing them off like flies. The landlord stood behind her, split between wanting peace in his house and glad to have good trade at this early hour.

A moment of silence.

The crowd swung as one to survey the newcomers. There was a loud clap of laughter caught up and bandied from side to side, hiccups, the odd groan.

‘It’s John Constable, isn’t it? From Bergholt.’

‘What are you doing here, John? Didn’t see you out with the hounds this morning. We were walking the new pups—’

‘A fine day—’

‘Yeah, yeah, very fine I say—’

‘Come on, John. Have a drink with us.’

‘Yes, come and join us. Whose round is it?’

A pause, the young gentlemen becoming silent. One stepped forward.

‘He don’t look too keen; what is it, John? We not good enough for you?’

'What, don't he drink? He don't look too keen.' A round red-faced young man thrust to the front, waving his tankard in John's face.

'Good day, Gerald.' said John. 'I see you have had—'

'Aah, come on.' He threw an arm around John's shoulders. 'Come and join us.' He swung John round to face the crowd. 'You all know John, don't you? Miller's son at Bergholt.'

'No really—'

'What, won't drink with us?' Gerald swayed, hiccupped and sat down with a crash on a chair.

'I've come for a bite—'

'Here, John, what do you carry in your bag?'

John retreated to the door. One man grabbed at his bag, tugging at the strap. Dunthorne stepped up beside John and stared at the young man, who let go and retreated.

They fell dumb. Looks of surprise and shock.

A slow appraisal of Dunthorne rippled through the crowd, his clothes, his manner. John wondered what they would do, and what he would have to do; perhaps if he kept still, avoided all eyes…

'What? Would you? Shall we throw him out, chaps?'

'Yeah, yeah. Less throw 'im out, com'on!'

A swaying crowd advanced on Dunthorne. There was more laughter but a note of malice had crept into the room, unseen and infectious. Dunthorne did not move away, folding his arms casually. He seemed huge, impassive, gazing over their heads as though they were not there. John wondered how far they would take it; he remembered other occasions when he had been at school and some boys had created mayhem in the town, beating a poor mad boy and breaking windows. He was grateful for the presence of Dunthorne who looked as though he was hewn from the trunk of an oak. But what could happen, he thought, if Dunthorne was obliged to curb an unruly young man with a blow? Rumours tended to get around, ruin a man's reputation. He had known it. My God, it could be a call on the constable and the end of Dunthorne's business locally; the gentry would never suffer to be beaten by a tradesman. I know; I've seen it happen from time to time and it always ends in some poor man being wrongly accused, leaving the parish with wife, children and all. He edged forward in front of Dunthorne.

There was a pause; they shuffled about.

'Send your man out. What's he doing here, John?'

'He doesn't eat with his man, do he?'

'Shall we throw him out?'

A long pause. Some of the young gentlemen were flagging, dropping back to the bar; but a hard group around Gerald were holding their ground.

'Now, gentlemen. Can I be getting you some food?' The landlord was clear, his voice ringing above the drunken muttering.

Dunthorne caught the eye of the landlord, a mutual nod. With the landlord on one side and Dunthorne on the other like piers, solid and unmoveable, the drunken crowd swayed, rotated, muttered threats and curses and, slamming the door open, picked up momentum and spilled out into the street where they burst into song, a loud raucous noise, and went away down past Church and shop to the other pub.

'I wish I could warn John at the Old Oak. He will want the constable before long. They should throw them in the Cage, genl'men or no.' The landlord was dour, but greeted Dunthorne and John, sending the maid for food while he pulled beer.

'Do you have much of it?' said Dunthorne.

'No… no, not so much. But there seems to be more idle money around, profiteering from the war no doubt and the young gentlemen don't have the responsibilities of their fathers. And they have no respect for the village people and none for their own families, it seems. I'm sorry that they treated you so, Dunthorne; I won't have such talk in my house if I can avoid it.'

They sat back in the bay window, drink washing away the sour taste of aggression. Dunthorne was hungry but John was slow to eat, sunk in thought.

'I'm sorry, Dunthorne. They had no call to treat you so.'

'You knew them?'

'Yes, yes, I'm afraid so. Some of them were at the School, you know. Gerald, the round fat one, always a trouble-maker, used to draw us into all sorts of scrapes, and then—'

'The others? Where do they come from?'

'Oh, I believe they all live round here; I have met a few. The sons of landowners, farmers, businessmen, lawyers, you know. Many were away at school, and now… now I suppose they will join their fathers or the Army… or something.'

'It's a common enough pattern, isn't it? For a son to follow into his father's business. Particularly if there is work enough for all. Why, I'll be wanting a son to follow me, build the business with the two of us. I could do with an apprentice even now, but I daren't take on the responsibility for a young man's life. And then a son would take some of the load when I get older and have a nice business to step into when I have had enough and taken to my garden and my fireside chair.'

John was silent, staring at the floor, food and drink ignored.

'I guess I've said too much, John. That wasn't called for, I'm sorry.'

John smiled sadly. 'I have tried. I know that I can run a windmill and understand the workings of the locks and lighters. But I am no businessman, my figures and sums don't work. I don't know what to do.'

'It's a problem, that's for sure.'

'My father has been good to me. He supports me while I try to become a painter; I only work some of the days for him. I am fortunate.'

'You are the most fortunate young gentleman I know. But then I know few young gentlemen.'

'My mother has been talking again. She would seek an apprenticeship with a lawyer in Ipswich; I had difficulty deferring the appointment. A lawyer! I should be as bored as a pig, asleep over the papers while the law runs amok.'

'Is it possible? Could you ever be an artist, a painter? How do these gentlemen support themselves?'

'Oh, I have learnt a little. Some have no need for an income, it is there already. And some have patrons who sponsor their art. And then some provide the paintings that society values; they sell for huge sums, to collectors and… anyone who would pay such money.'

'What paintings does society value when it is at home?'

'Grand paintings of battles, myths, scenes of classical subjects.'

'Not your interest at all?'

'Well, the artists that I admire paint landscapes, ships and people working. They are real to me, the things that one sees, things that I can understand. I had no education in the classical myths. Or none that I remember.'

Dunthorne stretched; he wondered; does he bring John to the point? Is there really a living to be made as a painter? There's the family business, surely a place within it for "the merry miller". He wondered briefly and not for the first time, what it would have been like if he had joined Golding when he made the offer six years before. No worries about an apprentice and perhaps working more amenable hours as well as more interesting work. But then I wouldn't be out on a fine day like this walking the fields with John, sketching, dropping into the Sun and such like. I have a good life; my time is my own, I am my own master. He pulled on his beer, and drew the back of his hand across his mouth. A contented sigh.

John asked him why he set up by himself, with all the responsibilities on his own shoulders and now a wife with two boys to support. Dunthorne had never spoken of it.

'You know, John, I'm a master plumber, not a miller. Your father has been generous, I can never repay him, but he has no need of a master plumber. He set me up, you know, found the workshop for me, gives me work.'

'That's all very well, you know. But you would have made a good assistant to my father and I believe that you know it, know it well. Perhaps regret your decision, on a late rainy afternoon, working on a dull roof in freezing temperatures.'

'Why John, you sound quite impassioned.'

John was silent, he felt guilty. If Dunthorne had been employed by my father, he thought, there would be less call for me to join the family firm; and I could pursue my life as an artist without doubts or fears… or concerns for my father. What if he was to become ill, or worse? How would we all survive? We all depend upon him, for all that we have… perhaps, I should bend my will to his. He looked at Dunthorne; there he sat, legs stretched out, a large piece of pie in his hand and a mug of beer in the other. A great look of satisfaction, a man who knows his place in the world.

Dunthorne was thinking of Patty, not Sarah his wife. He had met her by chance, six months or so after first meeting her, in a quiet lane at the top of the village; he had wondered what she was doing so far from home, but didn't dare ask. He had said how good it was to meet her and she smiled and asked him how he was; and before long they were talking, all interests, wide and free. When they parted, he said that maybe they would meet again by chance and she said it was possible, she had business with a farmer up that way; she would be there the following Tuesday. And far from work, he found himself there, settled in a bank, waiting. She came by and greeted him with surprise, a warm smile. It was a warm day for late autumn, and she sat down beside him. They talked, more intimately than before, she asking and he also, until she fell silent, head down. And gazing at her he dared to brush his lips across her forehead gently, a touch like dandelion blossom; she opened her eyes and gazing deep pulled him down to kiss her. No word was spoken, looks only, and he was lost, perhaps she too.

He could never tell John; he didn't know what he would feel, but it would be back to the family, a word, a hint, some small presage of disaster that would lead to the loss of his work, his workshop, his good terms with Mr. Constable. And what would he say to his Sarah?

9

JUNE 1798

Lead shot rattled against the boarding. Close, too close. Dunthorne ducked and fell to the ground, dropping his mallet. Where was it coming from? Who was firing a gun up here on Pitt's Farm? What the… how can this be?

Is this what it's like for the boys who went to war? My old friend Sam; he and a few of the old boys escaped farming, all the poverty and harshness, and went for soldiers; swapped their lives for the King's shilling. So this is what it's like on a battlefield, to sink into the ground like that worm there. Mud and blood. What a life! God, how awful. Mind you, it ain't often that one envies a worm. And what happens to the wounded? How can they earn a living, wife, children and all? Seen a few in Ipswich, hobbling around on crutches, cared for by a grateful country… I don't think.

His face was pressed into the ground, his heart beating; a sharp smell of crushed grass and wet earth. He examined his body for wounds. Nothing, and listened for an intruder. Overhead the sails continued to turn at a gentle pace and he could hear the gears groaning inside, over the grinding of the stones.

Life hadn't stopped after all. Anger flowed through him like a fire across dry tinder. Dammit. I'm under fire. And it ain't right.

He stood up, roaring. A howl of fear and rage. Here I am, working on the windmill fitting a new cill in the doorway and I'm under fire. Bugger, it don't do, it don't do at all. He did not think of bolting into the mill. The miller shouted, came to the door.

Dunthorne strode around the mill to where the shot had come from. A lanky young man was standing there, reloading his fouling piece. Smart coat, a hat with feathers and fishing flies. As he put the butt to the ground, tamping the wadding down, he looked up into Dunthorne's eyes. A lazy smile spread over his face.

'Did I get you?' he said. And laughed.

Dunthorne checked himself; he had been prepared to berate some youth or careless farmer. He would have wrested the gun away from the fool, threatened him with the constable and warned him of dire consequences. And if he had received some cheek, he might have struck him to the ground, stood over him. He had not been known as Bull for nothing; in his youth, there had been a few occasions when his strength had overcome his common sense and he had sent some young lad flying, always for a good reason. But it was not popular, this type of behaviour. His "mother" had had words with him on more than one occasion; he always felt deeply ashamed and humbled. She had told him to put his strength to better purposes, to helping others or earning some money.

But this was a different matter. Oh God, he thought, why me? Everyone knows this young man: Mr. Constable's son Golding. And everyone knows about his shooting on fields and gardens and homes, even the Church; he is a danger to us all. I don't know why Mr. Constable can't control him; relieve him of his guns, limit his movements, somehow…

'Good morning, Master Golding.'

'I say, I didn't hit you, did I?'

'No, Master Golding. You didn't hit me.'

'Well, then all is well. I shall leave you.'

'But, may I ask, what had you in your sights this morning up here? It looks quiet to me.'

'Ah well, you know, just a bunny. I thought. A scut among the grasses. I fired. Damme if it didn't disappear. I never miss, you know.'

'Your father didn't tell me that I would be under fire.'

'Oh really? Well, must be getting on. Game to shoot and so on. Do you like my piece? It's new you know.'

'You won't find any game around the mill.'

'Oh really?'

'It's the sails. They frighten the bunnies. And the birds.'

'But I have often—'

'You won't find any game here.'

'But I have seen—'

'No.'

And Dunthorne turned away, round the mill back to work. He was aware of the young man close behind him, mouthing words. Images crossed his mind, scenes of mayhem created out of the stories that circulated about this young man. Why he had not gone into his father's business, why he had not gone into any business at all but spent his days shooting and creating trouble. And, dammit, he was still talking.

'You can't speak to me like that, you know. It's… it's not right.'

'Right? It's not right to shoot at people, master, but—'

'I'll speak to my father, it's not right, not right at all.' And he strode off over the hill, talking to himself, muttering and kicking at tufts.

Dunthorne sighed; he had no fears that Mr. Constable would take action. Though it would be a good thing if he did and remove his son from the village. Did he not know that there had been a number of incidents? A villager's prize cockerel, shot outside his own cottage; the Church windvane rendered useless after a lucky bullet shattered the shaft, and the rumour about a young girl, stopped on the way to school. We never heard what happened to her, he thought, but girls don't care to walk alone anymore. It's a crying shame, that's what it is; a good village like this one. We look after our own and have no need of the constable, wherever he may be; wouldn't want his nose sticking in where it's not wanted.

He watched a pigeon fly through the sails and smiled. Went back to his work, dressing the lead over the cill.

The miller came down for a quiet smoke and chatted.

'What was that I heard?' he said. 'Sounded like a bang, and I was a'lookin' over my gear but couldn't see no wrong. What was you a'gettin' up to?'

When Dunthorne told him, he said, 'Waal, it ain't right, bor, and that lad should know better. Would you be having a word with Mr. Constable? It's about time, that it is.' He knocked out his pipe and disappeared inside.

The sun shone. A rabbit sat up, ears and nose twitching, and settled to feed.

A new century coming. Ideas beyond the limits of this village would change life, in time. There would always be work for me, he thought, but perhaps I ought to have accepted Mr. Constable's offer to be his right-hand man and see the world, London and trading and inventions and new ways of doing things: weaving and spinning machines of all sorts, improvements in farming with rotation and selective breeding, the Watt steam machines, even talk of making machines that can fly.

There's time yet to make my mark, if only I could see some of these new inventions. I could escape the old slow ways of doing things. These local boys, good workers all, good company too; but damme, they make me riled when they sneer and turn their backs when I suggest they find a better way, whether it's winnowing or simply loadin' a hayloft. Manpower, that is what it is all about they say. And if we don't do our work, if you find machines to do our work, what would we be a'doin' for our bread and beer, tell me that.

And Dunthorne would be silent. He had read of the factories and mills that had sprouted from innocent farmland all over the country, less in Suffolk and low-lying farmland. And of the new farming machinery, seed drills to replace the seedsman, threshers to replace the flail and winnowing. But he also knew of the violence elsewhere, mostly in northern towns, violence arising from the fear of no work, and no bread. The smashing of machinery, sometimes with the farmers' approval. The towns were growing, not shrinking, there must be work for all. But yet there's poverty, in Ipswich and elsewhere. Poverty, fear and violence.

There could be no way to hold back the future; machines and power would come, whatever they said or did. Or didn't do. But he could not tell them, had no way to explain it to them; how they should all have work, bread and beer. Probably, they would never see it in their lifetime, this change, even though it was coming into agriculture and every branch of life. No, there was no way to tell them and he kept his peace. No point in falling out with them.

He finished the work, noting that the lead he was using was poorer than it should have been. Perhaps he should find another supplier than Wheelers. They made good lead sheet, but he felt that they were selling him the dross. It would not do. Perhaps they resented his freedom, the way that Mr. Golding had bought him out of his contract, released him to be his own man. And perhaps they resented the way that the best leadwork contracts around fell into his hands, not theirs. After all, he was the best leadworker in the Hundred.

It was an irony really. While he dreamt of inventions and advances in mechanical means, his work was the most traditional craft around. More even than making lime; he had seen the new kilns, producing a mass of quicklime in one burn. He was a skilled repairman when it came down to it. Using the skills that had developed when they built the churches, or even before it. And if he had taken Mr. Golding's offer, he would have been involved with the new age of machines, and steam, and coal…

He stood up, stretching his back, looking over towards the village. His Sarah would be preparing a good meal; she had been on to him again about having a maid. And a cook. Did she think he was made of money? Marriage had not been as he had imagined it, a meeting of minds and mutual comfort, a quiet haven for retiring after a hard day. No, his Sarah was restless. She had been widowed young with two small boys and a piece of money that had bought them the cottage near Bergholt House. She liked to walk out with the ladies, pretend that she was one of the landowning class. But he wished that Sarah was more content with her lot and gave him a bit of peace. Maybe he would slip down to the pub later, sit in his corner of the settle and allow his thoughts to mellow until bedtime.

I shouldn't have married her, he thought time and again. But Patty will never be my wife, I know that an' all. And when Sarah came along looking for a husband with a bit of go to be a father to her boys, and with a bit of money to buy the cottage, it made sense, gave me a home of my own and a place in the village.

There were times when he felt he should give up his sketching with John, out for hours at a stretch. He thought Sarah might resent it if he were not working, not making money. But she liked to think that the Constables were her neighbours, as they were; that they would share time and interests together. Daft. They owned land and a great deal more; Mrs. Constable would no more share time with her than she would with her cook. But, like a foot in the door, Sarah welcomed John Constable into their home and had even given up a room, a studio where John could paint and Dunthorne could keep his sketches out of the children's hands. He smiled. Giving herself airs had brought a little benefit for him. And he looked forward to his next walk with John.

Ah, Patty. I'll never have her out of my mind, out of my heart. He had no way of sharing his joy and sang aloud at his work, that only brought down calls that he join the Church choir. And he a Chapel man. He would smile, turn away to conceal his grin, pure and undefiled joy of Patty, and dream of speaking to Mr. Constable, demanding her hand, claiming the right of joined hearts and judging it a fine thing that he might earn his place in the family. Until he thought of Mrs. Constable and drew back and knew that Patty must bend her will as home demanded. Occasionally he wept.

How long is it until we are together again? Only three days, our Tuesdays, in that private place where we can be man and woman. She's no shy maiden, that's for sure. And as we lie together, we talk of things that can never be and how we will carry on as we are. As long as nobody knows; and that's hard in a village like Bergholt.

She knew of an empty cottage, owned by her father, far from lane or road, a payment by a poor farmer for monies owed. She had told him where to find it, the hour of their meet, and he bent his way one Tuesday; the door was open and wandering in he found her in the kitchen putting flowers in a old jar which, without a word, she took up the stairs to a warm room set deep beneath the roof beams, walls plaster white and dusty. A bed remained, a tumble of bedclothes all clean and dry; he suspected her care. She looked at the bed and at him; he was touched and did not care to take advantage but laughed with embarrassment, of which she did not show an iota. She approached and ran her hands over him, lifting his clothes and feeling his muscles, arms and belly while he stood mesmerised and lost to her charms. He had known a few village girls, a tumble or two, maybe more but never such slow attention, more the thrusting as in a sty. He bent and kissed her neck, and gently teased her hair loose to fall about her shoulders, and she laid her hands upon his belt, his britches but he placed her hands on his shoulders and released his own britches, before lifting her apron, smock and kirtle free. She laid down in her slip only, watching as he shrugged free of his jerkin boots and all underthings, standing bare, before her eyes roamed around his legs. Had she ever seen a naked man? He wondered. He lifted her hand, the pleasure it gave; she said to him, how should a woman take in such a size? Then kneeling, she pulled off her slip that he might admire her body, full grown breasts smaller than some village beauties, and a soft belly.

He would come to her, but she held him off, a slow smile, taught him to touch and pleasure her. And so he learnt the ways of her body, what she liked and what excited her, so that she came when he had never known such a thing; no village girl this. He held still within her, until she incited movement and brought him to an early climax, flooding her and spilling upon their bed. She laughed, became housewife, wiping him and the spill as she kissed him. And told him that it was her first time, but that she had learned from the mares and stallions on the farms, from dogs and ducks, and new novels such as he had never read. And she liked it well; she had felt no pain and did not know why but maybe riding hard had broken her maidenhead.

And that became their haunt on Tuesday afternoons, about the hour of two – no message could pass between them so they found a simple way to let one know; a chalk strike on a post near Bergholt House told him nay or yay.

And then there was John; they would go out in the afternoon, after his day's work when John was looking for an escape from the dust and silence of his studio. John said the light was better later in the day. Lower, creating shadows that brought out the shape in things, shadows that were darker with rich colours. Dunthorne had always thought them black but now he saw the greens and blues, even reds on occasion. He remembered how he had been content to sit with John, watch him draw and splash a bit of colour on. Ask questions; sometimes there would be an answer, sometimes silence. And he would chew a stalk of grass, and watch the birds, the hawks and jays after the smaller birds, hear the anxious calls and conversations in the hedges. Fat pheasants waddling over the young crops; stupid birds. Swallows on the rising evening air, soaring and swooping to feed. And he would fall asleep in the late warm sunshine.

John was strange company, changeable in mood. Sometimes he would be as dark as a low cloud, almost wordless, struggling to finish a sketch but often tearing up the paper as he stared out into the distance, no words, grim. Dunthorne had learnt that there was nothing to be said; at first he had played the elder brother, a gentle chiding, suggesting setting work aside, walking or drinking, any distraction. But John stared him into silence, turned his back and, on one occasion, walked off into the distance, head down.

At other times, he was light gaiety, a song on his lips or a tuneless humming, inconsequential chatter over a dozen different subjects, and his work would be light, almost instantaneous, bright colours, challenging ideas, a magical land portrayed. They would talk, sharing a close knowledge of everything before them: birds, crops, animals, ways of ploughing, draining the land, building a lighter, constructing a mill. And he would listen to Dunthorne, answer questions, lightly suggest games, puzzles, random ideas so foreign that Dunthorne marvelled at John's knowledge. John told him about the different clouds, what each one meant, what weather was coming sooner or later. Sometimes, they would seek shelter under a stack or hedge when a squall came rolling up the valley, dark shadows chasing over the fields and a rising cold breeze. John would laugh, having seen it coming, and tell him to wait five or ten minutes. And it would be gone, rolling over to Nayland or Mistley. They would shake the rain off their coats and stride out into the fields again. On occasion they met a man working, hedging or ploughing, and they would exchange words, a few minutes distraction. Once or twice they had to leave a pasture in haste, herded by inquisitive young bullocks.

Occasionally, there was a sternness of being, a studied approach to a painting that included small sketches, his pencil placed precisely upon the paper, a few marks that were always right. He would teach; Dunthorne noted the change in voice. This was the working painter, no time for frivolity or chatter but concentration on observation and detail, reading the view like the study of a serious painting, drawing from it what was necessary to suggest a statement, a considered arrangement with a message.

One day he found himself restless, leaning over John's shoulder, watching every stroke of the pencil, brushmark and splat of colour. He wondered why John chose a particular colour; it wasn't the colour he could see, too bright, not right. Until John told him and explained how the colours were combined, how a painting could never be reality but was a like a poem, a statement about what they were looking at.

'But John, all that Truth and Reality. I don't understand.'

'The image on the paper; it's not the land in front of you, is it? It's paper and pigment, a figment drawn from your imagination.'

'But reality; you tell me you paint reality. And that colour there, out there, is real, isn't it?'

'And you think that I could reproduce that colour? And how many colours are there in 'that' colour? Your eye selects what it wants to see, to focus on. And so does my painting, focus on what I select.'

'But the colours?'

'I told you; there are more colours than you can see. And my colours have to be harmonious, to work together.'

Since that time, Dunthorne had carried his own sketchbook, a present from John, and his own pencil and brush, borrowing colours as he needed them. John had let him be, not interfering unless invited but pointing out the views, the surprises and the way of seeing something so well known, so accepted without question, that it became something new, different, fresh.

They would work down at the mill at Flatford on many occasions. It was a good place to be when the weather was not fair: too wet or windy or cold. John loved the lock, drawing sluice gear and the rotting boarding. Dunthorne liked the buildings and the machinery. He would sit inside the mill watching the stones turning, the gears locking mechanically true as they followed the turning of the cogs. He could hear the river sloshing in the paddle and the shaft turning overhead, a continuous easy groaning from a wonderful constant source of energy that he never failed to admire, to exult in. Now and then, Mr. Constable would come in from the counting-house next door and stand with him, talking of the gear, how damp affected the mill, where he would sell the flour. And Dunthorne would go silent, enjoying the conversation but reminded of an alternative life that he had not taken up. One day, a fresh thought arose: would he, Dunthorne, have taken the place that was John's and released the young man for a life of a painter? It had not occurred to him before. And if it had, would he have made a different decision? Well, it was too late now, too late to throw up his business. There was a pride in his work, his own business. He was not one to go back on his decisions, to rock the boat.

His wife knew of his debt to Golding Constable but did wonder why he spent so much time in the company of young John Constable. It was all very well, this sketching and walking about the country, but why did he not spend more time with her, if he was not working? He had answered her questions and knew that she would not understand. She had everything she needed, he made sure of it, and he spent enough time with her and the company of her family, a mass of brothers and sisters and cousins; like a rabbit warren all living in a tight group of cottages. He did not come from a large family; his mother had died when he was very young and she had come from outside the village. His father had been an only child, grandparents long since dead. He had to leave the village just to get away from his wife's family.

Sometimes he would go across the road and prevail upon the housewife at the Farmhouse and draw the great fireplace, half a tree alight beneath a kettle. And look up to find the smoke-hole that had served before the chimney-breast was even built. Or sketch the solar staircase, one of the oldest in the country they said.

Willy Lott's House. He had been there; it was close enough and John had sketched it often. It sat on the edge of the millpool, a stone's throw away, fading limewash, peeling paintwork, a sunken ridge. John said that it had been there long before the present mill building. An old farmer lived there.

But he could never go close. Not after he had walked past one evening as light was failing.

Swallows were wheeling overhead through the low sunshine, a rich harvest of flies shared with bats that emerged from the eaves of the houses and the mill. The ground was warm from the day, felt through the soles of his boots. Odd calls and shouts resounded in the still air. And there was the smell of straw from the fields, chaff from the mill, and the sharper whiff of horse droppings. John was away the other side of the mill with his beloved lock; recording aged gates or chatting with any lighterman who would tie up for the evening below the bridge.

After, he was not sure of his own eyes or his memory. He had glanced into Willy Lott's House as he walked past and seen it for but a moment; the staring face of a young woman dressed in rags, her face drawn with horror, crying out without sound and tearing at the window. Two paces on, rigid with anticipation, he had stopped, snorted in disbelief and turned back. Looked through the window. A storeroom, barrels and boxes piled high, no room for a figure within the window. Nobody there, and the door closed.

Walking up the hill, he was shaken against his own common sense. There was no logic to it. After all, ghosts didn't exist, did they? But he felt a shade hanging over him. He asked John about Willy Lott's House.

'Willy Lott? He lives there alone. Sad really. He's a bachelor, will never marry I think. Too much alone. Farms Gibeon's, the land behind that runs down to the river.'

‘Nobody stays with him?’

‘I shouldn’t think so, I should be surprised. It is hard to have a conversation with him you know. He becomes silent, looking at the ground. Takes the first excuse to be away. Sad really.’

‘And no maid?’

‘Oh no. Who would want to work there with him? I mean, I imagine that he is not a violent man, but… you know, it would not be easy. And I doubt that he has the means. Why the interest?’

‘I was walking by. That’s all. Occurred to me I’d never seen him except at a distance.’

Dunthorne tried to put the image from his mind and did not mention it to anyone, not even his wife. But he could not forget it. Who was the woman?

10

AUGUST 1798

He lifted his eyes from the papers and rubbed them. Man wasn't made to spend all day looking at figures. He called his clerk and asked him to check the list again. His clerk looked at him; he had checked them before putting them on the desk. He said nothing and took them away.

Golding sat back. How life had changed. Once a tradesman, he had been a younger son obliged to leave home and seek his living elsewhere. But he had been lucky. The inheritance from Uncle Abram had bequeathed him the Mill and some trade, as well as connections with the local farms and landowners. He had worked hard and built up the business and more connections. More successful now than his elder brother in Bures, who had inherited the family business, years ago just after John's birth.

And what did he get for it, he pondered? A life of figures. When he had wanted to be a miller. The time for that had passed; he sighed as he looked down at his waist, an easy spread that came from a life of sitting at a desk, and the middling type life that his wife Ann pursued. A handsome house, good meals, parties, visiting, frolics… Well, at sixty-one years of age, aren't I allowed some relaxation?

It always brought on thoughts of his men and the villagers. Henry Crush, his miller, would be busy the other side of the wall, checking grain delivered, the quality of the flour, and worrying about the state of the millstones now that French stone was hard to come by. Odd name, Crush… perhaps his family had always been millers; never asked him. A good man, worth encouraging… a box at Christmas at the very least… must hang onto him in spite of the poor supply of grain. And the men; I don't want to lose men to see them picked up for the press gang.

Ah. The war. It didn't affect us much until you considered that damned Income Tax that Pitt introduced to pay for it. Pushed up prices and the poor suffered, as usual. There have been bad harvests and meanwhile the daughters are adopting expensive habits, dresses and romantic novels. I will have to reduce their allowances. And as for Nancy and her riding…

And there's the Vagrant Act, the Government's excessive attempt to put crews in fighting ships. I'll have to be careful about my own men on *The Telegraph*… particularly sailing into the Port of London. Must remember to have a word with the Captain, see whether there is a way of keeping them onboard. I'll surely lose them if they go ashore after the fleshpots and the press gangs, whether it's Queenhithe or Puddle Dock. Time they completed larger docks. It don't pay to have ships waiting to unload, and it increase the risk of losing crew. Thank God my cargoes don't go bad, as long as they give the grain some air.

And there has been no threat to the sea lanes down to the London River. Not that I have heard; French ships haven't been seen in the North Sea. No losses reported apart from the usual ones, wrecking on the Gunfleet and Barrow Sands, or storms blowing them ashore. Occasionally, there's an unexpected loss requiring a payout from the insurers. That makes me angry, the loss of good seamen and the greed of it, all for a large insurance payout; it's a scandal. Not surprising really, the huge investments in canals. Why, my banker was trying to persuade me to place some money there. I'll stick with my business; better to invest in new millstones and repairs to the paddles.

London; they'll be wanting our grain. There have been riots at the price of bread. I read of loaves thrown at the King and Queen. Perhaps it would be better if John didn't spend too much time with his artistic friends in London. For a while.

Ah, John.

He couldn't help it; old habits died hard. He stood up, stretched his back and went outside. A bit of cloud coming upriver, the weather was on the change. He hoped they wouldn't suffer the equinoxal floods like the ones that had carried bridges away on the Severn last year. The sun was warm and he leaned on the wall, looking down at the outflow from the wheels. Strong. Too strong? Should he bring Mr. Crush's attention to it? Ducks gathered around the mill house, barging for position. Mrs. Crush came out, a basket of crumbs; for a moment, seeing the master, she paused and dropped a brief curtsy before sprinkling bread upon the water. She looked worn; they had lost a child in the river two years before, a little girl dragged down in the flow from the mill.

He turned and looked into the open mill door. The noise and dust was normal, welcome; he breathed it in with satisfaction. A man saw him, tugged his forelock and continued tying up a sack. It was hard to see the shortfall in wheat from the poor harvest; it was more apparent in those damned figures. Still, prices were up and trade was good on the river and he was building lighters at the yard, some for other owners elsewhere. The Stour was his, all the trade that moved from Cattawade to Sudbury. And it was no great labour being a Commissioner of the Stour. Some might say that he had it too good. Well, he had earned it. Two watermills and a windmill near home at Pitts. And he had ended up a farmer in a small way, interested in the recent improvements, particularly from a man called Robert Bakewell who had recently died and left a fund of useful knowledge for improvements in harvesting and farming income. Improvements like machinery and crop rotation; they weren't popular with some farmers and there had been violence, destruction of threshers and drills, but how could man stand in the way of progress?

He strolled round the corner towards the boatyard. The old farmhouse, on the other side of the road, looked in poor condition. He was glad that it had not been included in the bequest; he should have been obliged to live in it and the house in the village was much better. Modern. Comfortable rather than that damp old timber house. Of course, they had to live in the Mill House when they first came, back in 1764. But he had been the miller then. How hard life had seemed, the work in the mill while presenting himself to the local farmers and landowners, building up connections, increasing trade. Time that old farmhouse had a coat of limewash.

Past the old granary and he paused at the boatyard. A lighter lay in the dry dock; the men were completing the top strakes, bending timbers to shape. They didn't notice him and he stood silent, partly behind an oak to observe them. It was another skill that he wished he had been able to practice. He had picked up as much as he could from the men but knew that he couldn't tell if the construction was poor. Until it was on the river and leaked or cracked. He determined to question his captain about ship construction and make notes in his chapbook.

He turned and walked back to the Mill. And the problem of his successor came back to him again.

Young Golding. Like a millstone round my neck, he thought, with his expensive tastes and reckless behaviour… and yet he will throw another of his fits and his mother will be gushing to care for him, refuse him nothing… and what did he want to do? For God's sakes. Shoot things: birds, animals, weathervanes… an expensive habit and he seems to need a new fowling-piece every other year… I have no idea what will become of him.

John. Now twenty years old; no, twenty-two… how the years do pass. Does he not realise that as oldest responsible son he has a duty to support the family business? Dammit, life depends upon a man doing his duty, don't it? As his grandfather and great-grandfather passed down their businesses to their eldest, so should I. And yet his mother will get wild ideas to improve him… she was in favour of contacting a lawyer in Ipswich. I had to convince her.

'My dear, you must recall his years at school. He never flourished, did he? Always slow with his exercises, and his numbers remain abysmal. Why, in the counting-house the clerk must always check, I should say, rewrite his entries.'

'But Mr. Constable, must he remain a merchant? He should be the equal of the squires, who lord it over us as though they own us.'

'My dear, I am a merchant and I am happy with my lot. And though you see "the squires lording it over us", as you say, we own our land, we have our own men and a good deal more. John is a capable mill man, better at reading the skies than many a miller and he would be a great benefit to the business. As you know—'

'My dear Mr. Constable, you cannot be thinking that John should remain a miller? Have we not strived to give our children a better education and introduce them to a better life?'

As though her husband is a humble miller… not a landowner, the owner of three mills, a ship, loading wharfs at Mistley, a lighterage business, and… but not as she would have it. A middling type she says we must be. No need to work… but employ others and be there for tea parties and other delights.

What can I say? There is no sense in these discussions; Mrs. Constable sets aside all practicalities for the sake of appearance.

And John; he tries; I'll give him that consideration. He is a good miller and he knows it… up at Pitts he is the best man for reading the clouds, telling the weather, and thorough with his grinding… he looks after the stones and all the village knows it… his reputation goes before him. As a miller. What does he want a painting life for? Is it not possible to spend the better part of days working the business and do his sketches at other hours? But he tells me that sketches are not the thing; it must be great paintings as I have never seen. Not even at the grand houses around.

He shook his head, as though to fend off thoughts that crowded his mind like a swarm of stormflies.

As he wandered back to the Mill, a door banged and John Dunthorne came out of the old granary onto the lane before him, his hands full of tools and lengths of lead. He stopped abruptly. A brief bow.

'Mr. Constable. A fine morning, sir.'

'Dunthorne, a good morning to you. May I ask, have you…' He paused. He really couldn't ask him when he had last seen John. Why John wasn't free to be working at the Mill as he should. He coughed.

'Er… have you any work to complete for me?'

Dunthorne smiled, an unsure smile. 'No, sir. I finished that last window at Pitts last week. And there is a cill that I have just completed here.'

'Good. That is good. You are most prompt; I am grateful. Could you cast your eye over the overflow in the dry dock? I fear that they are sometimes careless when flooding and taking lighters out and damage the top of it.'

'I'll take a look now, sir, while I am down here.' He gave a nod, half a bow, and went down the lane. Golding watched him go.

He didn't tug his forelock to me, he thought. But that is correct nowadays, is it not? Dunthorne is his own master, deserving of respect. Yes, that is how it should be.

But, if he was employed by me, would he tug his forelock? I suppose it would depend upon his job, his importance… and I would have him in my employ if I could; he is a most capable man, well organised, writing and reading skills and many others… and perhaps, he would delay my concern for a successor, play the part of a family member. Could he… I wonder… could he have married Patty? No, I can't see Mrs. Constable agreeing with that; marry a tradesman, she would say, Good Grief what are you thinking of I don't know and I try to introduce them around show them how to live. Good Gracious marry a tradesman! Oh what a pity; Patty was quite taken with him, once. But I am glad I set him up in his own business… he is useful to have at hand.

It is a pity that Ann does not share my liking for the man; I know, there have been the odd incidents and she believes he behaves above his place in society. Rubbish. He is his own man with his own business and a skilled man at that. But I cannot shift her opinion which is more like a barnacle on a ship's bottom.

Oh well. What can I do? I must wait, must I not, for John to wake up to his responsibilities. I do not doubt that he will, in time. Perhaps when he meets a young woman…

Back in the office, his clerk was waiting for him, looking worried.

'Oh, sir. Please, sir. There has been a note from Mistley. That farmer, the one that caused the trouble last week, he is again… I mean sir, he has done it again.'

'What has he done, if you please?'

'Dumped his ballast on your wharf. He was told. He has no right. But he—'

'Thank you, Justin. I shall attend to it.' He went back into his room. The harvest was almost all in; a few cartloads of grain to come from farmers either still flailing… the old-fashioned ones… or caught out by storms, those who did not employ enough men to reap the wheat while it was dry. There were always a few, some who would bring in grain so damp that he would be bound to refuse it, good for nothing but animal feed. It was a shame; he did not like to do to it, not to his neighbours, and had even purchased poor grain and set it aside in the past for feeding his own animals. A charitable deed, that rankled with the book-keeping. Offended his clerk to whom he preached good business.

But it hadn't been a really bad harvest; he was glad of that. With trade so poor with the Continent, it was as well London would be glad of the flour. And they would pay the price.

He took to returning home earlier than usual to look over the garden behind the house, discuss what had done well that summer with the gardener and what might be planted for next year.

Ann, Mrs. Constable, had prevailed on him to accompany her and the girls to Tendring Hall for tea. What a palaver; the girls had dressed in light floating gowns to be met by a fresh shower when they arrived, hurried into the Hall by servants with umbrellas. Golding had wanted to stay outside, survey the Hall and park, enjoy the air and see the animals. He had read that deer were a better park animal, smaller than beef cattle, and enhanced the view; cattle loomed too large but were more profitable.

But his hosts had invited him indoors where he had spent an agonising two hours listening to talk of dancing, dress and popular fashions, all matters that bored him. And sipping tea; he would have preferred ale. He watched his daughters; Patty and Mary were quiet, perhaps awed by the surroundings but making light conversation. Nancy, as usual, was too strong, almost arrogant, quizzing the young men on fowling-pieces and horses, happy to argue the finer merits of one type against another.

Golding sighed to himself; she will never find herself a husband, not like that. Any sensible man would look elsewhere rather than live a life of continual challenge. The younger two? There was every chance that they might attract husbands and then there would be a great gathering of dowries… it didn't bear thinking of. At least young Golding was not with them; they would be spending their time deflecting his barbs and watching his behaviour.

Once home, he retreated to his study. He had to come to a decision: what to do about John. He felt unhappy, pushed to a decision that should never have fallen to him.

Mrs. Constable had continued with her demands; John must become a gentleman, rise above the merchant types and enter a profession. The law would be the most suitable. Possibly the Church, though she did not really favour this alternative. The Rector was not a nice man and the thought that John would be mixing with his sort was not pleasant. No, he must go into the law and she was sure that chambers in Ipswich could be persuaded to take him in. Show him the ropes and introduce him to the right sort of person. What nonsense!

In his study, he gazed out of the window. What comfort I have assembled, he thought. Look at this house, the parts of it, the aspect and land… it must be the envy of many. Why could John not want it all? For goodness' sake, what did I have at John's age? Was I married? I don't recall but I had no business of my own, no wealth or practice that I could fall back on; I worked for my Father with no expectation of inheriting; my elder brother went before me. Thank God for the inheritance from my Uncle. I must lay Golding aside, though he is the oldest, and this will be John's house in time.

I wonder.

If John attends a School of Art, and there is nowhere nearby, he would be removed from his mother… removed from her desire to enter him into a profession in which he could never be happy or successful… would fail, I am sure of it, become a disgrace… well, removed from here, he will spend no time with Dunthorne. Good man Dunthorne but I am sure he does not need to be spending time with John when he has much work to do. And Mrs. Constable will have less concern for the friendship… and he may even move in such exalted circles, patrons and such like, Sir George Beaumont at Dedham, others that he has met… his mother will be envious of him, proud and envious in turn.

Unless, God forbid, he is taken up by a press gang… pressed for this accursed war… I wonder; how do young gentlemen, particularly those with too much time on their hands, evade the press gangs?

At a remove from an art school as he is now, he will continue to think it the most marvellous place, full of dreams and accomplishments. But when he sees the life of an artist, corrupted no doubt by the demands of society, with little reward and a life of hardship, the dissolute life of Londoners, he will have the truth blind him with common sense… and after all that, surely, he will come to see reason, come to a maturity… and realise his responsibilities. To be here, where he belongs, and to return to the life that he loves… he loves it, anyone can see… and take my place, here in this house, in the mill. He will be cared for; there are always men for that… the bailiff, my clerk, others. Good men.

Yes… yes, it is the way to manage this problem. I am sure of it. I must speak with him, enquire as to his aspirations. They may match my own.

The following morning, as they sat at breakfast, Golding said to John, 'There is a matter that I wish to discuss with you; please to attend on me at the mill at midday.'

John glanced at his mother and nodded. Ann Constable looked up, a sharp question on her tongue, but seeing her husband's expression bit it back. Without further explanation and ignoring his wife's unspoken questions, Golding departed for work.

Midday passed, the bells of Dedham Church sounding down the valley. Golding Constable rose and looked out of the window onto the front of the mill. The sun shone warm on the red brickwork and an occasional blast of flour emerged from the open door with the sweet smell of fresh grinding. A crowd of squabbling birds had gathered, picking at the flour and chaff on the ground. The water in the millpool was calm, hardly broken by the outflow from the mill, a subdued stream reflecting the dry past week. Away over the water, Willy Lott's House looked as lifeless as usual, the limewash faded, the old ridge sunken, not even a trickle of smoke from the great chimney. He strolled to the corner of the mill. No traffic in the lane, no sign of any person. He sighed, and returned to his desk.

Ten minutes later, there was a commotion in the outer office; he could hear the excitable voice of his son, the low murmur of his clerk, a pause and a tentative knock on his door.

'Father, I do beg your pardon; I know, I am at least ten minutes past the hour. And I had intended indeed,… but the walk down, an exceptional morning and I looked over to Dedham, the tower glowed… just glowed in the sun… I had to stop, make a few notes… sketches of course… can I show you? A later painting in my studio… it serves very well and I'm glad to have taken the air, of course, and…' He faded as he noticed his father's closed look.

A blackbird called, sharp outside the window; John whipped round and settled into a gaze of rapture at the sky, the sun, the warm brick of the mill…

'Sit; yes there. Now tell me,' said Golding Constable. 'Please if you may, tell me what your aspirations are. For the next ten years, if you would be so kind.'

John gazed at him; he felt like a rabbit caught in the stare of a fox. He assembled a few thoughts. I must convince him of my serious artistic intentions… and thank him that I have not been driven to serve him, not all the time… and say that of course I will be happy to work for him in some fashion but he must know, must see that I am not suited to the work; no, not at all. Oh God's teeth.

'Well, Father, of course I wish to continue my artistic studies, you know, and it is thanks to your generosity, I am aware, very grateful. I would be happy to help you more, though you know, my figures do not bear scrutiny, and… and—'

'You speak of continuing your artistic studies; I assume, though I know little of the matter, that you refer to your visits to Mr. Smith in London and Beaumont in Dedham and… and your sketches. But I do not see paintings, not paintings like the ones that I see when I visit Tendring, or Old Hall, or any other great house.'

'No sir, that is correct. I have tried, a few poor examples, but I am learning, trying to find my own way, because it is not the Truth to copy the great paintings, nor to emulate the styles of their painters. Except, of course, in exercise. I need to express what I know, what I love, the country here and all it means to me.' He gasped as he ceased; he had never spoken of such things to anybody apart from Dunthorne, who would chaff him and ask him why he didn't paint with moss and rotten timber and cow droppings.

Golding blinked; what does this mean, he wondered? Express what you know? Do I express what I know? It is more a question of practice, is it not? I note that his aspirations do not include working with me, working for the family business… oh well. I must move forward, achieve some sort of deliberation; I cannot continue as at present, waiting for a decision from John… it is not going to come, is it? He is caught between a sense of family duty and this artistic urge that I do not understand… and yet… yet, he has pursued it since he was breeched and I cannot frustrate his natural instincts. He is no businessman, which is for sure.

In a gentler voice, he asked, 'In what way, may I ask, in what manner might you proceed with your artistic studies? To put them onto a more serious standing?'

John stared at him; he had never thought that his father might have considered his future in painting. Was this some sort of trap, well meant but leading me to a life of duty and… if I were to say that I would study half the week, and work here the other half… or should that be that I would help at the busy times of year, harvest and thereabouts, and that the winter might be spent painting? Would that satisfy him? And me? Oh, I am considering myself only. He ages and carries the burden of the business on his shoulders… no son to stand by his side, nobody to step into his shoes should he fall ill. It is not fair. I have a good life, I must play my part, bear my load.

'Father, I am aware, too aware, that I have not been a faithful son, not helped you as I should while living a good life supported by your great generosity. And I am not a child any more, have lived long beyond achieving my maturity. Father, I believe that I should work with you to the best of my abilities. You must judge in what way I can help you.'

Good God, thought Golding. What is this? Does he mean it? I never thought to hear such an avowal; he has surprised me… and laid the whole problem in my hands. Well, well. What would he say if I accepted his offer? I suspect I would see the lights go out in his eyes; the "merry miller" as they call him in the village would be merry no longer.

'You mother, as you know, would have you adopt a profession; not the Army, thank God. I could not have raised the price of a commission in a respectable regiment. I have not persuaded her but I do not believe that the Law would suit you at all. I foresee calamity there. And the Church; I suppose you could become some sort of curate in a far-flung parish, with time to sketch as you will. But how you would support yourself and a wife in a seemly fashion I cannot imagine. Have you considered the Church?'

'No, Father. That is to say… of course, Mother mentioned it but I could not, in faith, consider it. If Mr. Rhudde is the picture of the Church, it does not attract… I mean… I cannot see myself in such an exalted and learned position.'

Golding smiled; he sympathised with his son's instincts. Mr. Rhudde was not an easy man; any conversation was always brief and he left the impression that he was intended for a higher position. The parish knew him as a devil driver; his sermons flayed the congregation.

'So… to repeat. How may you continue in your artistic studies?'

John looked down; he had had ideas and talked of such matters in London with other young artists, the few that he had met. He wasn't sure whether he could give a well-judged answer. And a comment from Beaumont came into his head.

'Father, I believe that it is to ask much, perhaps too much, and I don't know—'

'But nor do I know, unless you tell me.'

Oh well, thought John. In for a penny, in for a pound. He can always refuse me.

'Father, I believe that the place to go is the Royal Academy Schools. There, you can receive an education about the history and practice of art and pursue one's own painting with painters, I mean well-known painters, known throughout all serious circles, fashionable and—'

'And this would help you advance in a proper manner?'

'Yes, Father. I have met young men who study there and spoken with others. They all say that that is the place upon which to base own's business. The painting business.'

'I'm glad to hear you speak of business. May you expect to sell paintings, to make a living from your work? That is my understanding of business.'

'Well, it would take some time to become an artist, in the fullest sense. But then one would—'

'Then? And how long is "some time"?'

'I'm not sure, Father. I have not the experience… I don't know.'

'I don't know, then, how long I should support you.'

'Support me?' John was dazed.

'You must educate me; I am only a humble miller. Would you give me a picture of the painting business to which you refer? What do they paint, what is bought and sold, how do they place themselves in the marketplace? What are the capital costs, depreciation and overheads? Do the products gain in value? What is the proportion of sales in the product?'

John stared at his Father; is he hazing me or are there some aspects of business that I do not understand? he wondered. It would be hardly surprising; I never get the idea of it when the bailiff spends some hours trying to explain it to me… how money is made and lost… the costs of purchase, production and sales… and tells me it is all as clear as daylight in the figures before me… and it is all Greek to me. Oh God, as bad as the Greek that my tutor at Lavenham tried to bully into me. But come; the painters I have met, they do not talk of "product" and "depreciation"… they sell what they can and I know it is only a few of what they paint… I have seen the other canvases stacked in their studios, awaiting… God knows.

'Father, it is not the way of it at all. One must paint many pictures to sell a few and fashions change; so that other paintings may sell in a few years time. If your name is high, fashionable and esteemed, many of your paintings will sell; it is in the nature of things. But one must attain those heights.'

'And what paintings are fashionable? What paintings may be more likely to achieve a good market?'

'At present, Father?'

'Yes, yes, at present, my boy.' Golding was abrupt. What nonsense John talked; the very idea, painting a lot of paintings that do not sell and selling only a small part of your product… why, that would be like selling only a quarter of the mill flour and how would I pay the overheads, the men, purchase of wheat and so on? What sort of a business is it that has no idea of the turnover and the profits?

There was a knock at the door; his clerk begged a few minutes of his time, if he would be so good. A matter had arisen, not serious but demanding Mr. Constable's attention. Leaving the business to be discussed, John wandered outside raising his face to the sun, breathing in the fresh air and casting off the anxieties of the office; he smelt the sweetness of the flour dust, a reminder of Pitt's, and the rank smell of the millpool. He looked into the mill; the miller was binding sacks of flour and turned to him with a greeting.

'Master John, it is a good while since I saw you. Are you here for milling?'

'No, Amos, my father wished to speak with me. But how go things here?'

'It's that damned war, these Frenchies getting beyond themselves. Look at these stones; we have been buying them in France this last century and now we have to mend and make do. It is a crying shame.'

'And does the war have other effects?'

'Not that I know of, Master. Apart from the price of everything... disgraceful. It was not a good harvest and your father gets a good price in London for both grain and flour. He is even selling on coal there; have you not seen the collier brigs at Mistley? And of course he is selling upriver at Sudbury, both grain and coal. We don't do too badly here but who knows what will happen if them Frenchies invade? I did hear from my nephew that they have been building castles around the coast. So there must be some truth in it.'

'Castles?'

'Yeah, bloody great round castles, like the olden time ones. Mind you, I don't know what the Frenchies would do with our flour; Master said that they don't like our flour and all their bread looks funny. They must have a different flour, but I don't see how that is, considering that flour is only grain ground fine. But how are you doing, sir? Do you work at Pitts like you used to?'

John started to speak but caught sight of his father at the door and left the miller with a nod.

Back in the office, Golding settled at his desk again. 'It was a difficult matter; one of our farmers who brings in grain had a fall; he is in a bad way and needs help. These matters will not broach delay; our business must have consideration for all our farmers. Where would we be without our farmers, our grain?'

'What is to be done, Father? Would you like me to—'

'It is taken care of. Now, where were we?'

'I believe you were interested in the fashion of paintings.'

'Yes indeed. How would you make a living as a painter?'

'At this time, Father, I cannot say. I have not been to the Art School nor attempted to—'

'Then tell me; what paintings do you see that may have been sold in the last year or so?'

'Well, sir, many history paintings. The War has a great effect and great victories are always popular. A recent history, if you see what I mean.'

'And can you paint these history paintings?'

'No, sir. I do not have the experience or the skills. But things will change.'

'Change, John? It is painting, is it not? There will always be portraits, and… and… Oh, I don't know what.'

'Much painting is old-fashioned—'

'A young man's words; I hear them often. Throw over what is good because it is old-fashioned!'

John was silent. He felt confused, unable to answer his father's assertions, and at the same time, convinced that he was pursuing the right path for his life. No, he would not be beaten to being directed to some sort of false situation, to painting "fashionable paintings"; there would always be painting and, in time, his kind of paintings would become popular, would sell. It was a matter of being strong. Father will not support me if I am not strong.

Golding coughed and looked grave. 'I have been thinking of your future, perhaps more than you. But I need to know how serious, how committed are your ambitions in painting.'

'Father, I have lived and sketched this valley since I was a boy. I cannot see another way of living; no, that is not true and an insult to you, sir. But I cannot see one that has as much meaning or truth as the one that I have pursued. Of course, I have not sold paintings; have not tried to sell, judged that they were not good and required improvement. But painters I have visited in London do better.'

'So, London is the place, is it?'

'It would seem so, Father. Unless it is the Grand Tour that our titled neighbours take, returning with such marvels by no means modern but truly great.'

'London. I have concerns that you may be persuaded into a dissolute life, money wasted on drink and gambling and, above all, caught and pressed into the Navy. Or aboard some deep sea Indiaman.'

'But Father, how could that be? I should not wish to be away from here for too long. This place, this valley, it is my soul, the source of all my painting. In future years, I may wish to be further afield but for the present… and I would wish to be a help to you…'

There was a silence. Golding reflected that this was not what he had expected; he had thought, beyond doubt, that John, a young man, would wish to be gone from here… living a good life in London with his painting friends, Smith and others… and become subjected to a violent sustained dose of the City that would turn his stomach, rebel against the London painting life and make him long to be back here with us… in the mill by his side.

And now, he speaks of returning often. And yet, would I not wish it in all truth? And will his mother not be glad to see him? I have gone too far with him today and I would not wish to frustrate his leanings… God, I feel tired, aged beyond my years; why is it that my sons leave me like this? Perhaps the young one will rise to the task? The girls… no, that is not possible.

'Very well, John. You must apply to the Royal Academy for a pupillage or whatever; of course, they may not want you when they see your… sketches.' A pause as Golding looked hard into his son's face. 'Well, we shall make arrangements for accommodation at your aunt's house and you may go by sea, if you wish; I shall speak to the Captain, ensure that there is space for all your belongings. Now leave me; I have many things to attend to. Good day.'

'Good day, sir, and thank you.'

11

AUGUST 1799

Some days no drawing was done, not the briefest sketch, and they would wander back to the village. Sometimes not even talking as though their own affairs weighed so heavily that they dislodged all sketching, painting and company. They would separate in front of Bergholt House with a brief farewell, no promises for the next day or any other.

Dunthorne was never clear as to why it happened and had been sure that many fine views had presented themselves. Only to be passed by as though they were blinded by their own thoughts. Some days, it was true, they had dallied in the pub too long and any effort for working had dissolved into happy reminiscences or tall tales; he would ask John what London looked like, smelt like, tasted like, and John would fall back on stories that he had been told; it seemed his knowledge of London was not great but his imagination made up for it. And Dunthorne pressed him about the Royal Academy; what he was learning, what the other artists were like, how was life now? But John said little; he did not enjoy being away for long, did not spend time with the other students, who loved gaming and cock fights. He was working hard on drawings and a painting but not the things that he did when here; he was obliged, exercises and so forth. He was sure that he would learn much in time.

Some days, John would appear to sink into a quiet state from which Dunthorne could not lift him, morose, uncommunicative, occasionally plaintive.

And on other days the weather would close in, dark clouds rolling in from the east, cold blasts of hail as they cowered beneath a hedge or in a field shelter, sharing it with horse or cattle. But on those occasions, John would become ecstatic, dragging Dunthorne out to see the clouds. He would stand, arms wide, staring up into the heavens, face running with rain, his old coat dark with wet, a grin that defied the darkness.

From time to time, they would fall in with a shepherd or a horseman and talk farm talk, the way of the beasts, how the harvest had gone, the state of the gear, friends in common. Dunthorne was always surprised at John's knowledge: who owned the land, what the crops were and how they fared, the type of harness on a horse, the design of cultivators and ploughs, timber mouldboards or the Dutch iron ploughshares. And John's readiness to challenge the men on their gear, point out weaknesses, discuss links and straps, admire and criticise. Dunthorne was sensitive to his words, sometimes worried that John had insulted some good ol' boy, criticised his gear when he might know no better; but there were few occasions that a man took offence and the talk generally ended in good cheer, farewells, looking forward to meeting again.

Late August. The week had been stormy, showers sweeping over the valley interrupting a late harvest, men sent home at all hours and sheaves wet after a dry cut. The land was hard to work and the mill ran low on wheat. Mr. Constable had expressed his concerns at breakfast, concerns for the business and for the village men who would be short of money and bring poverty into their homes.

John and Dunthorne settled one afternoon in a high bank; a small field surrounded by hedges, only partially harvested, a stand of wheat in the centre surrounded by stooks. Bold wandered into the field, sniffing the rabbit runnels in the hedges.

'It's interesting,' said John.

'How so?' Dunthorne was tired, ready to go home. He couldn't bring himself to think and keep up with John's enthusiasm. Why, where does he find such energy, he thought, such keenness? I'll be glad to be home to hot food, wife and warmth… enough of this wandering the fields, sitting in wet hedges, wet clothes and a wet dog for company. John is the true artist, is he not? Such dedication and earnestness that sets aside creature comforts and would have him carolling the virtues of a thunderstorm or full moon, or… whatever, while honest folks would be tucked up in their beds… here he goes again.

'Look at the shapes, the shadows, the contrast with the hedges behind. And do you see it? The shape of the standing wheat; not unlike a grand piano. How about it?'

John was working fast, drawing to emphasise the shapes, overlapping and interlinked. His pastel flew over the paper. A discarded start; he tore off the top sheet of his home-made pad and started again. Shadows as shapes, stooks as sculpture, a background of wheat and stubble.

Dunthorne pulled out his book, glanced over at John's sketch and wondered at his speed. How do he see it? The simplifications in creating a pattern; he tried to think of the shape of a grand piano. Couldn't say he had ever taken much notice of one when visiting the grand houses for repairs to roofs and windows. Probably hadn't ever seen one, come to that. An odd shape for any instrument, if it was like what John said; not at all like any in the village band. Though perhaps like a giant harp laid on its side. He sighed and started to make a few marks, through the drips running down his paper from the ferns that crowded his arms. And glanced over again; how was it, dammit, how was it that John's paper was dry?

There was a clinking in the lane. A four-wheeled hay wain rolled down into the field, a pair of Suffolks and a team of men. They looked over; a few nodded, a silent acknowledgement, and set to loading the sheaves, chatting to each other while they moved over the field with a gentle but inexorable pace leaving a clean carpet of stubble. Behind them, three men waded into the last of the standing wheat in line, a synchronised sweep of scythes.

Dunthorne felt John moving beside him and looked at him. He couldn't repress a bark of laughter; John was furious, glaring and mouthing words. An unusual mood, thought Dunthorne; never seen him like this.

'What? All ruined. Hoy! And it was so interesting, don't you think, like a room in some great house? And now ruined! Hoy!'

One of the men came over, stood below looking up. He looked confused, a quick nod to Dunthorne and stared at John.

'Do you have to?' said John. 'I mean must you harvest at this moment?'

'Well, sir, that's what we be told to do and that's what we be doing. Master never said to hold up or nothing.' The man stood, hands on hips, and shrugged.

'But, I mean, can't you do that bit over there? While I finish this drawing?'

'We…el, it's been a bad week, sir, not a whole day's work through the whole week, an' we must be getting it in while we can. It's a late harvest, you know.'

'Thanks, Tom, you be getting on.' Dunthorne raised his

hand as John started to speak. 'You can't be keeping them from their work, John. It's not a good week for money, their earnings will be well down.'

'Oh, what a pity, what a pity. The pattern of it; did you see it? And all lost, lost to the harvest. One day, one day, there may be automatic drawing machines that will capture it in an instance. How I would like one now.'

'And one day,' said Dunthorne, 'there may be machines that will thresh as they harvest and you won't find half cut fields like this no more.'

They started to pack up their things, John casting looks at the field as though to memorise the shapes. The standing wheat shrunk away as the men cut, scythes swinging in time, a concerted felling followed by others who bundled the sheaves, bound them with straw and stood them in stooks. The sheaves were loaded, an easy swing of pitchforks up to the man on top of the wagon who stowed them one by one; a golden harvest. Bold circled, sniffed out animal trails, alert, ears pricked, a paw raised as he peered into the remaining stalks.

A rabbit appeared, leaping out of the wheat. It hesitated as though seeing the men only one by one, unable to decide on an escape. And bolted, springing through the stubble, a sleek brown shape, ears back, sanctuary a deep grassy bank twenty-five, twenty yards away.

Bold saw it; head up and gave chase, low and fast zig-zagging in the rabbit's path, closing.

The loud blast of a gun shattered the peace.

The rabbit halted in mid bound as though hitting a wall. And slumped to the ground, shapeless, legs kicking. Close behind it, Bold leapt and fell, a sharp scream.

A frozen moment, all standing and staring, mouths open. The horses had their ears back, heads turned, eyes white.

And John running as though for his life. The men dropped scythes and pitchforks, turned to help him. As he reached his dog, they came up all quiet with shock but talking among themselves, offering advice. Bold lay on the ground, whimpering, a foreleg bent out at an impossible angle: bloody knee, eyes white and pupils large with pain. There was a small hole through his right ear; the pellet would have missed his head by a miracle.

Nobody looked to see from where the shot had come.

Dunthorne watched John reach his dog. He stood, looking around; he could see no sign of a gun or hunter. A moment later, a young man strode through the gateway; smart clothes, a fowling-piece on his arm, a slow smile, cocky.

'My rabbit, I believe.' His voice was sharp, a clear demand.

Dunthorne stepped down from the hedge, strode over to him and stood in his path. He knew this man but could not think what he could do. Except to keep him away from John.

'Stand aside, my man. My rabbit, I believe.'

Dunthorne stared at him. He was speechless, unable to come to terms with his arrogant air and the harm to John's dog. He, Dunthorne, was not a dog owner and felt that too much attention was given to them but he was aware of John's love for his animal, the importance of it. He closed his eyes, not wishing for confrontation; he wished only to stand between this man and John. There was a possibility, too, that a hot-headed man from the farm might be tempted to put Golding in his place, knock him out or remove him from the field in a rough fashion. That would not do. He had no idea of what he should do or what Golding might do to him.

'Who are you? How dare you impede me?' Golding was loud, demanding. 'Tell me, speak up, you fool, what is your name?' His face was red, eyes glowing with anger, spittle upon his lips. 'Do you presume, sir, to obstruct me? I am sure that we can arrange some occasion when I can whip you like a dog. I can't duel with you, one simply does not duel with your sort, you… you yokel!'

Dunthorne turned over in his mind what he could do; he could turn his back and suffer any blows that might fall. Or he could grasp the young man by his arms. And take the consequences. Or he could leave him, go to John, be near him.

'I'm sorry, sir, but his dog has been hit.' Dunthorne stood sideways to Golding, not meeting his eye, still obstructing him.

Golding stepped to one side to pass Dunthorne. Dunthorne took a step forward and then back, blocking the young gentleman. Who now frothed with frustration and anger.

'I hit his dog? No, not possible, I never miss. Why, I saw the rabbit fall. Now, stand aside, you impudent blaggard.' He raised his hand as though to strike Dunthorne; thought better of it, dropped his arm, muttered under his breath, stamped.

'Is that not my brother there?'

Dunthorne stood still, large and immovable.

'You must allow me words with my own brother, surely.'

'He must attend to his dog; I must help him. Please.'

'Well, really. We shall meet again. I shall find out who you are, you impudent dog.' He turned and strutted out of the field without looking back.

As he joined him, John was gathering up the dog in a coat, cradling him, bent over him like a mother over a new-born child. He was talking, a low moaning monotone, an attempt to comfort the dog that was now silent, eyes turned up to his master. Apart from the fractured leg, a bone shattered by shot, the hole in the ear seemed to be causing little pain.

Dunthorne gathered up John's bag with his own and spoke to the men, assuring them that the matter would be dealt with; there was no need for them to speak to Mr. Constable. A mood of unhappiness hung over the field; it wasn't right, treating a dog like that, they said. You don't go shooting a dog; why, a dog could be worth more than a wife, one man said, and was joshed and teased. All the same, he said, you always looked after your animal, come what may. And you don't expect some man to come shooting your dog. Yes, it was said, it weren't right shooting in a field full of men; who knows, it might have been me or you?

John and Dunthorne walked back to the village, a short walk up the lane, leaving the men wondering at Golding and gathering in the harvest. At the House, Dunthorne left him, leaving him and his dog to his family.

A few days later, they sat in the pub. Bold lay at John's side on the settle, his front leg a bundle of rag.

'It's not too bad, really,' said John. 'At least, it could have been worse. I suppose Golding never meant to harm him. Perhaps he didn't see him. I don't know.'

Dunthorne was not sure that he had heard him right. 'How can you say that?'

John was quiet, avoiding his eye.

A man came over from the bar. 'I was there, I saw it, Master John. It weren't right; he shouldn't have been shooting in a field full of men. We didn't see him, warn him off.'

'That's all right, Tom,' said John. 'He didn't see us, didn't see the dog.'

'How could that be? We all saw the dog and the rabbit, and… there were so many of us, he might have hit one of us.'

Dunthorne leaned over. 'It's all right, Tom. There's nothing to be said. We all know Master Golding.'

'It ain't right, and that's that.' Tom left them, went back to his friends; a muttered conversation, glances cast at Bold and John.

'Are you going to tell me about it?' Dunthorne asked.

'There's not much to say. There never is when it's Golding.'

'What do you mean?'

'Oh, he could shoot a man and it would not be his fault.'

'Not his fault? A man? Now you're talking—'

'It's not possible, we are told. He has fits; he cannot be responsible. At least, some of the time.'

'But he has a gun. It might be you next time.'

'Oh, I don't think he would go that far.'

'Come, John. Matters could go too far too fast. What does your father say?'

'If it was only my father. But it is my mother; she will not have a hair of Golding's head touched.'

'Is it something she has done? Is she feeling guilty, do you think?'

'What? What about?' John was mystified.

Dunthorne wondered. Wondered whether there was some reason that Golding Junior behaved like he did. Some reason from his birth or early days. There had been Miss Hambleton talking of one of my schoolmates, he recalled… a rough tough little boy, always biting, fighting, punching… could never sit still, always restless, off his bench, put in the corner… Teacher was lost; couldn't handle him. Miss Hambleton went out and learnt about him, about his parents and his big sisters, and it turned out he had a hard time… bullied, put to sleep in a shed, no shoes, no tea, old smock, a right ragamuffin. And she told me, this boy can't help it, can't control himself, don't know how to behave… give him space, help him… don't fight him… don't pick arguments. It was hard; don't come natural to a boy to let another do him down. Bugger me, it worked in the end… last time I saw him, the lad was working on a farm, happy as a sand boy, left on his own. Hedging, ditching, whatever.

'Oh, I don't know. Maybe there was something about his birth…'

'But,' said John, 'what has that to do with the way he behaves? His life has always been soft, easy. He has never had to—'

'No, that is not it, is it? But, you never told me, what happened at home when you took the dog home?'

A pause.

'I don't like to speak of it. My mother… Golding… it's not right.'

'Well, I think you had better tell me what is not right.'

John looked down, took a pull of his beer, sighed, and looked at Dunthorne.

'Golding said that you abused him, dared him to shoot.'

'He said… what?'

John was apologetic, pleading. 'I know, it's absurd. An insult to you; I told them that you were sitting by me. My father, he will not hear a word against you. My mother, she will believe my brother Golding, will always back him up. Told me once that I didn't know how lucky I was with all my life before me and Golding is trapped in the mind of a boy.'

'But the gun… he's allowed to shoot, everywhere, anytime…'

'Well, Dunthorne, what age do you think most young men are shooting? It is rare in a shooting family that a son does not have his own gun by the age of ten and is free to shoot alone by the age of twelve. The age of responsibility, I suppose you could call it. And Mother will have it no other way; Golding is responsible, even if within the mind of a boy.'

Dunthorne was shocked. 'He can do no wrong.'

'Just so. But it was wrong; he blames you for inciting him to shoot when he was passing by peaceably. I could say nothing to bend her mind and my father… my father sat there; he must support Mother in all things, I suppose.'

A dark cloud passed over Dunthorne; a shift in his life leaving him breathless as he turned a corner into some unknown threat. Good God, he thought, the hours that I have spent with

Mr. Constable, talking over work and about lead and timber and machines, farming improvements and new ways of building… I thought we understood each other, valued our opinions and knowledge? Is it worth so little now? I could probably get by without Golding's work… if I travel further afield but life wouldn't be the same… and here I am in Golding's premises; a peppercorn rent, but a rent… not my own studio. What will become of me? He stared at the table, lost.

And there was John. Speaking, as though to himself, staring into his mug, some words lost.

'Perhaps I have never told you; it is not something that I like to speak of. You see, he has always been the older brother and I have always been the younger. That is a nonsense in a way. But you see… he has always treated me so, while my mother is not present. A kick or cuff, usually the thing. But sometimes I have carried the blame for a wrong that he has done; he would tell Mother. That was all; the older caring brother ensuring that his little brother was corrected. And I endured punishments for crimes not my own; no point in complaining, learnt that at an early age. It came to it at home I would be in a room, reading or drawing, and he would seek me out. I would go rigid before my drawing was plucked away, torn, ruined, or a book thrown out of the window. He would spank me, beat me at bedtime. They thought to save me from this meaningless beating; so they sent me away to school. Where beating was the habit. Can you believe it? Hah! Thank God they moved me to Dedham. Before I was… But Golding. A boy, he is just a boy, and I can never change in his eyes, will always be the younger brother to a bully and even if the blows have become less, the mental blows remain the usual thing. For him. And yet he is family. My family. And I love to be here, in the village. Where I belong.'

12

SEPTEMBER 1799

Evening sun. They drifted downstream.

The surface of the water glowed, broken by deep shade beneath the willows that stretched their branches low. All was still, warm, dust a light scum on the surface. Gnats hovered in clouds and fish rose, a gulp, expanding rings as they sank. Swallows swooped between the banks, low and fast, gulping flies, soared up and out of sight. Now and then the distant call of a cow, a dog barking and an alarm from a bird.

They lay back, paper and paint set aside, one at either end, with a slow conversation of childhood memories, work, the land. Houses visited, pubs explored, old men and village girls. There was a bottle of porter and a seed cake on the thwart.

It had been John's idea to take a skiff from Flatford and pull up to Dedham. A floating studio to view the world with a low viewpoint across the river meadows, cows looming, trees like monuments. He would point out fish rising, rats swimming to their holes, ducks squabbling over food. And swan nests; at one point, John had had to bend to the oars, outpace an angry pen who flew at him, feet treading the water, an aggressive defence of her realm.

'They say a beat of the wing can break a man's arm,' said Dunthorne. 'We used to come here as boys, making rafts from branches. The odd soaking; well, quite often. Had to watch over those who couldn't swim. I used to tell them, this was the Amazon or the seas of the Caribbean but they never got it.'

'Yes, I used to do that too. Even with Golding when he was young. How did you know of the Caribbean and… what was it? The Amazon?'

Dunthorne looked at his young friend and was surprised. Did he not know of the River Amazon? What did his teachers try to push into him? Why, even in the village school, there was a bit of learning about the world, not that it sunk into many a head… I suppose all that Latin and Greek that he has mentioned left no room for real things like what the world is made of, how machines work and stories about old villagers… things that matter in the village. Seems there's a bit of a gap in his learnin'… why, where would I be if I didn't know what missy was courtin' who and who was sharp about a debt owed and who to avoid in a fight? As well as how to construct a gate and repair the road outside our house?

A pair of ducks broke the peace, a noisy splashy squabble into the reeds. The skiff drifted beneath the overhanging branches of a willow, startling a drinking bullock that stared with white eyes and bolted backwards, barging against other beasts, starting a rout, stamping, a cloud of dust.

Silence settled upon them once more.

Under Fen Bridge and a man leaning on the railing, smoke from his pipe drifting on the air. A nod, a smile in return and the man turned for home to the cottage. Further downstream, they met a lighter coming up, a patient horse on the tow path with a boy asleep on its back. The man at the rudder waved, steered clear of their meandering boat, laughed and turned back to his task.

'One of my father's,' said John. 'He will be taking coal up to Sudbury. Shouldn't think he will make it tonight.'

'Why, John, you seem to know the business well. Now, you could spare a day or two for your father, and—'

'No, Dunthorne. Please. Don't start on that again.'

They landed by the Mill sluices and walked slowly up the hill back to the village. Neither seemed in a hurry and the warmth lingered, heat rising off the hardpacked roadway.

Near the Hall, John halted, laughing.

'I had quite forgotten, Dunthorne. The day has been too good, I had quite forgotten.' He stood, looking over the valley, nodding slowly to himself. Dunthorne stopped, looking at him.

'It was a good day,' he said.

John turned to face him.

'Yes, I had forgotten, and now… well, now it seems ungrateful, unfriendly. But I shall soon have no need of the use of a room in your house.'

'No need?' Dunthorne was shocked. What was this now? First he goes off to London for his painting and wotnot and now he wants no more of our house. I don't know what my Sarah will make of it, she is so set on him coming often, gives her airs, keeps her happy.

'No… no need. But please Dunthorne, it is better than that. I have been grateful for the loan of a room. You must tell your wife; it has been generous, very kind. And I could not prevail upon her longer. Or not much longer. It is an intrusion upon your privacy.'

'Well, where will you be?'

John looked at Dunthorne; he looked shocked, like a slap in the face. John asked himself, what have I done? Did it mean so much to him? I shall still seek his company, discuss my work with him, go sketching. What have I done?

'It is not a simple matter.' How could he explain it? I'm sure that I have hurt my friend and I never saw it coming, the hurt. But they have such a small home, they must be glad of the space and Mrs. Dunthorne, she was not one to discuss art; she must be glad to have the home free of this distraction. Dammit, what have I done? What can I say to him, tell him that it doesn't change anything, that I can still go sketching? Oh, why do I always say the wrong thing? Never seem to get it right though I thought with Dunthorne, we always understood each other... how many years is it now, and there is nobody like him for understanding me. He gazed down, kicking a pebble.

'But you are leaving?' Dunthorne's voice was hard.

'Leaving? The village? Never. I could never leave this village. It is the soul of my work.'

'But... oh, I don't understand you at all.'

'You see, if I can... no, the other way round. My father is seeking a studio for me in the village. The girls, they complain about the smell of oil paint; it is good of your wife, she has made no complaint. But now that I am a student with work and tasks to complete, my father wishes me to have a studio of my own. Where patrons may visit. And the work can stand all around.'

'Oh, you are leaving. And you are mistaken about my wife; she was always happy to greet you.'

'Was she? I didn't know, always thought that... Won't you come with me? Must you remain at your house? I would want you to work with me as you always have. Is this not the best solution, a good studio for both of us and away from the women?' He added, quickly, 'If you want.'

Dunthorne remained confused. 'But... well... I don't have time to travel away from home and work. Where will you be, this studio?'

'Near, very near, I assure you. My father is looking at the lease for the building near the shop, a barn of a building; I don't know what it was used for. Perhaps a smithy or a stable...'

'Do you mean the one the other side of West Lodge?'

'Just so, the very one. And there is a large window facing the South. Of course, I shall have to manage a blind of sorts, cut the glare, moderate the light, but it would...'

Dunthorne smiled, a wave of relief passing over him.

'Well, thank you, John. That is good of you. Yes, I can see that you should have a studio, a workplace as I have my own workshop. And if there is a corner for my humble work, I shall be grateful.'

'But,' said John, 'it is not a simple matter.' He paused, twisting his fingers together.

'So you said.'

'It is a sort of contract. My father, a businessman, he would see it as a contract. Even within the family. And I must satisfy it, I mean him. He is so good to me, pays my way in London. And I give him so little in return.'

'But you could, John. You could spare a few days or hours for him, could you not?'

'I could, indeed I could. But if I did, I would be falling behind. You see, I find it difficult; I do not know when a painting is finished. Who can say? It is not like painting a door; I am sure that a decorator knows when the door is finished. But a painting is not the same thing at all; it is a matter of knowing the right moment. When the effect has been captured, when the painter has expressed the truth of the subject, when—'

'Thank you, John. I think I understand you.'

'I do not have time to set my painting aside, not for one day if I am to continue at the Academy. My parents understand the issue. And my father wishes to drive me, no that is unfair, wishes to help me to complete a painting in a reasonable period.'

'Well, I am no wiser. It sounds like a quart in a pint pot or a pint in a quart pot. I am not sure. Perhaps time for a drink.'

John ignored him, looking out over the valley. He felt the tower of Dedham Church beckoning, dark among the trees in the low light; my God, he thought, this is the time, the hour. I should be painting now on this very spot; look at the shadows. What colour are they in this warm light? And the tower, which yellow, that Lincolnshire stonework? While the oaks are going black, and beyond, the rise to Stratford Hills, blues, warm blues, not four miles off… he started; how could he set his friend aside like this?

'It is quite simple.'

'Now, there you have me. You said, twice I believe, that it was not a simple matter. And now you say—'

'My father will lease me a studio when I have completed a painting for him. That is the nub of it; how long will I take to complete a painting? I have no idea, it is all so new. He has only recently talked to me about it; earlier today.'

'The painting; it is a portrait, I assume. Your mother I should imagine. That would be right. You have little experience with portraits I suppose. A difficulty.'

Dunthorne adopted a serious manner, frowning, stroking his chin. John stared and burst out laughing.

'No, it is not that at all. You are cruel. But correct; I should not like to have to paint a portrait of my mother; she would never forgive me, I'm sure. It would hang in a dark closet, out of sight. I have never drawn a face, not even at the Academy; it will come but I must draw the body first.'

'A naked body?'

'Life class, they call it.'

'Is this… excuse me John, I know nothing of it. Is this quite suitable, you know, correct? Drawing a body? I assume a body without clothes.'

John laughed again.

'Yes, I see. It must seem strange to those who have never heard of such a thing. We start on casts, great dusty plaster casts of gods and things. And when we can make a reasonable rendering, we are allowed in the life drawing classes, one or two life models.'

'Life models?'

'Men and women.'

'Now you are teasing me. It sounds like a brothel or a house of amusement. All these men staring at a naked—'

'It is hard work.'

'Hard work staring at a naked woman? Come, John, you are losing touch with real life…'

The conversation dragged on for a time, Dunthorne not believing and yet believing, John working to keep a straight face and not give in to the teasing, the rude suggestions.

At last, Dunthorne interrupted him.

'Tell me, what painting does your father want if it is not a portrait of your mother?'

'An altarpiece for the Church. St. Mary's. He wishes to make a gift, a donation from a notable member of the village. And my mother will be pleased; she believes that it will place her with the landowners and she always—'

'But you are landowners.'

'Yes, we are. But we are not squires. And never shall be.'

Dunthorne shrugged.

John stared at the ground. 'Did you say a drink?' he said.

13

MAY 1800

John had come down to the boatyard, sat on the bank and suggested a walk along the river; there was a heron fishing he said. Dunthorne had been finishing a small job, the drain to the dry dock. Yet again. It drained under the river to the meadows below the opposite bank; a lighter had fouled the outlet, crushing the leadwork. It happened from time to time.

On the south bank, they walked down the river to the big bend below the mill. Dunthorne felt the weariness of the day lift, content to let John go ahead. Behind them, the sun cast long shadows over the river meadows. At the bend, the heron had flown. Before them, the valley ran flat to Manningtree and Harwich, the way to the sea.

Still evening air. The smell of fresh cut hay. Distant calls from the hamlet. Birds were active, swallows swooping to catch flies. The river ran slow, the surface occasionally rippled as fish rose to feed. They dawdled. John wondered aloud how he would capture the low light, the warmth in the colours and shades; would it not seem too dramatic, deep shadows against the warm lights? Dunthorne sat down, rubbing his knees. The trees on the opposite bank were in full leaf, chestnuts flaming. John wondered when the harvest would start.

Dunthorne was silent. He said that he was tired, looking forward to getting back; he had to stop by the yard to pick up his tools. They turned back towards Flatford, stepping over the lock gates onto the island and back to the yard. All was quiet, the men long since gone home; an old lighter sat on the bearers, a board out in the chine. A plank of oak lay below awaiting the new working day.

The lane, deep beneath its banks, was warm and dark, close air until they came to the top of the hill. There, a slight breeze and the sweet smell of flowers. Near the village, they paused in the shade of a great oak looking out over the valley. An occasional sound broke the calm: a door slamming, a mother calling for her children. Below them, a lighter, a single sail hoisted, was taking advantage of the evening air to drift upriver towards Dedham; they could see the horse and lad on the towpath. A lazy spiral of smoke rose from the chimney of Fen Bridge cottage; a man working the garden dropped his spade and disappeared indoors. John and Dunthorne turned for home.

There was a cry, shattering the somnolence. Piercing and abrupt. A woman, distressed.

They paused, looking at each other. John was shocked; such things never happened in the village that he knew; perhaps in London, quite possibly, but not here, not in his home village. He could not understand Dunthorne's expression, a mixture of alarm and determination. What was he going to do? Please, might there not be trouble. They peered through the hedge.

In the driveway of Old Hall were two people, a man and a woman. The man had his back to the hedge and appeared to be holding the woman, pulling her to him as she struggled. It was difficult to see the lady, just the swing of a dress.

'Unhand me, you brute. How dare you!'

A lady's voice, educated, not a village girl. And her dress. Yes, a lady.

A harsh male laugh. 'But, missy, you asked for it, didn't you?'

'What do you mean? Don't you know who I am?'

'Yes, I know who you are. And no call to be adopting these high falutin' airs with me. You're a young maiden trailing her tail, a young peahen, hoping for a bit of attention from a male like me. A huntin', shootin', fishin' sort of man. A proper man, not some saloon dandy. I've hunted you and… and now… and now I'm fishin' you, hauling' you in.' Another coarse laugh.

John and Dunthorne knew the voice. Young Golding. How was it that they encountered young Golding when they went out sketching and only wanted peace? It stung John like a curse that the thing he wanted most was spoilt by his brother, who corrupted his home, his village, his family. Dunthorne pulled John back from the hedge and whispered that it wasn't his, Dunthorne's business, to curb the young master. In fact, it could be trouble, couldn't it? He didn't want to fall out with his father. John was worried; he saw that his friend was confused, indecisive. He would have to intervene himself, he thought, and rescue the lady, whoever she was; it was time to stand up to his brother, put him in the right of things and try to explain to the lady. That it was all a mistake, his brother was not well and he was sure that a proper apology would be made. And dammit, it had gone on long enough.

He turned to Dunthorne to tell him that he should stay out of it; and even if it meant a beating, it was better that way. But Dunthorne raised his hand, stopped him before he could say a word; he said he couldn't stand by and let the brothers come to blows. John was a strapping young fellow but he would be powerless before his elder brother. And what would Dunthorne look like watching his friend being beaten?

'Help, help me. Oh, you brute!' A sob.

Enough.

John started forward. 'You don't understand. I must explain—'

'You keep out of this, if you please', said Dunthorne. 'It won't do you any good, not with your brother. Just stand back behind this hedge here.'

He stepped round the corner. John could see the young woman but didn't know her; her clothes were pulled awry but her dress was of such a quality that one only saw in London. Young Golding stood behind her, grasping her arms, a glazed triumphant look on his face, spit at the corner of his mouth.

'Let her go, Master Golding. If you please', said Dunthorne, with a brief bow to both of them. The lady froze at the interruption and tried to pull her dress straight.

'How dare you. I suppose you want her for yourself, don't you? Well, keep away from me, you… finders keepers!' A leer. The lady strained against his arms, tears running down her face, a look of horror.

'Now, if you please.' John saw Dunthorne step up, solid in front of Golding who continued to wrestle the lady, twisting this way and that, a manic expression.

'You… you stay out of my affairs. Why, who do you think you are? You jumped-up little…' There was a note of fear in his voice.

John stood behind the gate pier wondering how he could help his friend, for whom he felt more concern for than for his brother. Golding is impossible, he thought, a danger to polite society; he should be put away. I couldn't see it before, defended his behaviour but it is clear now. I must tell Father and he must persuade Mother that no good will come from leaving him to run free in the village. And for goodness' sake, I mean, molesting ladies. Something must be done. But still John hesitated out of sight.

Golding looked dazed as though he couldn't be aware of what he was doing, or the consequences. Dunthorne looked at him. The village knew of young Golding and generally avoided him. Though he had heard that a few young men had gone shooting with him. Once. Never to be repeated and returned with tales of how he shot at anything that flew and rambled across any land, cultivated or pasture, breaking down fences, smashing through hedges. He didn't know the lady and wondered with which house she was associated and how much trouble would wash over the Constable family. Perhaps it was one of the squires; poor Mrs. Constable would never live it down. And it wouldn't do the master much good. He sighed loudly. Golding jerked up, staring at him.

'Now,' said Dunthorne. 'Who is that coming down the drive behind you?'

Golding released the woman, turning slowly as he wiped his mouth with a handkerchief. To swing back, a vicious light in his eyes, gaping with anger. Dunthorne had taken the woman by the arm and placed her behind him.

'You tricked me, you bastard. Now… now you'll pay for it.'

Golding struggled with his coat, throwing it to the ground, tore off his neckpiece, eyes wide, frothing at the mouth. Dunthorne called out.

'See this lady home, would you, John? Now. At once.'

John emerged, embarrassed to be discovered. He hated that a stranger had witnessed it and wondered which family would hear of the Constable sons and their bad behaviour. Good God, Golding must be curbed!

Golding glared at him. 'Brought your little friend, have you?' And to John, 'Why John, do you have your man protect you?'

John ignored him. 'Dunthorne, I am concerned for you—'

Dunthorne cut him off. 'John, it is a sad thing, this. But you would be better taking this young lady home, taking her away from here.'

John took the lady by the arm gently and retreated to the gateway. But he could not leave and hovered behind the pier, his back turned while she rearranged her dress. He felt sore; the pleasure of the afternoon had drained away leaving a thin skin of frustration. An emptiness scored by futility and despair. He knew that for Dunthorne it never paid to tangle with the gentry; there might be a few coarse jokes in the pub, a clap on the back or two, but his friends would know where respect must be paid, who owned their homes, their labour, their very lives. And with a young wife and children, he could be no longer a free man. John didn't know what to do. A blackbird flew low over his head, shrieking an alarm call.

He could see his brother rolling his sleeves, carefully one after the other, his tongue in the corner of his mouth like a child doing laces, Golding with the strength of a brute and the mind of a small boy. How was Dunthorne to avoid hurting him? But Dunthorne just stood there patiently in the driveway, his coat on and his arms folded.

He sounded exhausted. 'There's no call for this, Master Golding. If you will excuse me, I should be heading homewards. It's getting late.'

'Oh? A coward, are you? I should teach you a lesson, not to interfere with your betters. About time too, getting above yourself.'

He started to flail his arms about in the direction of Dunthorne, a clumsy imitation of gentlemen's boxing. When Golding came too close, Dunthorne stepped back. And again. He turned, as though to walk away. Golding struck him on the shoulder, knocking him forward.

John flinched; he didn't know whether Golding would hurt his friend or whether Dunthorne would respond and irrevocably ruin his position. Oh God, he thought, why does it have to come to this? Should I run between them, stop this farce? I can't leave now, I can't leave Dunthorne… Oh… the lady; she seems all right, standing as though waiting for me… about my age, I think… a strength in her eyes and the way that she stands… Who is she? She gave him a timid smile and suggested that they walk away. John hesitated, wanting to see his friend released from the violence.

'Running away, you coward, you country dolt, you bastard. I dare say your mother was a sow, reared in a filthy sty, and you were spawned…'

John knew that Dunthorne's mother had died when he was young and was furious. He watched Dunthorne close with Golding, ignoring the blows that fell on his chest, place a foot behind Golding's heel and push.

The last he saw before turning away was his brother, arms waving at the sky, a look of astonishment as he fell back onto the ground. He left at once hurrying the young lady up the lane. Dunthorne was following, shaking his head.

A few days later, John called on Dunthorne at his workshop.

'I wondered whether you would like to walk, sketch perhaps, down Fen Lane. I was going to try…' He stopped.

Dunthorne looked up from his work, a leaded light for a house. He looked at John, a wary look. John stared, wondering at the change. And thought of the incident at the Hall.

'Oh… oh yes, Golding.' said John. Damn, he thought, I haven't been to see him, explain that all is well. What a fool I am.

'I must be getting on with my work, John. I expect your family—'

'No, no, please. It's not like that at all. You don't understand.'

'Well, I'm not sure that you do. When you are a craftsman in this village, you have to keep in with people, those that give out the work.'

'Yes,' said John. 'I do know. I do understand, and I have to tell you, what they said, what has happened, and… but, please, won't you come out for a while? Can I buy you a pint?'

So Dunthorne had been afraid that the word would go round and that he would lose work and his family would suffer. And even have to move away. What an idiot I have been, thought John… and I would lose my companion who means more to me than all the young gentlemen around and my blasted brother… but hasn't Golding apologised, for putting him in that situation? Poor Dunthorne, he must have heard nothing and feared the worst… estrangement from my father and me if my mother has anything to do with it. That's the way of it; I've seen it before, even a bit of cheek from a servant to a family son… they disappear and God knows what references they have for any other position… and where would Dunthorne go, for goodness' sake? A village can be a tricky thing; I have found that with workmen who can be friendly at the mill but humble themselves in the street… and if you fall out with your neighbours and those you work with and for… it must be hard.

He felt a twist within him, frustrated that he did not have the power to make everything well, to sweep all trouble under the carpet. Dunthorne sighed, looking John up and down.

'All right there, John. I'll be with you at the Red Lion in ten minutes; I must finish this soldering.' Half a smile, waved him away and bent to his work.

In the pub, Dunthorne nodded to Walt and made to buy a pint but Jem told him it was pulled and paid for. Over there with

Master John. There was bread and cheese and a pickled egg too. John sat on the settle, looking pleased with himself.

'Can I get you anything else, Dunthorne?' He stood, waving him into his usual corner of the settle. Dunthorne sat, stretched his legs. John wondered where to start, embarrassed and overflowing with explanation.

'I owe you an apology; I ought to have come to you days ago. I would have but my father said that Golding should make his own apology and should make amends for putting you in that situation. But he hasn't, has he? Oh, I'm so sorry, I wanted to, I should have really, but—'

'I don't quite follow you, John.' Dunthorne sounded wary.

'Well, it was like this and you see, and of course my mother but Golding was… and then it happened that—'

'You mean, your father is not getting the constable on me?'

'Good gracious, Dunthorne. How can you think that? No, no, not at all. My father was sorry that you had been put into that situation; I told him all, explained how it came about, what happened. And the lady. He understands very well how you had to act, how… I would have, really, I told him, but he said that it was probably better that you were there rather than two brothers having a brawl in front of a lady, not that I would have brawled, if you see what I mean. Oh, it's so difficult. He would like to make amends, to show… but Golding was meant to, did say that he would… oh, it's so difficult with Golding. He bullies me, you know. Always has done. And now, I think he hates me because of Maria… You need worry about nothing; my father thinks highly of you, is grateful that you were there and stopped any fight. He was disappointed that you wouldn't work with him, he thought that you could help him, particularly since I left.' A pause. 'But he is good to me, never makes me feel that I should have stayed. How I hated the counting-house. But you, you need not worry; he understands that you must be your own man, your own master. He understands that well. You will do work for him now, won't you? He would miss you and he always has some job for you.'

Dunthorne chewed bread and cheese, slowly. Then he smiled, pulled on his beer and wiped the back of his hand across his mouth.

'Well John, you do put a different complexion on things. And there… I thought I was for the Cage.'

'I'm so sorry I didn't come myself. But my father, he said that Golding must—'

'Your brother a bully? Yes, you have told me before.'

'I don't know why; he is the oldest, he has always had his own way, and yet… I can't put a reason to it. There is none. But you know he is not always quite himself. My father has never had him in the mill or counting-house. He can't do it, has to walk out after a few minutes or set the men to doing something else, not their work. It's difficult but my mother looks after him, won't have a hair of his head touched and he goes around like a young lord, free as the birds that he shoots. Everywhere. You wouldn't believe the problems we have had with the farmers; Golding will shoot over any land that takes his fancy.'

'Well, you can get away to London now, can't you? Be your own man.'

'Oh, I'll never be away from here for long, you know that. This country made me. The fields and the river, the wind and clouds, the workmen and boats.'

'I'm mighty pleased to hear it,' said Dunthorne.

'And now there is Maria.'

'You are walking out with someone? You have kept this from me, I dare say.'

‘No, no… I don’t know if it is walking-out in that sense. Perhaps there is no sense to it all; I cannot afford a wife, there is too much work to do, and… it’s difficult.’

‘It is, for sure. You never know what they are thinking, women. You have to watch them like a hawk and then it’s too late. You are trapped; and sometimes happy to be in the trap.’

‘No, no, you don’t understand. It’s more difficult than that—’

‘I don’t know what is more difficult than that, but I—’

‘She is Dr. Rhudde’s granddaughter. Her father is Solicitor to the Navy.’

There was silence. They became aware of the murmur around the bar; a few men were looking at John, whispering to their friends. Perhaps his “walking-out” had been seen by a few inquisitive eyes. John saw none of this but gazed at the table, his face twisted, his glass hanging from his hand, food ignored. Dunthorne looked down at him with affection. Was John old enough for a wife? Not in years but in other things? He couldn’t see him settling down, not for a long time. There he was, sitting in his old clothes as usual, that worn coat, stained with linseed oil and God knows what else, frayed cuffs, breeches look as though they haven’t been washed in a long time; and the boots and stockings. Why, he dresses like a poor farmer. And wishes they would treat him as such.

‘Watch your beer, John,’ said Dunthorne. ‘He is not an easy man, Dr. Rhudde. I wouldn’t wish to cross words with him.’

‘I know, and I… but, it’s not like that, I can’t afford to marry, not yet and… well, she is good company, you know. Witty, and… well, I don’t know that I can explain it. We get on well, always conversation and…’

John stared into the fireplace, oblivious to the men around it who chuckled and looked at him. Dunthorne cleared his throat, turned a few stares with his own hard look. John had never been taken this way before, he was sure; it was remarkable, this change. What might it bring? Less sketching time and more courtin'? But the lad was struck, that was sure. First love; that was it. Couldn't say he had ever suffered it hisself, but it must be that.

'Well, are you going to tell me when you met this paragon of virtue?'

'But… you know, you were there.' John's eyebrows rose.

Dunthorne frowned. 'I can't think of a time when I would have been able to introduce you to a lady. No, most unlikely.'

'Oh, but you did. Well, you didn't introduce her but handed her into my care.'

Dunthorne stared at him. And remembering the struggle, young Golding, John behind the hedge, a young lady in distress…

'You mean… ?'

'Yes, Dunthorne. The young lady you released from my brother that evening, the whole business with Golding… Do you not remember her? Well dressed… well, until Golding dragged at it… but good-looking, attractive and an intelligent person with great qualities—'

'And you say she is related to Dr. Rhudde? The Rector? How can that be?'

'I took her home, as you said. She is his granddaughter and her father is—'

'Solicitor to the Navy.' Dunthorne spelt it out slowly. 'My, you are mixing with quality, I'm thinking, John. You'll be getting yourself a smart house in London, a carriage and four, and—'

'Please, please, Dunthorne. Don't tease me. It was quite by chance. And she was grateful for your interruption.'

'I have heard nothing of it.'

'Please, don't take umbrage. She asked me to tell you, she has no means of reaching you.'

'No. I meant I have heard nothing of this walking-out. And you say she was grateful?'

'Oh, indeed. Very grateful. She was quite shocked, you know, and had not expected such an assault in our quiet village. Indeed when approached by a gentleman, she thought that he—'

'So you spoke to her, introduced yourself.'

'Well, it was a bit difficult. Because of Golding. We were talking before any introductions, of the village and the church and a little of painting – she is quite knowledgeable and she said she was Maria and I said I was John and then I saw where we were going and she bid me leave her at the gateway and—'

'And you never told her your name?'

'Well, I did, we were Maria and John from the first. Which is not quite correct, I am sure. There were so many things to talk about—'

'And she never learnt your name, your brother—'

'Oh no, I mean, oh yes. She does know my name now.'

John was silent, gazing at the floor.

'She wasn't happy when I told her. Who I was and my brother, and everything,' said John.

'I should imagine not.'

'But… but it was only a temporary thing. She does understand, I am not my brother.'

'You meet often?'

'No, not often. More by chance, really. But I know when she walks out, in the afternoon. Usually with an errand. And I… well, we meet here and there. She will not tell her grandfather, she cannot. He… well, I'm sure he means well but he tells her that there is no person of consequence in this village, all farmers and—'

'But your family are no farmers.'

'It was difficult; she did not like to speak of it. She said… she told him, she had met a Constable family, sisters of a suitable age, a large house near the church. And do you know what he said? Perhaps not farmers but very like.'

'Very like?' said Dunthorne, with a grim smile.

'Oh well. Must life be like this? Do I have to choose to be gentry or villager? But it is all hopeless; I have no money, cannot marry with no prospects or position. It is galling; a callow youth from a Hall around could make his respects to her, be entertained at the Rectory. But I may not.'

'Come, I must be back at work. Shall we walk tomorrow? I have things to ask you. And you must tell me more of your friend.'

14

JUNE 1800

Out of the bright sunlight, Dunthorne stooped beneath the lintol, peering into the shed. The brick floor stretched into the gloom, worn and uneven, and he could make out hay bales at the back, floor to roof. John was standing in the centre at a table scrubbing at a panel in a cloud of white dust; he paused, frowning. A swallow flew out over his head.

'Watch out for my friend; he's teaching the young to fly. How are you, old friend? You see, I'm getting into my work, all this preparation as I have been taught in London.'

'What are you doing? I thought that panel was good for painting after I had butt-glued it and planed it.'

'It's a miserable workplace, I know. But the girls can't stand the dust any more, and I was banished from my room. I had to clear out this stable; there were a lot of old fruit trays and Nancy's saddles and stuff.' He paused, standing back from the table. 'These panels need a lot of work. But I couldn't do it in your house, not at all.'

'And what of your new studio?' said Dunthorne. 'You're right; my Sarah wouldn't care for all this dust.'

He hesitated on the threshold; the dust lay thick on the floor. And what of the hay, he wondered; would his sister want it after all this mess? John's not a practical boy, when it comes to home and hearth. Look at him now. And I was going to take him to the alehouse, what would Jem say? Why, even when the good ol' boys come in, they don't bring the fields with them.

'It's not the wood; your work was good, a good start. But you have to build up a ground for the painting, a hard level backing, and you rub it and rub it – it's only chalk and rabbit-skin glue – but it has to be as smooth as a baby's bottom. How smooth is that? I don't know, never seen a baby's bottom. Maybe the rabbit-skin glue has gone off; can you smell it? At the Schools, they said that if you can smell it, it's unusable. But I can't smell anything, my nose is full of…'

He sneezed, smiled and brushed on another layer of ground, standing back to let it dry. Dunthorne looked at John and his clothes, the dust, the floor, the panel, and backed out, breathing in the garden air. He didn't tell John that Old Wally at the boatyard had given him chestnut rather than oak, told him it was better in damp conditions; he wondered if John had noticed the difference. He would hear about it soon enough if he had.

Behind him, the garden stretched away, well-tended fruit trees, herbs, vegetables; it was like a small farm, large enough to supply a few households. He wondered how Golding disposed of it all, whether there was a large family elsewhere to feed. Maybe he sent a box to the relations in London on the ship. Typical of Golding to have such a well-organised kitchen garden and put to good use. A lad was weeding, standing up to stretch from time to time; he caught Dunthorne's eye, smiled, nodded and bent to his work again. A robin hopped near him, head on side, looking for worms. The kitchen maid emerged from the house, emptied a pail and turning, saw Dunthorne; she waved and then put her hand over her mouth before running indoors.

White clouds sailed over in a blue sky. Swallows hovered around the stable door.

John emerged from the shed. He clapped his hands.

'I never knew it was so much work; I've only painted on canvas and paper before.' He shook himself like a dog, whitening the yard bricks around him, and coughed.

'I wondered whether you would like a bite at the Red Lion.'

'Are you not working? Yes, I would love to leave this for a while; let the dust settle.'

'I could do with a break. How are your sketches coming on?' said Dunthorne. 'You told me that you've been visiting a good number of collections, Tattingstone, Dedham, and goodness knows where else. But how is your own picture coming?'

'Ah, if only you knew the business. It's a queer world, the art business. There is so much to learn at the Schools. I am doing what many generations of painters have done, looking to the great painters, the Italians and their like. I'm much taken by the Northern Italian paintings; I've seen a few in London and houses here. It's a good way to learn the business and there's always a market for good copies... No no, I don't mean "copies", rather new paintings in the style of, if you see what I mean.'

He stepped into the shed and came out shaking a sheaf of drawings. And coughed again.

'Leave your dust and come away to the pub, John. We can look at them there.'

'A minute or two, if you please.' John disappeared into the house; a clamour of voices rose in the kitchen.

Dunthorne stood in the fresh air. Was this what it was like to be a painter? Did the painter have to consider the sales, their taste and fashion, before he started a painting? It didn't sound much different from his own work. Both involved with the design and execution, designer and tradesman in one. And working to a customer's requirements. When releading the aisle window, he had had the sense to re-organise the panels to tell the story, rather than refix the jumble of coloured glass left by some craftsman a hundred years ago or so. Rector had been unhappy, wanting to keep things just as they were; it wasn't Dunthorne's place, he was informed, to decide whether "there was a story to be told or not".

A blackbird called a sudden alarm as a cat crept around the bushes; too slow for the bird that took off with a loud complaint. Bold was lying by the house against a warm wall; he ignored cat and bird, and yawned. John appeared, a clean jacket, his hair standing up, a wry smile.

'I'm surprised your womenfolk allow you to go abroad, looking like that.'

John laughed. 'I didn't see them. Well, not Mother. Came out the back way. Come away, Bold.'

In the alehouse, Dunthorne exchanged nods and words with friends and neighbours and they sat in silence for a while. The beer was good, a fresh barrel. Bread and cheese; a pickled egg for Dunthorne. Bold circled and settled near the fireplace, ignoring offers of food and drink.

After a time, John spread out his sketches. They were simple: pencil and watercolour, rapid confident marks, splashes of colour, suggestions of private intentions. Dunthorne snorted.

'I hope you didn't try these out on the Rector; he'd be concerned, wondering what your father was up to, encouraging you to be an artist.' The last word was drawn out, mocking.

'No, no… but… they're only my ideas, you know. I wouldn't show them to anyone, not these. I thought… I thought you might understand. Perhaps at a later stage.' And he started to roll them up, turning his back.

Dunthorne laughed. 'Come on, John, stay a while. Here, have another pint and tell me about them.'

'Well… they're only ideas, you know. To place things in my mind, what I will paint. Of course, a painting like this, it must be traditional, a Bible scene, a painting that will be accepted, recognised, understood. I'm following the Italian painters; the big houses round here, you know, they all have Italian paintings, holy paintings. Wonderful work; it is the thing, don't you think? They knew how to do it, what to show and—'

'What is this here?' He was pointing at the centre of the sketch.

'Adoration of the Magi. It was one of the most popular things, you see, central over the altar. And the Church is St. Mary's; I don't know which St. Mary but I thought—'

'Is it always a… what was that word?'

'No no, not at all. But it is common, quite usual, to see an Adoration. Of course, there were other scenes, the Annunciation, and—'

'But, John, these paintings you see, you find them in houses hereabouts?'

'Well, most of them, it's true. But they were painted for churches, holy paintings. There are some in English churches. And I thought, how grand it would be if—'

'So, bear with me, John, what sort of paintings are painted for churches now, these days?'

'Oh, I have not seen many… well, not one, I believe, that has been painted recently. But there are so many, there would not be the need. And then—'

'But there is the need for a new one for St. Mary's, you say. No old painting hanging in the Rectory or Old Hall, that will do.'

'But you forget, Dunthorne. My father. His gift. I must honour his request. And then I may have a studio; he promised.'

'I do forget.' A pause. 'These Italian paintings; you favour them, you think they are the right thing?'

'I do, I do. The ancient and holy themes, the right thing, as—'

'But John, what has this to do with you and me?'

John stared at him. What does he mean? I'm sure Dunthorne cannot understand churches, the rules to be followed, a serious commitment to the religion and tradition, what you have to do. Yes, that must be it. But what does he mean by "you and me"?

'I… I don't understand you, Dunthorne.'

'Yes, you and me.'

'You mean, us? What could we have to do with an altar-piece?'

'Why, now you do confuse me. I always thought that the church was about the parish, about us and—'

'Oh. That "you and me". Now I understand you; I think. You mean the village, do you, or are you—'

'And there is the other matter, of your painting. Now, I don't know much about painting as you know. But you talk about Truth and Reality and I am confused I confess.'

A pause. John racked his brains. What was Dunthorne talking about? Really, I must put him in the right of it. Somehow. When I can understand what he is talking about. Ah, if only the Rector was here, to give guidance… but actually, no, that wouldn't be the thing at all… we would sit in silence watching our feet, wishing him away. But Dunthorne; what is he about? He doesn't understand and that's an end of it.

'Confused? Really I don't know what you may be confused about I'm sure and if you think that I can simply—'

'Now John, calm down and be straight with me. You talk of the right thing and what all these grand houses have and it doesn't hold with what you tell me about what painting must be.'

'Must be?'

'Don't turn into a puppet there will you, John? Just repeating what I say. You can't be wanting a hearing horn, not at your age. But sometimes, I do wonder whether you haven't filled your head with ideas from London so you can't think straight and then there is Mary and I'm sure your head must be turned with thoughts of her—'

'Hold, please hold. May I remind you, her name is Maria. Let us not muddy talk of Maria just now. She is too precious, too—'

'Precious? Is that so? Well. Right then.' He gave John a hard look and smiled. 'So that's the way of it. Now, what am I to make of your Truth and Reality? I've heard it often enough when we are away painting our views of the fields. You tell me, see, I've learnt it well that all must be Truth and Reality when we are painting.'

'Truth and Reality?'

'Here we go again; your head must be blocked with something, John. You don't hear me too well. It must be all that dust, clogging up—'

'I'm sorry, I was thinking of… but you speak of Truth and Reality?'

'I mean, what you sketch when we are out on the valley, the hills and fields and Dedham Church away over in the distance and the clouds that come rolling up from the sea in the afternoon. The Truth and Reality you talk of then.'

John was silent.

'Isn't that your Truth and Reality?'

'Indeed it is. You know it well.'

'Well, I don't see where copying an old Italian—'

'Not copying, please. But in the style—'

'And what you talk to me about, this valley where you belong and how it is the spirit of your painting, how you don't wish to paint these court paintings, these fancy mythical things that you have seen but want to show where you live, the land and all. The Truth of it.'

'It is a more complicated matter than that, I assure you. It is a question of…'

But Dunthorne had left him. He went to the bar, chatted awhile with Jem, asked after his missus, bought a pint and came back to sit gazing into the hearth. He was not used to talking at length with John; where did the words come from, about the fields and Dedham Church and the clouds and so on, unless they came from John himself? Before he went off to London, mixing with all them teachers and painters and so on, there was none of this complication; I understood him… nay, he taught me and now here I am teaching him his own words. Truth and Reality! I thought I knew what he was talking about but now he confuses me… I don't know what he gets up to in London but it don't sound the same John to me… all mixed up. But he belongs here, told me often enough and I'm hoping that these Schools that he talks of can't have too much of a hold on him just yet.

'How are your sisters?' he said. 'I saw Nancy out riding yesterday; that's a fine mare she has there.'

John took a sip, staring straight ahead, a slight frown.

'It's not like you think, Dunthorne, not at all. I can't hang my landscape sketches in the Church, they wouldn't do. This is a different kind of art, a formal thing. You have to do the formal thing, the accepted thing. And you see—'

'These Italian paintings. What do they have in them?'

John looked at him, coughed, looked around the room and sighed. He shrugged.

'Well… the holy scenes, the ones I'm speaking of, they will have an Annunciation or an Adoration of the Magi or a Crucifixion. An important religious scene.'

'And what is around the holy scene?'

'Around? I don't understand—'

'The people, the background, the view.'

'Ah, well, you see.' John paused, recollecting pictures that he had seen, mostly in London, some in the Royal Academy that was new, barely thirty years old and held some fine paintings. And there was talk of a national collection, whatever that would be. But there were fine private collections in the great houses; he had seen a few.

'I suppose, really I mean, it is what the painters thought the Holy Land looked like.' He paused again. 'But they couldn't have seen it of course, not even the same country if you think about it, and I don't think that they would have committed the sacrilege of transferring it to their own homeland, though I don't think that would have been such a bad thing, not in a painting if you see what I mean but please, Dunthorne, don't tell the Rector I said that, I would be in awful trouble and any painting I do would be rejected out of hand and my father would—'

'My goodness, John, you do go on. It was a simple question, what the paintings looked like. But if you think that I am just wasting your time…' He started to gather himself to leave.

John stayed him with a hand. 'I suppose they painted a mythical landscape; and the people around…' At that moment, he faded, staring at the table. 'The people around…'

Dunthorne watched him. And did not speak.

'I don't know,' said John, throwing his hands up. 'But that is what the paintings are like, like Italian towns and people, a few hundred years ago when the painters were working. Though I'm sure that they were painting the Holy Land, only they didn't know what it looked like and used—'

'The towns and people that they knew.' Dunthorne took a long pull on his beer, drew the back of his hand across his mouth. Sat up.

‘But… but, you are forgetting the circumstances of the matter.’ John stirred himself and looked at Dunthorne. ‘My father, he asked me to paint it, an altar painting. Wants me to finish something and he wants to make a gift to St. Marys from a leading parishioner and his family. And so on. And I won’t disappoint him; he does much for me already and I know he was counting on me, depending on me to take over his business when he retires, and now… I’ve let him down and he promises me a studio.’

‘Let him down? Maybe. They call you “the merry miller” in the village. Say you learnt the trade well, could read the sky, taste the grain; they don’t understand you, the farmers. They valued you, saw you standing in your father’s shoes.’

John looked down, frowning. Oh God. He’s right, he thought; what am I doing? I could be working in the village, using my knowledge to run the mills, wind and water… taking my father’s place by degrees, managing the business helped by the bailiff and clerk of course. Would life be so terrible? Forget painting; I can never paint the perfect painting, the painting that means something to me; it was a dream and dreams are always beyond Reality. Aren’t they? Why paint at all? Why face an uncertain future with no money or home? I should settle where I belong. As I have often said. The life right here if I choose it.

‘You’re right… yes, you’re right. I can see it; you think that this is what I should do, don’t you? Art, it’s all nonsense, I should be with my father and Abram. They could use another foreman. I should have taken over the bailiff job when old Revans passed on.’ He felt drained and slumped in his seat.

Silence.

Dunthorne was torn, angry with himself. Perhaps I should have considered Golding’s offer longer, he thought; it might have benefited both John and myself… though I don’t know how I would have been able to take time off for sketching, even with the owner's son; what would that have looked like? And I wouldn't have been no more than a bailiff anyroad. I've had an easy introduction to an apprenticeship through my father, learnt the trade and business and now here I am running my own and blow me down, Wheelers come to me when there's a grand roof to be done or any high quality glazing… that's worth something. Not a bad business and time to go a'sketchin'.

There's always enough work to feed the family, as long as I work from Ipswich to Colchester; it's not a bad stretch… and maybe one of the youngsters will step into my shoes, keep me in my old age… I've been fortunate; true, Mother died young – I can't put a face to her now – but Miss Hambleton raised me up; what an education she gave me in manners and knowledge. I can mix with the gentry and such when called for… it do set me aside from my old mates, those that I shared the form with at school; they think me too smart for my boots but they… what of it?

I always thought that young John would take on his father's business and keep it in the family way; hasn't he told me that Golding would never take a partner and young Golding's not capable? There's enough business there for John and young Abram when he comes of age and enough mouths to feed, the sisters and all. It's a family obligation, ain't it? Following in your father's shoes… and this painting business can remain what it is, sketching and the such… we would find time; I will always welcome it. Yes, John should be glad of the family he was born into, the advantages and all… he should stay here.

He bought more drink; his work could wait this afternoon. John was staring at his sketches.

'There's one missing; I thought I had it… I can't lose it, where…'

He started to push the drawings around on the table, chalk dust settling in the puddles of beer. A muddle of rough sketches that told Dunthorne nothing.

A small painting on thick paper appeared, sliding from beneath the larger sheets. It was an Adoration of the Magi, fully coloured in antique style, precise and entirely without the life that Dunthorne saw in John's sketches.

'Do you see now? I think I captured it.' John's face was alight, an innocent pride.

Dunthorne turned it over in his hands, holding it up to the light. He glanced at him; a quiet weight settled upon his heart. He spoke slowly.

'I see what you mean now, very close. Just as you have said. And this is what you want to do?'

He watched John closely. Would doubts arise in him?

'Well, this is the thing, don't you think?' said John. 'It should do, shouldn't it? Yes, yes. I know what you have been saying; it is not the sort of thing that you have seen me do before. But I told you, that would not serve, would it?'

'I don't know, John. It just seems odd to me to call this your painting. Did you not tell me, no, lecture me on the artist's eye and truth? I don't see where this fits, it don't seem right to me.' He cleared his throat and gazed out of the window. 'But you don't want to listen to me; what do I know about the painting business?'

He nodded to Abe, an old ploughman. He had known him all his life.

John was sitting in a daze. It was clear to Dunthorne that John had studied and worked hard but seemed to have been persuaded away from his own convictions. He, Dunthorne, was not used to dealing in doubts; he told his customers what he thought and, almost always, the work went ahead as he had planned it. Yes, he thought, it's a matter of black and white, yes and no. Mr. Golding is the same, I've seen it, no mucking about; he makes a good decision and sticks with it. One of the best men I've ever worked for and he must be a good master, no blaming happenstance on his men. Why, now I recall, he has even spoken of John on occasion; what was it? He didn't spell it out rightly, but I guess he always spoke as if John would take his example from me, the responsibility to family and village, and that he would bend his will towards the family business. And why not? He could go sketching now and then, do his painting, as long as business allowed. No reason he couldn't have a studio for it.

John sighed.

'What do I do if this won't serve?'

He looked lost, like the time he had fallen in the river, a full river in spate. As though his heart had shrunk and his will evaporated.

'I can't say that it won't serve, no, not at all. You know that, John. But if you want my opinion, well, I—'

'Please, Dunthorne, please tell me what you think.'

'Well then. What did you see in those big houses?'

'Oh, grand paintings; Italian, German, Flemish. There was one, a triptych, you know, early Italian from a small hill town, I should guess, a number of—'

'What is this… triptych? Was that the word?'

'Three paintings together, hinged. The centre one usually bigger with a central theme like an Adoration. And one either side, all relating to the centre picture. It gives a sort of panorama, a spread across the altar, but I like a panorama of views, like…'

He drifted into a dream of memories, gazing out of the window. A dog barked and a thrush flew past.

'I do recall you speaking of a… panorama. We were sitting on the hillside and you—'

'But Dunthorne, I was speaking then of a landscape painting.'

Dunthorne sipped his beer, shrugged.

'Don't see much difference when it come down to it.'

John looked around at the people in the pub, out of the window, at his dog. Bold came to his knee and submitted to a stroke. A panorama, he thought. I'd never thought… never… no, it won't do, I don't see it. All the difference in the world…

Dunthorne coughed, pushed his glass away. This would never do.

'Now John. You spoke of panoramas a number of times. The catching of the nature of a place, a wide view that might show all which one may see. This triptych of yours: sounds a bit like a panorama to me.'

'If it is allowed, permitted by the Church, that would be three paintings.'

'Aye, you could spend years on 'em, I dare say. Years and years.'

'No that is unfair, Dunthorne. Not years and years. If they were planned, there was a theme running through, it might be as a big painting in three parts.'

Dunthorne looked at him, frowning.

'You might be able to do it then? Same as a big painting? Well, it would be a fine piece of work. I've never seen such a thing meself, I dunno…'

His voice faded away. John was smiling.

'Yes, yes, I think I could. Of course, I would have to work everyday and… oh, I think it could be done. I wonder—'

'It would be a wonderful thing then, would it?' Dunthorne did not sound convinced. 'Well, there's not much to be said then, is there? I should be—'

'Another pint, Dunthorne. You have turned me upside down and I believe I like it. Tell me, tell me again, how do you see it?'

'Well,' Dunthorne spread his hands, gazing down at them. 'How do I see it? It may not be the right way, the proper way, the way that you would see it.'

'No, no, please Dunthorne. Don't play with me, I have always listened to you, learnt much.'

'Well, and I'm not a painter, as you know. But I see a spread of this village land here with your three religious scenes in place. Wouldn't that be doing what those Italian painters were doing?'

'A triptych!'

'If you do come to like it, you don't need to worry about the extra panels. I'll have a word with the yard at Flatford, they'll have something I can use and I'll fix the hinges when it is finished. Why, I might even give you a hand with all that rubbing down, whatever that is.'

'I would have to start again. And my father was hoping to present it this year in time for Harvest. He said something about a sign of providence and fulfilment. And he might not like it, you know, if I was to paint my own work, make the triptych my own.'

'Now then. I wouldn't want to be upsetting the master, John. It's not my place, you know it well. I'm not saying you are not to do a religious painting; that is your decision, but I do believe that you are talking of a holy painting. It's true I don't hold with the Rector and his religion; I'm a Chapel man as you know. But I am not saying that at all. Now, where am I? I'm all of a kerfuffle; I don't know what to say.

'You must do what your father wants. But a panorama... that would be wonderful. I never knew it possible. That's a wonderful idea, John; I congratulate you.'

'It would be a lot of work... I don't know...'

'Well, if you put your mind to it, John, anything is possible. Particularly with you. So, what religious scenes would you paint?'

'Oh, normal important scenes. Adoration, Crucifixions, things like that. Scenes from the Bible, and—'

'But suppose, just suppose, if you had local scenes for the background, like the Italian painters, what would fit? What would work well?'

'A local scene? Your "village land"?'

'It's your country, isn't it? It's what you always come back to, what you know.'

'Oh, I don't know. Do you mean local scenes, this village? And local people? They would laugh, wouldn't they, mock me for bringing it all down to local scenes, to—'

'But John, what did those other painters do? The ones you were telling me about? You wouldn't want to be just copying them, would you? Just painting local people of somewhere else?'

There was silence. John gazed at the table, his food ignored in front of him. Bold stirred and gazed up at him. Dunthorne sat back chewing on a crust. He nodded to a few friends, smiled did not speak. After a while, he stood up.

'Well, I must be getting on. Work to do. Let me know if you want the extra panels; I could get them to you in no time.'

He searched his pockets for coins. John laid his hand on his arm.

'I hear you, Dunthorne, I hear you. You have been taking me on a foreign passage, well out of familiar waters. Please, tell me again; what do you see?'

Dunthorne sighed, sat and stared ahead.

'I see three local views, perhaps a single view split into three, each a holy scene with local people as the holy people.'

'The Flemish painters painted local scenes with local people; I saw the painting somewhere, London perhaps. An extraordinary painting; you could see farmers and cobblers and dairymaids and—'

'And what scenes might you use with local people?'

'A Birth; I've always wanted to do a Birth. An uplifting local scene, animals, ordinary people, straw, cold, shade, a lamp—'

'You could use the Bellcage for a stable…'

John gulped. Dunthorne watched him come towards a new way of seeing things.

'Before the Birth, on the left side, what comes before?'

He wanted to say it, felt he was leading John by the nose, laying ideas before him to pick up like a hound following a trail.

'Of course. An Annunciation,' said John. 'But not in some precious building, not with Mary on her knees. She could be in the fields, taking cider to the men. Nine months before Christmas; March. What could they be doing then? Stoning.'

'You'll get it, John. You're almost there by the sound of it. That leave the other side.'

'A Sermon on the Mount, at the top of the hill below Old Hall. Oak trees, a crowd of men coming in from the fields, stopping to listen, looking up at Our Lord. I can see it now.'

'Can I go now, John?'

'Oh, it's a new world, I don't know. I must try.'

Dunthorne walked away to his home. He was confused. Here, have I not been telling John to get back to the mill? And when I hear of the painting he is to do, of the new studio and all, how can he not do what he must? Bugger it, I am confused; is he to be a miller or a painter, or both?

In the pub, John glowed. Dunthorne was right; what was he doing, painting an old painting? What a marvellous thing this would be, a triptych of a panorama… what a good idea I had; it was mine, was it not? Though thinking back, I cannot be sure whose idea and whence it came; but no matter… now I shall paint a painting to conquer the world… well, my world. And the Mill? I don't have to think about it, not just now. I have a painting to complete for my father, for the Constable family, and it comes first; my father would agree... and... and... and I shall put in all the local people, the village people; the village will be proud. As I'm sure the Dutchmen were proud when they saw their friends in those great paintings. Religious scenes, all local people. Yes.

'Oh, thank you, Jem. Did I call for a pint? I don't rightly... no, leave it, leave it, and please, pour one for yourself.'

15

AUGUST 1801

Golding stepped down from his trap in the yard and handed the reins to the lad. He sighed and turned to look over his kitchen garden. I wonder, he thought, only August and the evenings are drawing in, damp air, the end of the harvest though I'm sure there's some wheat still standing in this parish… it will be in a ruinous state, hardly good enough for animal feed… and now a running downhill to Christmas; or so it seems… though, come to think of it, a third of the year to pass, grain to sell, coal to ship… and the fruit is still on the trees, apples and pears, quince and medlar; it looks a good crop… must make sure the gardeners don't pick the medlars until they almost falling… never can get it into their heads; an early picked medlar is of no use to… another poor grain harvest, violence in London, all at the cost of flour… thank goodness we seem to look after ourselves in the village… well, I hope we do… must have a word around the mill and yard, make sure that their homes are provided for. Charity at home, eh? Must look after my men… I wonder if the squires remember… and now for the family… oh dear, when I could do with a small ale and a soft chair.

Behind him, a murmur from the kitchen and sudden music, perhaps Mary at the square piano, another romantic composition or a bagatelle. He was not musical, had never had the need to sing or play an instrument. It was good to hear his daughters well occupied. But he felt tired.

The harvest; how come it was so poor? Yes, the winter was long and hard but we have seen that all before… is it the type of seed grain? Grain price is up but there's less to grind, less to carry… perhaps it's a good thing; *The Telegraph* is tired, old timbers strained by drying out on the quay at Mistley, and on the Goodwin Sands when the skipper times it wrong… I never checked how old she was when I bought her but she was a coastal brig, wasn't she, bumping in and out of shallow docks and off beaches, all kinds of cargoes… time to look for a replacement… as it is, she must be careened, scraped, the hull looked over, seams caulked, fresh tar before the winter storms work the old timbers again… perhaps I should look for a new skipper; no, I don't know… so much to be concerned with… need some knowledge to prevent some know-all dictating to me, telling me how to spend my money… no, I won't have it. I'll make a close inspection myself with the skipper… see if we can't make sense of it together… wish I could get her up to my own yard here; that would be a joke, her hull standing in that dry dock, taller than the cottages.

Mind you, the yard's not working to capacity; I own most of the lighters working up to Sudbury… and now those yardmen are employed to waste my time and money… tried them on other things… you would have thought, what with their knowing timber, that they could have felled a tree; just felled it… and what happens? They've no idea, no idea at all… failed to lop branches, felled trees so they snagged others or destroyed fencing, hedging, huts… shattered the trunks… useless timber except for firewood… let alone squaring, planking, and sticking out to dry… never make foresters of them and yet they complain if they don't get a clean butt in the yard, free of shakes… I don't know… have to find some work for them. Ha! I'll have them hedging and ditching yet.

He looked over the garden; bare earth with some remaining vegetables. Neat rows, the digging started for early winter planting. A robin bobbed over the furrows. It looked happy.

He threw off his coat in the back hall. Not for him the way of the gentry, the front door and a servant to take coat or cape. What a waste of servants. He could hang up his own coat. And so could the rest of the family though he knew the maids rescued boots, capes, hats, all that young Golding cast off in the front hall. Cleared away before his eye fell on them. He wondered whether they were fond of the young man; he could be a bore, treat them appallingly. He had spoken to him on a number of occasions, about how to treat servants. Girls, he had never understood them. It never occurred to him that the maids did it out of respect for the master, respect for his liking for a tidy hall.

He ascended the stairs slowly, for once not enjoying the mahogany handrail, the turn of the staircase towards the top, the panelled doors on each floor; good joinery had always pleased him but tonight he felt jaded. He entered his wife's boudoir with a light knock, a moment's hesitation only.

Young Golding was stretched out at ease in a low chair, complaining to his mother about village people, a hectoring tone, peevish, petty. Golding stood on the threshold; Ann came to him, a brief peck on his cheek, a small shrug and turned back to her son. Golding retreated all the way downstairs to his study where a hot toddy awaited him. Kicking off his boots, he settled before the fire and relaxed with thoughts of ships, lighters, farmers, grain, the Commission and trees, before he dozed.

Later, he settled in bed, weary and sleepy. His wife came in, ready for bed but awake, keen to speak. He gave her a brief smile.

'Golding tells me that he has been treated poorly, a lack of respect, worse, an abuse of his position.'

Golding said nothing. He heard too much of young Golding about the village, whether directly from farmers and shopkeepers or overheard in the lanes, from others who did not wish to upset his goodwill, his patronage. In some ways, he was more important than the squires, who owned land but employed fewer men and women; and then would lay them off when the weather threatened or there was no work.

'And Nancy; how is her new horse?'

'My dear, have you not heard me? Golding is upset. I have struggled to reassure him of his status in this village, his middling type and yet—'

'Must we speak of this again? And at this hour?'

'It is not the same. There is a particular problem. John Dunthorne. You know there was the occasion that Dunthorne struck him in the drive of Old Hall; and the time that he was positively pushed away from the mill when he was harmlessly passing by and then there was the incident with John's dog, which apparently—'

'Please. I hear your opinion.'

'But it is not opinion. Golding has told me all. This man Dunthorne holds a grudge and tries to put him in the wrong. I believe you must speak with him; he has received many favours from you, I hear.'

'Very well, my dear. Now—'

'You will, for my sake?'

'Yes dear. Now—'

'Now I really must sleep, my dear. I have a busy day tomorrow. Goodnight, Mr. Constable.'

She turned to one side, eyes closed. Golding took up a book, tried to read and threw it down after a few minutes. Turned down the lamp.

The next morning, as he was climbing into the trap, he stopped, hummed and descended. The lad holding the horse looked up, surprised; it was unlike the master to hesitate or change his mind.

'I shall be back shortly,' said Golding, walking away. He strode out of the yard and turned to the right, away from Flatford Lane. Before long, he came to a barn-like building near the shop. All was quiet, the sun rising behind him. He opened the door and stepped into the darkness.

Before him was an open space, full height with a loft at one end. Windows at the side were covered, long drapes and shutters. The brick floor was uneven, scored where horses and carts had been kept. The walls were finished a bright white, a fresh coat of limewash. He hauled back the shutters; sunshine flooded in, motes of dust dancing in the rays. In the centre stood a large easel; beside it, a long table, covered with papers, paints, a plate, glasses, a few bottles, canvas, brushes, bottles of turpentine, boxes, tools. On the easel was a panel, possibly part of a painting; looking round, he could see two more panels leaning against the wall, one larger than the others. Above them were sketches, washes of colour, drawings of characters, trees, cattle, stiles, the Bell Cage.

The panels were painted but only with an under-painting, broad areas of bright colour, suggestions of field and sky.

Golding stood in the centre, surveying the whole space in front of him. Apart from the table, easel, and sketches, it appeared to be empty. No rubbish from past ages, no bundles of canvas or timbers. He clapped his hands, his face grim, and turned, walking fast out of the building, pulling the door to behind him. Returned to his trap and left for Flatford.

In the counting-house, a boy was running through a list of figures; he looked up with a serious expression.

'Abram, dear boy, did you see John last night?'

'Yes, Father. He came in late.'

'Was he… did he say anything?'

'No, sir.'

Golding stepped into his office, closed the door quietly behind him, sat down and pressed his head into his hands.

I don't understand it, he said to himself. I don't understand it at all… they want for nothing, the boys… a good home and all that goes with it; why, oh why, do they not respect it? A family business, thriving… my God, I've built it from nothing… well, not nothing, but it is so much more now… a fortunate inheritance, I wasn't even the oldest son… there's room for all the boys to take their part. And yet I have two sons, two out of the three for goodness' sake who cannot and will not take their parts… and young Abram must take the burden… it is not right… not right at all. How has it come about? Have I been too considerate to them… and my wife? No, I cannot lay the blame at her door… but all the same… what shall I do… what can I do?…

He returned home early. The mill was quiet; he had sent Abram home in the middle of the day. Dropping into the boatyard, he came upon two men only; they had no idea where the other three were. They showed him their day's work, repairs to an old lighter. The keelson was rotten and they were cutting it out carefully, preparing for a new timber; a length of air-dried oak lay nearby.

'Do you not cover the timbers to be used? Why take more damp into the hull than necessary?'

'Sir, we were measuring it… this afternoon. Looking to see whether there where any knots to avoid.'

'Do you cover it tonight, if you please?'

The men looked up with surprise. 'Yes sir, of course. Do you see, there is rot in the bottom planking. I assume that you would wish it replaced.'

Golding looked at the rot, wondered when the lighter would be needed; there was a load of coal to be carried up from Cattawade in mind. No hurry just yet. And a rotten lighter, it would not serve if business picked up. He told them to go ahead but to have the timberwork completed by the weekend, no fussing and fiddling.

Back with the trap, he walked the pony up the hill, stopping to give a ride to the farmer's wife from Valley Farm. She sat in silence, not expecting such a favour, and descended at the church with thanks for saving her legs and a brief curtsy.

The village was quiet. A barn owl swept up the road and disappeared into the churchyard, a white spectre against the dark walls. Two small boys stopped to stare and ran off. A man passed going the other way on an old hack; he looked shabby, a stranger. Golding wondered where he was going, who knew him. He walked the trap back to his house, a glow of oil lamps in the windows. Briefly, he considered whether he would ever find husbands for his daughters or whether they would outlive him in the family home. He enjoyed their company but wondered whether they felt fulfilled in life; surely, they would want their own children and there would be no difficulty providing them with dowries.

The lad in the yard took the reins and he waited to see the pony given a good rub down before a feed. In the next stall, Nancy's mare stirred, rolled her eyes; she was a good sixteen hands and lively. But Nancy knew her stuff. She was coming up to thirty-three years old, a forceful strong woman who loved her horses and dogs. There had been no interest from local farmers in marrying her; he was surprised, she would be a good catch. Perhaps she was too strong-willed, too much of a handful, like her mare.

Indoors, he sat in his study and called for Patty.

She bobbed a quick curtsy and laid her hand on his shoulder.

'You look tired, Father. You should rest; shall I bring you a hot toddy?'

'Ah Patty, that would be good. But first, could you run a small errand for me? I want to have a word with John; he will be in his studio no doubt and it will be getting too dark to work. If he is not there, would you look in at the Red Lion? No, perhaps not. Be away with you, let me know.'

She was the easiest; he felt guilty that he gave her his errands, asked her to help with small works. And to what end? She was sure to marry before long. She was pleasing to the company who sought her at dances and frolics. She was placid, kind to John, easy with Golding Junior, considerate to her parents. The front door slammed. He stirred the fire and sat at his desk, pushing papers around. Affairs that he was in no hurry to attend to, small tenancies to be reviewed, the gardener's plans for next year, repairs to cottages at Pitt's Farm. The working mills and the yard, the lighterage and the shipping, all of that was dealt with at the counting-house. But owning land and property led to demands that never ceased.

John stood before him. His smock, an old shepherd's blouse, was dirty, streaks of paint and chalk dust. His expression was withdrawn, almost stubborn. His father surveyed him, slowly from head to foot.

'You have your working clothes. I had thought that they stayed in your studio. The dust, paint… well, do you wish to take them off? The back hall, I think.'

John disappeared. Time passed. Golding fidgeted in his seat, rose and went looking for him. He found him in the kitchen, scone in hand, hair brushed, a waistcoat, clean breeches. He looked at him, raised his eyebrows. John dropped his scone on a plate, brushed his hands together vigorously and followed his father back to the study.

'Sit down, sit down. How are things with you? I have not heard how your studies proceed.'

'Well, father, very well. I receive much attention from the teachers.'

'But you have told me that they do not care for your work, that you work on paintings that are unfashionable, will not make money.'

'That is true, Father. But they are the only paintings that mean something to me. They are about the land here, about our people, the river, the—'

'Must you be in London? You must know that I could use your work in the mills.'

'I need the teachers, sir. Whatever the fashion of the day, they will change. And I am learning a great deal about drawing and the construction of paintings. But I hasten back here as often as I can; my place is here, Father.'

'Well, I wish your place was in the mill; but I have said that often and do support you in your work.'

'I am grateful, sir. Without your patronage, I should be a sketching artist only, as Dunthorne.'

Golding frowned at the name; he had not wished to discuss that man but now he would have to.

'Tell me, how does your studio suit? Are you able to work well, move forward with your paintings?'

He saw John pull himself upright, look away, worried, tense.

'It is good, Father. I am grateful; it exceeds my expectations. To have somewhere so large, well-lit, so close to home. And I do appreciate that you have made it available before the commission is complete; I could wish for no more.'

'Well sir, I could wish for more, much more. I visited your studio this morning; you had not risen. I opened the shutters, let in the light. A good light; pity to lose it.'

'Yes, Father.'

'My painting. I did not see anything of it. Three paintings in preparation, not at all well advanced, and none that looked like an altar painting. To me. As you know, I wished to present an altar piece at Harvest, the appropriate time to present a bounty from the land, from the people; and had hoped that you would have completed it for me last year, at least. A twelve-month period to allow you your studies, your sketching, perhaps even some time in the mill… was that so hard an expectation?'

'No, Father.'

'Twenty-three months it is now since I asked you if you could spare the time to paint an altar painting for the church. Nearly two years. It seems to me that you will have nothing finished for this Harvest, will you? I assume that you have many other things to occupy yourself.'

'I have to do life studies and copying for the School. It does take time. But I assure you, sir, that—'

The front door slammed. Sounds of boots thrown on the floor. A whining growl. The study door was slammed open. Golding Junior came in, hose, breeches, waistcoat twisted, with a red face, muttering.

'It is too much, Father. Why should I put up with it? Your farmer at Pitt's? Told me to shoot elsewhere, sent me off his land. Do I not have shooting rights wherever I please?'

He wheeled round, saw John and scowled.

'Your friend Dunthorne. Yes, I know him now. He put him up to it I don't doubt. Dammit, how dare he? And you. Strolling around the countryside with a maiden on your arm, no doubt too busy to assist your father as you should. You pipsqueak.'

'No, I—'

'It's too much, Father. My freedom tampered with by your tenants, your workers. Who do they think they are?'

'Dear boy, a minute or two. You can see that I am occupied at present.'

Young Golding threw himself into a spare armchair.

'I… I was up at Pitt's. Rabbits and pigeons. Good for the pot, so they say. An excellent new fowling-piece; it is the envy of half the county. And then—'

Mrs. Constable appeared in the doorway. Golding looked up, a half-smile and a shrug, indicated his sons; John sprang up, rubbing his hands together. He said nothing. Young Golding sat up, smiled at his mother.

'My dear, I am surprised,' said Mrs. Constable. 'I had not expected you so soon. Is all well at the mill?'

'Yes, I have returned early to attend to affairs here. There are…' He held up papers, waved them at her as though to wave her away. She stayed in the doorway.

'My dear, I am glad that you have decided to speak with Golding. He has a true complaint, I feel. Opposition from all quarters, most especially from this man Dunthorne. Do you know him? What sort of a man is he?'

John turned away from Golding to address his parents.

'He is a good friend of mine. His behaviour is always reasonable, his manner quiet. He spares time to accompany me—'

Golding had sprung up and gripped John's shoulders, as though to thrust him down. 'I've never heard such rot in all my life. He is a bounder, above his place in society, always in my way. I—'

'It seems to me, John,' said his mother, 'that he is not quite suitable company for a young gentleman. Perhaps you could curtail your activities with this man; I am sure that your father would be pleased if you spared him some of your precious time.'

Young Golding crowed, leering with a light cuff to the back of John's head.

'That's the way of it, mother. 'Bout time, I should say. Young John gallivanting with—'

'Enough, Golding.' She swept away out of sight.

Young Golding laughed, gave a mocking bow to John and stalked out of the room, calling for a servant. John turned to make his escape.

'I wish he wouldn't do that,' said his father. 'The servants have better things to do than nurse Golding.'

In the doorway, John turned to close the door on his father.

'Come in, close the door, John. We were interrupted.'

John sank back into his chair, gazing out of the window. The sun was setting over West Lodge, a warm distant glow. Trees were dark against the low light. A harsh chiaroscuro; not his style. Now, if the light came from behind him, would that not make a good composition? He could imagine how the trees would appear, glowing in the evening light, that mixture of reds and greens… what colour do they make when mixed? I must try it tomorrow in the studio. An interesting experiment, since they are opposites in colour…

Golding turned and rang the bell. A maid came and he ordered tea.

'Now, John,' he said as the door closed. 'Tell me about the altar painting.'

He sat back in his chair, hands raised as though in prayer, a slight smile. John coughed, sat up, earnest.

'Well, sir, it progresses. Indeed, it progresses. But there are many studies to complete and a structure for the whole… er… painting. I hope that you will not be disappointed, Father, but it is not a simple thing. There are many aspects—'

'Do you wish for an interview with the Rector? I am sure that he would be delighted to inform you on the sort of thing that is right, appropriate.'

'But Father, I had thought this a surprise, a great gift.'

'Indeed. That was my intention. But if you are having difficulties, we could smooth the way, ensure that he will approve the design.'

John was silent, twisting his hands together.

'Which of those panels that I saw this morning is to be the painting?'

'All of them. I mean… they join together… it is called a triptych… I saw one in London, holy scenes, linked by the presence of Our Lord.'

'All of them?' Golding experienced a sinking feeling. Would John never finish this work? What had he started here when he was only trying to encourage the lad? And not such a lad any more… had hoped that the painting would be finished, presented, hung, a satisfied wife, and perhaps a pleased Rector… and now he talks of many studies to complete… what is a study, when it needed here… Oh, what have I started?

'All of what, father?'

'The panels, John. The three panels.'

'It is not so much, they join together. Like one painting.'

Golding felt the ground slipping under his feet. He felt a great weariness. It was worse than dealing with a farmer who had not delivered his wheat, or a collier merchant from the North who had cheated on the cargo. At least he could afford to ignore them, take them off his books; well, the merchant anyway though it would be hard to cut off a local farmer… not right to set your neighbours against you; it did no good in the village, no good to the village families. But John! Oh for some understanding… on my part, as well as his. What is his world? What values and aims? I am adrift on a foreign sea without a pilot.

'So, you have missed Harvest again. I particularly wanted it for Harvest, preferably last year. Or even this year. When, John, when?'

'When, Father?' John was standing now, before his father's desk. Golding was reminded of past occasions, when John had stood before his desk. School reports, always poor… sometimes reported a truant from Dr. Grimwood's… he couldn't altogether blame him then, particularly if he had been helping with harvest or the river warden… decisions and discussions about his future, suitability or otherwise for the Church, the law… such nonsense… look at him now? Where would we have been with a failure, an embarrassment to the family… his mother, for goodness sake… and when he was young, petty damage, always by accident I'm sure, neighbours' fences… steeplechasing with other young ruffians on foot, parish to parish… he appears just the same, even in his twenties… close to pleading, a supplicant.

'I shall not delay your departure; I can see that you are keen to be away. Please tell me when I may expect the altarpiece, however many sections it is composed of, in a state that I may present to the Parish Council.'

'Well… I mean, there is much to do—'

'Twenty-three months, John. You have had twenty-three months. Missed two meetings that I hoped for. Give me a date.'

'I think, possibly—'

'Not good enough, John. Closer, if you please. A date.'

‘Around the end—’

‘And what would the coal merchants of Sudbury say, if I promised them a load “around the end”?’

‘It is not the same thing at all, Father. No, I’m sorry. But I cannot tell how long I shall take to paint it.’

‘And is this so, in society portraits? Do they wait upon the weather, or the turning of the moon, for a completed portrait?’

‘No, sir.’

‘No, John.’

‘Well, I shall try—’

‘Indeed, you will. And I shall expect it by the end of February. Seven… no, six full months. And I’m sure that the Academy Schools are not open over Christmas.’

‘But the studio… it is cold over the winter. Water freezes, and—’

‘You shall have a load of timber. Off-cuts from the yard. I shall attend to it.’

‘Thank you, sir.’

‘Thank you, John.’

He did not see much of John over the next few days. His daughters told him that John went out early, before the family had arisen, and came in late to a hurried meal in the kitchen. Mrs. Constable had not raised the matter of Dunthorne again; he let the matter lie. And young Golding seemed happy to follow his continual slaughter of small birds and animals, bringing them into the kitchen for the cook and her maid to dissect the mangled shot-ridden carcases or dispatch to the stockpot.

From time to time he wondered about Dunthorne; I thought I knew him well… it’s always good to see him working on one of the mills, a familiar face, sound workmanship, never a problem with his work… more than I can say for others… even

Wheelers have been known to send me a poor carpenter… not a mistake they make twice, I'm glad to say… and Dunthorne, so interested in all industry and work… good man to talk to, even a good idea on occasion… such a practical man, and there's John, touch of the practical working man there but he is all but lost to me, with the will of his mother, I guess, didn't want her son to be a merchant and what am I? I asked… don't see really why Dunthorne cares to spend so much time with John… unless it's to be close to a good employer… but I can't see that in him, no, not at all… too straight, a man who calls a spade a spade, I reckon… no, not even if he reckoned on John being the boss but he must know better now. I don't know, John must be a good five years younger, a lad in comparison, never had to work for his living… not like me, back when I was his age and working for a friend of my father, any old work to pay my way… do I spoil my children, I wonder? Now, Nancy, she could be out giving riding lessons to young ladies, and Patty… oh, it's no good, their mother would have none of it, I dare say… and there's Dunthorne who gave John a room in their cottage and it's small enough, isn't it, with the two boys… could never make out why Dunthorne's Sarah was not more popular in the village… some history there… mind, John is never sociable, not in a local sense, always off on his own, away over the river or down at the mill… doesn't care to spend time with the other sons of his age, landowners, farmers, whatever… can't have much in common with them now, stretched the old bonds of acquaintance too far… you have to stay in touch with your neighbours, never know when a business contact is useful… the farmers and merchants who have been to our house, ridden out with me a few times, count as friends, all lost to John I dare say… you can't forget your roots, where you came from, but look at the boys, what business sense do they have? And I tried, God knows, I tried.

16

SEPTEMBER 1801

Dunthorne and John walked round the church tower; they could not agree whether to bear off down the Flatford Lane as they often did, or to stay in the village and go past Old Hall on the other side and down the hill to an enclosed valley. John had been speaking of it for months.

Harvest was over and the weather was unsettled. A crowd of unhappy restless men in the pub and around the village, muttering from lost income from a poor harvest, not knowing when they would be needed. Dunthorne was happy to escape them and walk out with John who was often in the village. John's London life was suspended for the summer months with no classes or supervision, tutors in far-flung places, hot classical countries and romantic mountainous resorts.

And it was hot in the City. John told him that, instead of a stifling journey in the stage coach, he had returned on *The Telegraph* in the cool of sea breezes, chatting with the seamen and staying awake through the summer night to watch the lights of ships and the coast slide past, the captain on deck at all times, as the man at the helm bent to the binnacle; sometimes a loud altercation with an unlit fishing boat, curses and swearing from both sides; occasionally a shouted greeting with a friendly coaster going the other way.

They stood by the churchyard gate, arguing the alternatives.

'The sky is not settled. We should not go far,' said John.

'Oh, John, what nonsense. We've survived many a shower; since when has a spot of rain resolved you?'

'I sense that it is more than a spot; more like a deluge. Do you see the clouds there?' He pointed away to the south-west, over the trees.

They turned through the Churchyard.

A door slammed, the clank of a latch. The Revd. Rhudde emerged from the Church porch, Maria on his arm.

Dunthorne and John halted, both parties obstructing the other. Dunthorne glanced at Rhudde and then at Maria; saw her gaze fixed on John, a slight flush, eyes sparkling. He was aware of John giving a quick bob of a bow with an awkward twist, eyes fixed on Maria. He looked again at Rhudde; there was a hardening of his expression, a gripping of the jaw, the eyes hooded. He thought how old he looked, his features becoming a caricature of solemnity. The minister at Chapel was a friend by contrast, warm and approachable.

Rhudde clasped Maria's arm more firmly within his. 'Come, my dear.'

Dunthorne and John fell back on either side. John gave a gasp and gazed after Maria. She had moved on, looking ahead and giving no further sign of their friendship. John turned back to Dunthorne.

'It can never be. Do you not see? I am a nobody, a vacancy upon the ground I walk. And she? She would have spoken; did you not see? She would have acknowledged us, greeted us. But her grandfather; he exerts a hold on her with the claw of a vulture.'

'There's nothing to be done at this time. We have spoken of it often enough. Come.'

And they walked on past Old Hall, past the bakers and down the hill. Now and then they met old acquaintances and paused, chatting until John looked up at the sky, tapped Dunthorne on the arm and they went away again, to the meadow at the foot of the hill and the stream that bubbled between banks carpeted in flowers.

'Do you see what I mean? You know I was speaking to you of perspective, the constructed perspective of an Italian architect. Alberti, that was his name. And here it can be much as a grand chamber, a single vanishing point at the horizon, and all flows towards it. But more difficult, for the land falls away; how do you show it falling away?'

'Yes, I learnt of perspective as a lad. But I see only trees and flowers and cattle, and… oh look, isn't that Maisie? What's she about now? Ah, I see now. Young Jim.'

'No, but… yes, it is all there. The shape of the place. Look.'

'That girl will be in trouble or in the church before long. I wonder how old that lad is.'

John had ignored him; sat and sketched rapidly, an indication of the lines that came to a point. A suggestion of space, an illusion of infinity, struggling with the falling land. Dunthorne looked at it, looked up and frowned.

'I don't see it, quite. There is an idea here but I don't quite grasp it.'

'And when you draw your glass designs, do you not worry about the perspective, the views and buildings as well as the figures? I don't understand, Dunthorne. You must meet this way of depicting things as often as I do. A daily way of seeing things.'

'Ah, well, you see, it's quite simple. It's drawn already, the old designs. I copy them from the broken sections to the new.'

‘Copy? But I thought—’

‘I don’t have your bare canvas, young John. Life is not so simple for me; I have to follow the rules, the right way of doing things. And I can’t go off making up my own designs. You know what churches are like.’

Dunthorne thought of his last work, a single window in a church, shattered by a stone; nobody could say how the stone had flown through the window. It was rare, they had told him… a stone. Occasionally a bird, confused and caught in glare no doubt, but a stone? Why, why would anybody have wanted to destroy a church window? Still, he thought, it was no matter to me; it was work, work that paid for the food on my table and shoes and cloth and all the other things that home and wife called for, before the alehouse. But it didn’t finish well for me.

The old glass was a horrible mixture, a real jumble of ancient glass set in old lead, some bits of beautiful faces, figures, animals. I wanted to make sense of it all, tell the story as the olden days glass-makers intended. I managed most of it. All except a few scraps of leaf and building. The old Vicar, he wasn’t worried, was happy to see the window repaired, but there was a sharp-eyed and sharp-witted old biddy who made it her business to put me in my place, remind me of how old the window was – as though I didn’t know – how I had no right to make alterations and who did I think I was to interpret the tale of the olden glass-makers? Well, when all was done, glass puttied and the light set in place, mortar dry, the old lady made a fuss, appealed to the Vicar who quailed before her, stuttered, dilly-dallied so long that she said she would go to the Bishop. Reckon the Vicar got a scare on; he told her that there should be no more delays or disruption but that they would look closely at any future work I may carry out for them and not allow me to make up me own mind.

He thought of telling John. But felt that he would not sympathise. Nobody told him what to paint, what to put in his paintings.

'Now, John, how does your altar painting come along? Are you getting the image of it? How is your perspective?' This last a teasing tone.

'Still on paper, working up the design. I don't know...' He sounded querulous.

'What, not working on those panels I made you? Why, they'll be getting all dirty, and—'

'I shall get to them when I am ready. But Dunthorne, for goodness' sake, how do you think I can portray our villagers? Do you think I can ask them to sit for me, like an artist's model? It would kill the thing dead. I could never ask Sarah, for example, to sit for the Virgin Mary. It would be around the village, I would be hounded before a brush has been put to panel. My studio would be compared to a—'

'Must they be so exact, John? It seems to me that you are wasting time; I wonder what your father will think. And it was to be presented this Harvest. But you won't be ready for that, now will you?'

'These things take time, surely you know—'

'Time, time, I don't know, you spend hours scribbling away, you spend hours mooning after an unreachable woman, and you have time to be walking out sketching something which is nothing to do with the altarpiece. I don't get it, John, you are wasting what you've got—'

'Wasting? You accuse me of wasting? You were keen enough to turn me away from the painting that I intended, a proper altar painting, steer me into troubled waters, a new course and stormy weather ahead—'

'And you are all at sea.'

A pause. John stared into Dunthorne's face, his eyes blazing, jaw clenched.

'If it is such a trial to you, I shall not trouble you again. I shall leave you to sketch in peace. I shall walk in another direction.' He turned with a sneer; his bag swung against Dunthorne.

'You won't get off that easily, young man. You have a painting to finish; get on with it, you lazy—'

'You accuse me of lazy? You… who takes time off to go wandering across the meadows and sit in the alehouse? I wonder what your patrons would say if they knew how you spent your time.' John clenched his fists, mind blown beyond reason.

'And what do you expect for the hours spent with Maria? I don't know; I'm sure she is charming enough. Though God knows there are enough village girls would have been happy to take you in hand, make a man of you—'

'How dare you… how dare you speak of Maria so? You don't even know her, you have no idea, you… you who was carried away by a widow girl, carried—'

Dunthorne gripped John by the collar.

'You speak of my Sarah? Why, she wouldn't pass the time of day with you if it weren't for your mother. She is far too good a person to dally her time away, far too good to… to… I don't know, but far too good for you. And she is with me, not some maiden floating around…'

John flailed at Dunthorne, light punches falling on either side. Dunthorne threw him down on the ground; John lay there, red face, tears starting, words gushing.

'Don't you… Maria… girls… lazy, I'm not… bugger it… you… you…' And subsided into silence.

Dunthorne stood staring down the valley. He cast his sketchbook aside, kicked at the grass, knocking John's painting water over his palette, his notebook and his jacket.

'Look what you've made me do. If you didn't scatter your things around the ground like a spoilt brat…'

John was on his feet.

'What have you done? You… you idiot, you clumsy oaf, you… How dare you speak of Maria like that.' He was shouting. 'She couldn't be more suitable; sensitive, such character… but then you wouldn't recognise it, you couldn't see it, could you, coming from… from…'

He hesitated. Oh God, what has happened, he thought. I feel dreadful…what have we said, what words cannot be undone? And I behaved like a spoilt schoolboy… how could Dunthorne speak of Maria like that… he doesn't know her, can't know her… and the painting, how can it ever be finished, how, how… and I owe Father so much, how can I repay it… how can I ever be with Maria… oh God…

He crumpled over on the grass, crawling around collecting painting things. Dunthorne stood over him, a look of confusion on his face as though he were waking from a nightmare.

A large drop of rain fell, bouncing off John's palette. A pause. Another heavy drop. A rapid increase in drops and a heavy downpour started, roaring and sweeping loose stuff away into the stream. The water began to rise, pressing against the banks and in no time overflowed.

John and Dunthorne picked up their things, helping each other but not speaking, and ran for a field shelter up the slope near the road. Inside, they dropped their bags and gazed at the rain. Small branches bent to the blast, the hillside became a sheet of water. The stream had grown to a torrent, carrying away leaves, twigs, turves, and John's sketch of the valley.

Above the roar of the storm, there was a cough and a sneeze.

From the road, a dark form slithered, slipped, fell and crawled into the shelter. A large dark cape, a huge sou'wester, light pumps, soaked. It sat up. A gasp. A hand wiped the face with a large spotted handkerchief.

'Oh, horrors, damnation and curses. Must we… is this our destiny?'

They stared. Who was this man, this shivering stranger in such odd clothes? And turned their backs on him.

The rain continued to descend, a deafening curtain of water carrying all before it. John and Dunthorne stood in silence, Dunthorne angry and not ready to give in to John's disorder. Why the hell couldn't he get on with it, complete a fair sketch and paint the painting? Why all the delay, the prevarication, the passing of wasted hours? He will never be a businessman, he would be hopeless. Look at him; wiping his face, side to side. Oh God, now he's smiling, and holding out a hand… I'm bloody angry with him… He took the hand, a single shake. They waited without talking for the cloudburst to pass.

A thinning of the rain; through the curtain of water, a brightness appeared shining off the wet hillside, leaves that shone as they dripped, the wet back of a cow. The stream, a full torrent taking the shortest route, continued to flood the field on either side. A vivid smell, wet grass and straw, rotten timber, soaked clothes.

There was a cough.

'Why gentlemen, this village will be the death of me. Such weather, I've never known it. In spite of all the cloudbursts that Cambridge suffers.'

They looked down at him; it was an odd spectacle. Obviously a stranger to both village and countryside.

'Aye, it was heavy but not unknown, these late summer months,' said Dunthorne.

'Heavy? Heavy? It was a deluge of water as though the skies were discharging all their debts. A punishment upon the land, a divine retribution. I have never known it so.'

'It happens.'

'It is testing me, you know. This village life. I am not sure that the cut of my cloth suits this rural residence. And I have tried; I have tried.'

'Would you be a Londoner? I visit there often… it never seems to rain as here; perhaps it is all the buildings… or something,' said John. 'The people are not like our villagers, not at all.'

'Why,' said the man, 'I have just come from the Rectory. The Reverend Rhudde. He is a distant man, is he not? We were both at the same learned institution within a few years, an overlap without doubt and he will speak to me as though I come from another country. It is impossible. I had thought, I had depended upon it, he would provide a source of sound philosophical thought, a learned man in this rural retreat. But no sir. He will not engage. Addresses me with a formal disdain, pretends to have no knowledge of modern philosophical thought and almost accused me, yes, I sensed it, almost accused me of some ancient heresy. I have no place here, I must submit and return to a city.'

'But, sir, have you not had good company here or at the Assembly Rooms at Dedham?'

'They have all been very good to me, I'm sure. Very kind; I am quite unable to return all their favours. We talk of many things, of geography and history. And literature.'

'But they will not satisfy—'

'It is a matter of my learning, my pursuit in life. I must seek other company.'

John looked at him; his sou'wester pushed back over his long hair, now bedraggled. The shepherd's cloak, huge and darkened with rain, and the pumps, almost ruined.

'Well, sir, I bid you well in your city. And now, will you accompany us to the Red Lion? Perhaps a hot toddy to warm the bones. Dunthorne?'

'The day is lost. Let's warm it with a drink. I wonder if Jem has a fire going this wet ol' afternoon?'

An odd triangle of persons ascended the hill. John and Dunthorne felt as though they were escorting an aged aunt, pushing her up the slope. They did not speak to each other; Dunthorne felt sore from his own words and a lingering feeling that he had been right, that John was wasting time and a suspicion that Golding would say the same thing. And that he, Dunthorne, might have added to the delays in John's work and appear to be in the wrong.

At the door of the tavern, Dunthorne stood back.

'I have work to do. I shall leave you, gentlemen.'

John looked at him, a mute appeal. But Dunthorne avoided his eye, gave a quick bow in the direction of the gentleman, swung on his heel and strode off. John held his hands up.

'He has carried away my sketchbook. Halloo, Dunthorne, my sketchbook!'

Dunthorne had gone, a distant figure, back turned.

17

DECEMBER 1801

Winter had come early.

East winds swept the land; the ground turned to rock, standing water to ice, and every living thing hunched against the blast. Trees stood bare and the fields were deserts of frozen furrows and frosted grass. A dusting of snow lay on open ground. At the mill, flour was still ground and on the river lighters moved, the men bundled in smocks and sacks. But it was hard work; Golding Constable lost a man who overbalanced lifting a branch clear and tumbled into the water, too heavy with clothing and too cold to fight a quick death. And now there was a widow with children to consider.

The meadows flooded, and after a week the ice was reckoned strong enough for skating. One evening, Golding was in the counting-house at the mill. A man came running; would he go over to the skating meadow? There was trouble with Master Golding.

'He looks to be in real trouble, master. Of course, we wouldn't have disturbed you, but with Master Golding… well we didn't know…'

Yes, thought Golding, with Master Golding, there were always considerations, allowances and measures to be put in place… there always had been… school was a useless experiment; the lad had lasted a week, before I was invited to remove him… there were complaints from boys, masters and parents… and parents, I was told, never complained; well, it was rare… and then a private tutor; what a waste of money. Anne's idea; I had no choice, supported her on the basis that any tutor must be more in the way of a carer, a strong silent sort of man who must lead him away from potentially disastrous situations, not allow him to be a nuisance, either to others or himself… And what happened? The tutors lasted, at the most, a month. They failed; and they were happy to admit it… some terrified, had been assaulted. Some had stood up to him, held him down by force, a physical experience that led to Mrs. Constable dismissing them with young Golding's complaints whining in her ears… what a pity, those were the ones worth keeping; if only she understood… like the old school sergeants we had, boxed our ears, silenced us when the master asked for it… oh, school. And there were some who left when Golding showed no interest in studies and they doubted that he was even capable of them… Mrs. Constable expected too much of her son; he could never be academic. One was frank in his assessment: Golding could read and write, but his reading and writing were those of a seven-year-old… his attention span lasted the flight of a fly across the room, his intelligence… Oh, I remember, what a laugh, the tutor ceased to comment before Mrs. Constable, unwilling to sacrifice his last payment, no doubt… and with that in hand, he left the village without bidding his pupil farewell, good luck, adieu. Can't say I blamed him.

'I fear, master, that there could be unfortunate trouble… very unfortunate.'

Golding Constable stirred from his seat, a silent groan as he pulled on cloaks, scarves and a hat against the cold. And followed the man along the lane past the yard to the flooded meadow.

The crowd appeared to be split. Close by the hill where the water was shallow, families and their friends circled on the ice; flying scarves, fur hats, chairs for the unsteady, a fire burning in a brazier on the bank, hot drinks, glowing lanthorns, toddy, laughter and cheers, the odd scream. He recognised most of them, neighbours and villagers, who waved to him, invited him to join them.

On the other side, by the river where the water was deeper, and trees hung over in near darkness, the crowd had a different hue. Backs were turned, a crowd huddled close around some spectacle; dark, hooded, a coarse laugh or two, a broken cheer, mostly silent.

He turned to the dark side, slipping on the ice, clutching his hat. He had no doubt that the spectacle involved his son in another loss of grace and dignity. He would rescue him, as always; perhaps be persuaded to pay damages to a few people. Dammit, is there no other way forward? Apart from committing him to some institution and Mrs. Constable would not consider that, not in any fashion or means… not that she has to deal with these situations… to be honest, I feel the same… it can't be right to commit one's own son. Where is he, what is he up to now?

He pushed his way into the crowd; the men fell back, now sullen and quiet. There was not a single woman among them. Typical; like bear-baiting. Not a soul turned to him and offered an explanation. As the last men parted, he saw his son, recognisable only by his clothes, in the arms of a man.

The ice came up to their chests. They stood in a pool of dark water, both shaking with cold, the water lapping around them, spilling onto the ice. It was hard to see in the late evening, the torches some distance behind him. He called for a light and a man hurried off. Young Golding appeared to be slumped, head dropped, no signs of movement or sensibility; Mr. Constable could not make out the figure behind him, dark in the shadows.

'What has happened here?' he called. No reply, silence from the men, a slight gurgle from the water surging black around the figures.

'You all know me. Who can tell me what happened here?'

Again, silence. The crowd was thinning as men slipped away into the darkness. The figures in the water appeared to be drooping; a man made an attempt at approaching but retreated at the sound of a crack, a sharp report that brought a shiver to the crowd causing it to retreat and fragment. Until there was only a handful, all known to Golding, all good men.

One went for a ladder, another followed him. A long wait during which no man dared to approach the hole and the two figures in the water seemed to be planted as one, unable to move apart from a swaying with a groan, from whom it was impossible to say. The torch arrived and Golding held it high, examining the face of his son. There was blood running from his nose and mouth; his eyes were closed but he appeared to be breathing. A hoarse gasping. Moving the torch, his eyes met those of Dunthorne.

For a time, they stared at each other until Dunthorne swayed and dropped his eyes, his arms around young Golding's chest. Mr. Golding shook his head. How could it be? And yet…

A ladder arrived, and a man with Mr. Constable's trap waited at the road. Over by the bank, the other skaters were watching, women with hands to their mouths, men standing apart, children staring. Golding led the way across the ice, a party of men bearing his son on the ladder, dripping mud and leaves across the scored surface. There were no words but at the sight of the body, there were low mutters, a groan, and a few sobs. He climbed into the trap and his son was bundled in next to him, smothered in rugs and sacks. They set off up the hill, a brisk trot, hooves echoing in the tunnel.

Dunthorne swayed; he had recognised the look in Golding's face: the incredulity, mixed with sadness and regret. It passed across his consciousness like a cloud, distant, irrelevant. The cold was shutting down his body and mind. He had lost all feeling in his arms and legs and when they pulled young Golding from him, he fell sideways as though to fold beneath the ice. A log was thrust against him across the hole and he hung over it, incapable of further movement or thought. Images of life floated before him… a man in his chair before the fire listening to a tale read by a young lad on a stool… Miss Hambleton shaking her fist at him… a pirate on the Spanish Main… hot bread… her soup… flowers… Patty naked in a shaft of sunlight… light through coloured glass… a woman, indistinct, beckoning, smiling… Mother… reach her, I must reach her, she was fading…

The ladder was hurried back from the trap and a brave man edged along it and grasped his shoulders. He was too heavy. A rope was fetched, turned under his shoulders and he was hauled out on the ice like a drowned cow, he was told later. Much later. Unmoving until they rolled him onto the ladder and bore him away across the lane to Bridge Cottage where he was laid before the fire, unpeeled, rubbed coarse with rags, wrapped around in bedding and propped up with hot food. He did not speak but touched the arm of the housewife and squeezed the hand of her husband. Wept with the feeling that he had been summoned from beyond death and failed by returning to a life of pain.

Word was sent to his wife. And the next morning he returned home on the back of a horse. He spoke to no one and the men around him were quiet as though they had bitten off something too big to swallow. For some days he was not seen.

His wife became furious. What was he doing there in the first place playing with those rough ol' boys, getting in the way of the gentry? And look what became of it; bed for days, no earnings, no new work, and all the questions she had to put up with, apart from putting up with him about the home. She had wondered what she was doing marrying a plumber and now she was learning the truth of it. Was he going to carry on like this? What an example to the boys.

They stood in front of him, side by side, the younger thumb in mouth. Silent at first, awed at the sight of their father laid up. They were difficult to shift when schooltime approached or bedtime called. An easiness grew between them; he read and told tales of the village, some unlikely, that they repeated to their mother and earned a slow cuff or two, giggling.

In time he went back to work. Neighbours avoided his eye, kept away. And he sought no company, kept to himself in the Red Lion and returned home early to his Sarah and the boys. She held to him, wouldn't listen to the rumours and stories about the skating, Master Golding and her husband. She had always been regarded as putting herself above her station, and now her neighbours had no difficulty in being distant, affording her the minimum of courtesy, the briefest of nods, scarcely a word in the shops and streets. The boys had the worst of it; playground scandal spread fast, of stories that their father would be in trouble with the Constables, that he had made enemies of his neighbours, the law was after him, he would be thrown in the Cage, their mother was a stuck-up pig and sounded like one, and they were born out of wedlock, bastards. Dunthorne heard all of it when he got home from work, saw the bruises and cuts from bullying and fights; he told his wife that she would get no satisfaction from complaining to the schoolmaster, that time alone would wash away the hurt.

Before long, he received no more work from Golding Constable or Wheelers and was forced to travel for all his work to Ipswich and Colchester. The builders there didn't know of his reputation and he had to take simple work to earn their respect. But there was always work; there weren't many who could repair a lead roof and advise on a church window. It kept him away, sometimes for the inside of a whole week while he completed a roof or plumbed a town house. And he would return with money, sufficient to keep his home running and his wife content.

The towns fed his old enthusiasms for progress and invention; at the docks, he saw machines for unloading the ships, steam cranes, rollers, grain chutes. The cargo ships themselves were changing, larger and faster, sleek lines, complicated rigs requiring smaller crews. There were some strange craft from Holland that could tack up the river, sail against the wind, leaving the brigs and ships waiting for a fair breeze. He heard talk of steam tugs to bring a ship in from the sea saving two or three days, perhaps a week.

Near the docks, housing had sprung up, tight narrow houses, three and four storeys high, leaning over narrow gutters of streets. He ventured into them a few times; housewives on the thresholds sang out to him, laughing and teasing. Children tugged at his clothes; bare feet, rags, dirty, some wall-eyed, crippled. And men lurked, cursing him on sight, calling out for work, threatening violence.

This was the other side of the future. He had not thought it, that mankind could stoop so low, a life without dignity and cleanliness, food and clothes. Surely, it was not the right way to move forward; machines were to lift man from the role of a pack-horse or a drudge, to give him time to live in warmth and comfort. Not to turn him into a slave to a machine.

A change in life, working away and returning to the village to rest. Occasionally, there was a small job for Wheelers or one of the squires, to be carried out without delay. He broached the subject of moving away to start a new life, to Ipswich, Hadleigh or Colchester, wherever she chose; Sarah would be furious, shouting and tearing at him, reminding him of her family just up the road and the boys at school in the village and their own cottage, neat and convenient, near the large houses where it was quiet. And she would burst into tears, standing in the kitchen surrounded by the warmth of her stove, the smell of fresh baked bread, her furniture and the few treasures hung on the walls; pictures that the boys had drawn, a sketch by Dunthorne that she favoured, a pretty cup. Dunthorne would hold her until the storm had passed, until she curled into his arms and lifted a tear-stained face. And his heart would sink that he must continue to tread his lonely road.

Being away from the village, he could not spare idle hours with John. Didn't even know whether John wished to see him. Constables; it don't do to mix with the middling types; they'll always get the better of you… and I thought that Mr. Golding knew me, would take the matter in hand… nobody has asked me what really happened, the truth of it, and know what it would look like if I told it straight out… where Master Golding is concerned, there's no winning nor never was… oh God, is this to be my life now? All that travelling and them roads, apart from the turnpikes, are worse than our own street, all ruts and holes and the haulier's cart… but I'm not telling anyone, not even my Sarah… though she is good, she does do well by me, never a poor meal… people can take me as they find me… I'm not puffing myself up… never does good…

He heard that John had called at the house a few times and left a note. He did not answer and he never saw him. He wondered how the altarpiece was coming on, whether John had held to his revised plan, the triptych. But he had no time to think of sketching or dropping in on the studio. He wondered why he had spent so much time with the painter. He felt adrift in the village, and had little contact with his old friends.

But John. Ever since hauling him from the river all those years ago, he had been glad to have a friend who could converse easily with him on matters above the common talk of the tavern; on new skills, on artistic ideas that fed his curiosity and his understanding of the church windows, on a knowledge of the countryside in which he had been brought up, the crops and men, birds and animals. And the weather; he wondered at that. He thought that the local boys must be the best forecasters, the ploughmen, shepherds and such. But John had shown him more, the height and speed of the clouds, direction and weight.

And John had introduced him to sketching, shown him how to use a brush and pen and how to look. He had never thought that looking was a skill. But he could no longer look at a view without seeing a picture or something unusual, a mackerel sky, a tree that had been struck by lightning and split to form an odd shape, an unexpected long vista across the river valley with Dedham Church standing tall. At least his long journeys were times for looking out on the crops and he could hear John's voice commenting on whether the corn was fit, or about the type of cattle or sheep.

One Sunday, a bright cold morning late in the year, he was walking with the boys to Flatford; he wanted to show them the repairs to the bridge and to look out for birds and fish. John came out of East Bergholt House as they passed.

'Dunthorne, I say, Dunthorne. Hold up there.'

He looked up, saw the Constable house with the young master and his trappings. And he saw his father's eyes as he held young Golding in the icy water, the shrug and dismissal. He recalled the absence of Constable work, a total cessation after years of working together. Hurrying the boys, he walked on to escape any embarrassment, giving John a brief nod.

'Father, father, he's calling you. Didn't you hear?'

'Father, what does he want?'

Dunthorne knew what he wanted, to wrap him up with Constables again, to bring alive the problems and conflicts. He had no time for them and wanted to keep his family with their type. He didn't turn but moved on. John stood in the road, gazing after him.

A few days later, arriving home late, Sarah greeted him, a smile and a letter in her hand.

'Dear, I had such a nice visitor. John Constable; he brought me some paper for the boys to draw upon, pencils, colours. And a note for you.'

Dunthorne dropped it on the mantelshelf.

'Do you have some hot food? I'm famished. It's freezing out there.'

'He says he is sorry that you are seldom here, that there is no time for sketching, for his company. Is there a problem, dear, something you have not told me?'

'This travelling; I do wonder when they will improve the old road to Ipswich.'

'You never said, when work around here dried up; I assumed it was a shortage as happens from time to time.'

'Aye, there was a shortage. Please, food. Are the boys abed?'

He escaped his wife who looked after him, frowning, hands clasped.

After eating, watched over by a silent wife, he took the note down and broke the seal. A ramble of writing at the top descended into a thicket of squiggles, various sizes until the writing became tiny as though to be sure of squeezing it all in.

Dunthorne,

I can find no words to express my SORROW my Disappointment that you cannot find Time for my compny. You are Away so often so long. I MISS our times tgether xcessivly & even if the weather is so inclemant to prevent sketching – why the water would FREZE in our beakers – we have always had much to Discuss whether in the Studio or the Tavern. But I see you neither There nor Here.

I questiond Father & Brother. Brother referrd to an Incident a jumble of Accusations & Rumours incredible unsavoury TALES that REEKD – I did not Beleive a WORD. You MUST beleive me – he is a LIAR often protecting his Wild behaviour with Falsities & Mother. She is ALWAYS taken in ALWAYS defend him. I don't Understand it. She told me once how ones own Children can do no Wrong how I Would protect my eldest Son. How after all I have been allowd to walk MY own path not assist Father & step into well-endowd Shoes – did I not see the Charity of it?

My Father will not discuss the Matter; he Sigh & Groan bid me to apply meself to Work asks searchingly after the Altar-peice. And I Beet a RETREAT for it is taking me a LONG TIME a Great Deal Longr than

I had forseen. Yes, I must confess it. I do Wondr at the Wisdom of following my own BELEIFS & not producing a Standard Altar-peice. I will not be Deterrd now. It Progress s. But Father will not visit the Studio. He say that it Pain him how long a Painting take how I seem to be Unable to compleat work. He askd Once whether it was yr Advice to paint a BIG Painting & I had TROUBLE Convincing him that I was Painting what I always Paint Landscape with Figures in the Old Fashion. Or so I Said. I thought He would Dispute the Truth of it. I did not wish for a dispute with Father & the Rector – he has THREATEND in the past to consult him – I had Great Trouble in Convincing him of the need for Secrecy a GIFT to the Church.

It HAS taken me into Strange Feilds & Homes in the Collection of Faces the Characters to people my painting. I did not like to ask your Sarah in your Absence – it seemed impertnent – but I have now a Cast of Contrastd Characters & do even now put them to Task. My Joseph a REAL Shepherd – how could I not – & I am sure that you would know him. & the Inn-keeper at Bethlehem – well there is only one Inn keeper that we know in this Village & I do beleive He was not even Aware of my Drawing in the Bar one Evening. The Women too no Trouble to draw – is there Something in a Women's Vanity? – a Good Collection all Ages to inhabit my Scenes.

I did have a small Outrage. I was drawing young Lucy for a Child's face at the Birth & her Father came upon me demanding why had I the Girl stripped bare – she was NOT I assure you but I could not have her Dressd in Bonnet & Smock not in the Holy Land though I admit that it might not be HOT at Christmas but I could not be sure – Great Trouble in assuring him that I was making a Drawing only no Intrusion upon her Little Person. And Of Course I couldn't tell him why I was drawing that it was an Artist's Calling & he was not Happy at my Words & did not wish to Beleive me until his Wife remind him who I was & Where he Workd – would you beleive it the boatyard?!! I offered him a florin for Beer – he didn't remember me perhaps he is new since my days there – at first he was Unwilling to accept until Lucy took it out of my Hand & ran inside.

The Baby Christ & Madonna has been a Great Deal Easy though I had to Undertake 2 Drawings & leave ONE with the Mother who Blushd at the attention – I had askd for a Suckling Babe and got ONE!! – was Overcome. I RAN.

The Scenes – ah I have had more Trouble. It is my OWN Fault or rather my Desire for Truth & Reality. For in the Construction of the Panorama I will cling to the Truth like a Leech & it does NO good NO good at all when the Bell Cage is on the North of the Church & Old Hall on the South until I Recalld that the Bell Cage was built on the South & only moved to the North at the Express Demand of Old Hall which Objectd to the Noise of the Bells the Joyus Ringing at Practise & Festivals & Sundays & all. As YOU well know though your Home is removd as is my Own.

If You can Spare an Hour or 2 I would be HAPPY to be in yr Company Happy to drink in the Tavern or talk in the Studio – although it is very COLD there.

Your Constant Freind
John Constable

P.S. Maria has been away for a LONG Time. I beleive that she visits the Village when the Weather is more Clement & keeps to the Town when it is Cold. She has told me NOT to Write that to receive Letters would embarrass & End our Freindship. I Await the Spring holding the Image of her close to my Heart.

18

OCTOBER 1802

On the threshold of the Parish Room, Golding Constable looked around. It was once a grand saloon but there hung an air of abandonment. Dusty, dark, the raw smell of damp woodsmoke that caught in the throat. Windows shuttered against the failing light. A poor fire of damp logs in an old-fashioned hearth.

How John has changed me, he thought. And at my age as well, a worker all my life. What did I know? Shapes and surfaces… yes, a well made millstone, fine baking flour, sound oak beams, the lines of a strong lighter, the frame of a windmill; the things that are important. But now I see colour everywhere, that creamy French stone in new millstones… if we could get them… and when is this blasted war going to end so we can get back to business free from the Income Tax, they promised…the honey of an air-dried oak beam, red oakum in the seams of a new lighter, yellow barley nearly fit, black pitch and hard coal, blue skies, even Anne's eyes, bless her, grey with a hint of green… I remember how she teased me when I noticed it… not so long ago… how the girls laughed, hadn't I seen it when I courted her, was I so blind except to business? Not that "business" doesn't buy them horses and dresses and novels and goodness knows what finery… bless 'em… three girls, three boys… ah, the boys. And thank goodness, one of 'em to take my place. The last. That was lucky.

The rug, a dirty red Oriental pattern with some blue, stretched away into the shadows. A huge brass oil lamp hung in the centre, smoke stained reflector; it spurted, a flash of lightening over the faces. On his left, a knot of farmers and traders, looking around and talking among themselves, some standing. They had come in their working clothes as though to emphasise their independence of will, their self-respect. He knew them all, was surprised at some present. And on his right, around the fireplace, three squires of the four manors, the landowners of the village, nicely dressed, sitting in silence, surveying the room like farmers at a sale. The dress all dull: browns, drab blacks and a few dark reds and blues, their clothes sunk back into the room like a coating of mud at low tide. Except for one of the gentry who had a bright yellow kerchief, bitter lemon cutting through the gloom. It was one of those rare occasions when landlord and tenant met on equal terms; at least that was the theory of it. The practice was a little different.

He had walked up the hill to the Rectory in the last of the evening light; still air, satisfaction of the harvest and a good day's work at the Mill. There was a depression in farming but he was holding off shortcomings of grain with trading, coal and timber. He would probably do better than all his neighbours, many of them tied to the land. The squires, they were always better off. Swallows dived through the trees, feeding on rising air; they would be off soon. After the swifts. He glimpsed a bat, early on the wing. His steward passed going the other way, touched his cap.

'Off to the Red Lion, James?'

A shared smile as James strode off down the hill. Would have been nice to be going the other way, he had reflected; an easy evening with neighbours in the alehouse rather than this ordeal. Not that he spent much time there.

The Rectory stood at the top of the hill on the left, an old ugly building, small windows, heavy roofs. He hadn't been there before. It looked in on itself, like the Rector himself. A dour man; never saw him visiting or about the village. A widower. Needs to let some light into his life, Golding thought. Needs a house like mine; new, light, practical.

He nodded to Squire Godfrey of Old Hall. The Hall held the copyhold of much of his property. The Squire bent his head and turned away. Golding frowned; as an employer, he felt uncomfortable caught between the villagers and the landlords. He was accustomed to visiting the grand houses locally; his daughters were always a useful adornment to dances and frolicks, his sons occasionally shooting with their sons. And he drank with the farmers and shopkeepers, sometimes, and exchanged goods and services. Bakewell the baker caught his eye and looked away; he seemed uncomfortable meeting his old friend in this uncomfortable place. But this was a public occasion, an official occasion, when Golding knew both sides and neither side recognised him.

In the centre of the room, almost below the lamp, stood a desk with a chair. It looked like a corn factor's stand or a schoolmaster's desk; the authority of the placing was unmistakeable. He went and sat down away from the others, near the door; he wasn't a member of the Parish Council, merely a guest. Next to him was a large wooden case, leaning against the wall; he had had it delivered by trap earlier.

Cobwebs hung from the lamp bracket and the walls were lined with bookcases, dark reds and browns, blacks, old leather covers. A painting hung over the mantelshelf, dark and cracked, hard to see. Was it a Birth of Christ or some other religious scene? He was surprised; he had thought the Rector a man of property and had expected a house of comfort. There was a strong smell of damp ash and decay, an air of neglect, despair.

The housekeeper came in, ignoring the company though some called out to her. She poked the fire, a slow smoking pile, threw on more logs; tendrils of smoke crept into the room. Golding felt suffocated by the cold stale air and wood smoke. Others were feeling it too, pulling their coats about them, heads dropping in fatigue. A few coughed. The conversation stilled. Chairs creaked. Squire Godfrey cleared his throat, a long commanding rumble.

The Rector came into the room, pausing on the threshold like an actor making an entrance. The shopkeepers, farmers and their kind, stumbled to their feet clutching their caps. The squires coughed and sat up and assumed an air of profound gravity. The Rector propped his spectacles on his nose and sat, drawing up the chair to the desk. There was silence while he re-arranged his papers. Then he stood, looked round the room and said a prayer. The gentry shuffled to their feet after he had started. The others had remained standing, restless and re-ordering their faces into semblances of rectitude. He sat and the business got underway without any welcome to guest or Council.

Golding looked at him; the Reverend Doctor Rhudde, clothes and all, looked as if he were carved out of some water-logged post; dull, dark, funereal. Yes, that was it, he thought, this was just like a funeral. He wondered, not for the first time, why the Rector's granddaughter Maria should choose to stay here.

The Rector read the Minutes at speed in a monotone allowing for no interruptions; it was as though he couldn't wait to have his home free of all these interlopers. At the end, he turned only to the squires for their approval; they bowed discreetly, one with a dismissive wave. He passed on to other matters, a new form of Service, clerical matters of which he must have known that no person present could hold any view. Or would dare challenge his authority. He spent most of the time addressing the desk in front of him, only rarely raising his head to look straight ahead. Maintaining a steady drone, he went on to an alternative arrangement concerning the schoolteacher, some reorganisation of the almshouses, and whether the verger should have his hours increased. The shopkeepers were in favour, the farmers and gentry against it.

'Who will stand the cost?' Squire Godfrey was abrupt; there was no answer.

Golding felt impatient. He had assumed that he would be given the benefit of early attention, like any important visitor… after all, it wasn't everyday that a generous gift was given to the Church. Why, if Mrs. Constable had been here, she would have been deeply offended by the lack of respect; she would have seen it as a snub to his rank and bridled, coughed and sniffed… he could just imagine it and wouldn't have put it past her to speak out. Of course, there were no women present.

Golding sighed loudly. He was ignored.

He would bide his time and dignity; let them talk of minor matters, vergers, organs, Chancel roof, the hanging of the new bell, and the waterproofing of the partially built Tower. Why, he thought, why have the manors of the village not funded the completion of the Tower as it was planned three hundred years earlier? I don't know why it was never built, but it's a shame, an eyesore, an insult to the village; who would want half a Tower? Why, the builders never even finished to a fair line unless a lot has been lost to the weather… I could never leave any of my buildings in that state, whether it's a cart shed, mill or dry dock… I don't know, it's as if time stood still within the bounds of the churchyard; no changes to be seen over a whole lifetime, only slow deterioration. It's shocking.

His head dropped and he snored. He came to with a start; nobody had noticed. What was it they were talking of now? The bells? Or the bell house? How long had it been there? Ridiculous…

The Rector turned to matters of re-ordering in the Church. He was offended by the suggested introduction of small pews for children at the back of the Church. And the new lights for the choir. He wanted to raise the altar and consider a gallery for the choir at the rear; he was tired of the small boys so close to him when officiating, they were always sniffing. Or whispering. There was much quiet grumbling at the suggestion.

A farmer stood up, a man who had not spoken before.

'With respect, Rector, Oi loike ter see the choir, Oi do. We know 'em all, they live 'ere. An' it's good ter hear the singin'. It's a right religious sound.'

He sat down with a look of determination, a mutter of approval around him. The Rector retorted that the choir was there to support the congregation and encourage them to sing, not to look pretty. He said this word with distaste. No decision was reached; the squires did not speak and the Rector appeared to lose interest in the matter.

One of the shopkeepers dared to suggest that his daughter who had a fine voice, clear and loud, should be permitted to join the Choir. There was a hush and a snort of amusement from Squire Godfrey. The Reverend Rhudde looked at the ceiling, quite still for a moment or two, and passed on to the next business.

Time passed. One of the farmers snored loudly and was nudged in the ribs by a neighbour. He woke with a loud gulp. Rhudde didn't raise his head from his Minute book. Golding wondered at that; was there not a Clerk to take Minutes? Did the Rector have to control matters so tightly that the Minutes were written as he would wish? Golding wondered how accurate they were, whether anybody present was concerned with a true record; he was sure that no note had been made of the suggestion of a girl in the Choir; Rhudde had not raised his quill. The air became closer, smokier and with an air of suppressed violence, of men held back from unforgivable actions.

At last the Rector rose and turned to him. Good grief, Golding thought, how sad he looks, gaunt, deepset eyes staring out on a world in which he has no contact… half-dead already… careful, maybe a bit too far… but look at him: unkempt hair, drab tired costume… he needs a good wife, he does, and there's not much chance of that, no, I can't see it at all… pity, really, it would do him the world of good… ha ha, the world… what does he think of all of us, I wonder… am I one of the shopkeepers, the uneducated? He will have had a university education; no doubt the gentry here have been to Cambridge, the "local" university. But what they do there and what they get from it, I have no idea… all those books of classical writers in their libraries, Virgil and Aristotle, and some English verse, Shakespeare and Milton. Does anyone read those books? Aren't they a bit old-fashioned? The girls read novels voraciously and poetry but I think it's all new… they sing and play the square piano… and they love their animals… even I read a little verse, after the newspaper and the trade business… how good it would be to be back home now, a deep chair and a warm fire and a hot toddy…

Rhudde was lost; he knew nothing of the new middling type to which Golding Constable belonged, the class that emerged out of the subsistence farmers and traders who lived a hand-to-mouth existence, to become those who had both time and money to spare: lawyers, businessmen, industrialists, traders, and even some men from the army and navy. He did not believe that they could have studied the Greats like himself, but they appeared to be men of enterprise and energy. They aped the gentry, built grand houses, held dances and assembled libraries. But he had no idea how to address them.

Do I accord him the respect that I am bound to owe the squires, or do I speak over him as to a shopkeeper? he wondered. He looks amenable enough, a gentleman at heart but perhaps… those clothes… is there flour on his cuffs… really, I don't know… it is all such hard work dealing with the village… give me strength, oh Lord… if only… but when I come to it, is this what I studied for at Cambridge? I think not… is it possible… and wisdom, oh Lord… might the Bishop put me to a better use, serving God in such a way that my future does not hang on the word of these… gentlemen… well, the squires… show me the way Lord, to be conveyed beyond this parish work to a higher calling… if it is thy Will… Maria… yes, I must remember her… but it is such relief when she is here… a lightness of heart… of spirit too… ah, let us be done with this meeting… with thy Help, oh Lord.

He sniffed and with a slight shrug of his shoulders, but not the slightest change of attitude, greeted Golding as though he was a stranger from afar. The shopkeepers stirred in their seats; farmers woke up, chatter among them, those standing shuffling. The squires smiled briefly.

Dr. Rhudde said, 'I see, sir, that you have something for us to examine. What is this?'

He looked at the timber case that Golding held before him and gestured vaguely towards the other side of the room. For a moment, Golding felt a fury of frustration that he had come to present something in a room so dark that it was almost impossible to determine the mood of the people present, let alone look at a painting in detail. And it was a gift, a substantial gift to the Church. How often did the Church attract such donations? Were they always treated so?

His old friend Bakewell stood to help him, pointing to a table in the shadows. Golding strode forward and, directing his friend, they dragged the table to the centre of the room under the light. Lifting the triptych onto it, they opened it upright before Dr. Rhudde's gaze; it was larger than the table and began to topple before Bakewell and another man grabbed the sides and held it in position. Rhudde glanced and sat up, a slight cough, frowning as he examined it more closely. Golding guessed that he was surprised. He had given him no knowledge of what was coming, merely a request to submit a gift to the Parish Council, a gift to the Church.

There was a long silence except for a polite barging as men moved around, trying to look at the altarpiece while avoiding the Rector and the squires, who stood behind Dr. Rhudde's chair. Whispers broke out, an odd laugh. The Rector neither rose nor made any arrangement to help anybody see the painting; it was as if he had neither interest nor concern for the views of the Council. But he was staring as though astonished and incapable of comment. Golding was forced off to one side, distant from the painting, making no eye contact with anyone; it wasn't the way he liked to do business, thrust out of the limelight. He was used to controlling affairs, ensuring that anyone he dealt with realised what he intended, what he would accept. The men were starting to talk.

'Oh, I say.'

'Oy, move along, Jem, Oi can't see ut.'

'What you be about? Stop shoving there.'

'What is it? What's it about?'

‘Whoa, look there! Do you see ut?’

‘But… can that be…’

One of the squires, not Squire Godfrey, spoke.

‘Good God, it’s a triptych. Haven’t seen one of those since I was in Rome. Dashed Popish if you ask me.’

Golding ignored him and spoke over the mutterings and comments rising from the crowd.

‘I had noticed, gentlemen, that there is no picture over the altar, as I have seen often in London churches. I wish to make a gift of this painting to our Church, to stand over the altar.’

There was silence. Then a subdued laugh, a grunted comment.

A log cracked in the grate and fell to the front. Golding sat down behind them all, and rubbed his eyes. There was nothing to be said or done at the moment; they would either accept it, or it would return to the studio. John had done a good job; he wasn’t embarrassed about the painting, the images looked good to him and he would stand by any judgement that John had made. He missed him in the mill, and John had never missed a day’s work when called on, but he could not prevent him from taking up the painting business. And John would have earned his studio in the village whether the triptych was accepted or not. That was right and proper; he, Golding, always kept to his word.

Squire Godfrey pushed forward, examining each part of the triptych closely. The Rector stayed at his desk, his bald head shining in the lamplight. From time to time, he looked up at the triptych; but for most of the time, he gazed down at the desk and made a few notes, his quill scratching over the murmurs of the workers.

Golding wondered what the villagers were thinking. Some were smiling, talking to their neighbours; others were pushing forward around the Squire to look closely. They exchanged comments, the odd laugh; someone pointed, his hand withdrawn hastily. The gentry, apart from Godfrey, stayed behind Rhudde; they had looked, sighed and adopted their customary boredom. One took a pinch of snuff, sneezing loudly and blowing dust over the Rector.

Golding could imagine their dilemma. It was not the same as buying a new timber wagon where the design came from generations of experience, and the only alternatives related to size, the number of horse, the material from which it might be built. It wasn't even like the furnishing of his new house where he had been happy to relinquish the choice of rugs, mats, wallpaper and hangings, furniture and linen, to his wife aided by her daughters. Some from overseas; ah, the expense. He had wanted a modern kitchen, a good range and ovens. Nothing to smoke out the house or threaten with fire.

But things of quality were purchased from afar, from artists and makers of repute, and therefore there was no need to make judgement. Here, the Council was being called upon to comment on a picture produced by a local lad almost young enough to be a child to all present. An unknown painter, no reputation and no authority.

For some time, there was shuffling and chattering as those near to the picture bent forward to look at the scenes and those behind pushed forward to see better. It was not much better than a stall at the Fair, good-natured shoving and pushing, a few laughs, suppressed comments, a single groan.

When the surging had ceased, some returning to their seats, Rhudde spoke. 'Well, gentlemen, you have all had the chance to examine this altar painting. May I have your views?'

Now the tenants could speak before their betters, express themselves without waiting for the landowners, their squires, to lay down the law. There had been trouble a few years before when the squires enclosed the common land in the centre of the village, and now the villagers would take the opportunity to have their word heard. After all, it was a democratic committee, they had been promised, and they would exercise their right. Even if their words were put in the balance. One day, perhaps, one day they would be heard.

'It's marvellous, a wonderful piece of work. Is that really John's painting? Why, you can see—'

'Blast, and I thought the lad was a miller. Not a painter. He did a good job on my grain last year. Or was it the year before—'

'Is that you there, Jem? I don't know as of anyone else holds his scythe like that. I reckon he's bin spying on yer.'

'Do you see? Can yer see ut? He's got my Daisy, right there, you know, when we was harvesting and she come down with the cider—'

'No, that ain't your place. That's the field down by Fen Lane, you know, the one—'

'Well, I'll be jiggered. Did the Holy Land look like that? And I thought—'

'Don't be daft, Smith.' The speaker, a broad farmer, florid complexion with hands like hams, stood in front of the picture dismissing the small farmer. 'I reckon that's a wonderful bit of work. Why, you can see our fields and the river. It brings it all home to us.'

The comments were well received by his side of the room; there was a murmur of support, a few "ayes" and smiles. He sat down with a look of satisfaction, a good job done. Golding smiled; he knew the man well, an honest and decent farmer, and he knew he spoke what he believed, not simply a blind support for the miller with whom he had not quite determined his contract for buying his wheat. "Brings it all home to us". Yes, that was well said; that was what religion should be like, shouldn't it? Real to the people, a way of showing holy things in a way that they could understand. Perhaps Dunthorne was not so far off the mark; he had always had doubts, hearing him talk, but he knew he was a man of principle, a man who saw God in the fields and workshops and in the workers who toiled there. It looked as if John had picked it up from him.

Dr. Rhudde looked up at the altarpiece.

'Gentlemen, I would appreciate your views. Squire Godfrey.'

There was silence. Golding wondered whether it was an opportunity for the landowners to make a stand, show their superiority by differing from the farmers. Or whether they were unable to express any opinion, as the picture differed so much from those brought back from the Grand Tours of Italy and France. He had seen such pictures in a few local houses, Tendring, Holbrook, Tattingstone. He knew that John had departed from the standard religious form, had used local landscape and characters like some Dutch paintings.

Godfrey stood. 'But dash it,' he said. 'It don't show the Old Hall, do it? It's not telling the truth, if that's what you are about.'

There was snort from the crowd. Golding made no comment. The other gentlemen looked to the Rector. A silence. Eventually, one said, 'It's a bit odd, isn't it? Should we look at our men every time we go up for Communion?'

Another spoke, a high bleat. 'Strange colours; it's very bright, don't you know?'

There was a loud rumble from the chimney.

Everyone turned and froze with anticipation. Golding stood up, watching the crowd. The gentry were lifted from their adopted boredom, staring. Some of the workmen gaped, horror on their faces.

A cloud of soot emerged from the fireplace, billowing out into the room; in the centre was the flash of wings. A phœnix. The soot continued to flow, settling on the rug and the chairs around. A rook appeared, flapping, turning this way and that to escape the fire.

'Broken his wing,' said a farmer. And he stepped up, treading soot into the rug, seized the bird, a quick twist to the neck and dropped it in the grate. The last squire to speak, a young man with foppish airs and a weak chin, stood open-eyed and coughed into his yellow kerchief. The farmer stared at him, turned without a word and went back to his chair. The soot settled over the fire extinguishing the flames.

Dr. Rhudde looked briefly at the fireplace and sighed quietly. He turned back to his Minutes, dismissing the interruption, behaving as though such earthly matters were of no concern.

One of the shopkeepers said, 'I reckon that chimney needs brushing, Rector. There's a lot of soot there.'

It was ignored though a few of the men exchanged looks, one whispering to his neighbour. Golding wondered; he recalled a discussion after Morning Service a few weeks ago. The Rector had wanted him to present a sack of flour for Harvest Festival. Golding had not been happy with the suggestion; the flour would deteriorate in the damp church and would be lost, an wasteful gesture. He had suggested a sheaf of wheat; no, the farmers were providing sheaves. What about a loaf, decorated, a wheaten plait? Mr. Bakewell would be supplying that. They had talked a while, separated without a conclusion; his wife had been impatient to return home, perhaps saw his frustration with the Rector. She had always felt a deep distrust of the man, resented the authority he practised over the village. In the end, he had supplied a bag of grain, open for display; he didn't tell the Rector that the grain was only the top two inches with straw and stones below. He was happy to give to the poor of the Parish but he could not countenance waste. The Rector had made no mention of it. Golding did not think he was a practical man.

He stood.

'Gentlemen, I am happy to present this painting to the Church, but only on the condition that it stands on the altar. If it does not suit, I shall withdraw it. I should not like to think of it standing in some corner of the Vestry or at the rear of the Church; it wouldn't be right at all. It is an altarpiece, for the altar.'

There was a murmur of support from the farmers; the shopkeepers stared and looked to the Rector. The gentry gazed into space. A silence fell over the room, broken only by coughing from the young squire who looked fretfully at the fire and pulled his cape about his neck. Golding felt the room chilling and sensed the mood of the Meeting turning; he felt that he should be elsewhere, that his time was being wasted. He looked down at his hands, clasped his knees, and resolved to be patient.

Dr. Rhudde rose from his desk and stood with his back to the fire as though he might gain some strength from it. His feet paddled soot into the rug, raising a small cloud that coated his shoes; he was unaware of it though one of the shopkeepers, a draper, beckoned and would have spoken. Rhudde addressed the meeting as though from the pulpit, a deep sonorous tone, little inflection, considered. Many a villager had fallen asleep under his delivery in church; here it was too cold.

'I do not dismiss it, not at this time. It is a good gift and we are grateful for it. But...' he paused. 'I have taken note of all your comments and there are a number of issues that I have to put to you. I am your advisor in all matters clerical and you must attend to what I have to say.

'Firstly, we have to consider context and tradition. It is not in my following to allow a casting-off of tradition and a despoiling of the Church, the portal of you all to the Highest of the High. It is a serious matter, one that should not be considered hastily. And one that requires a knowledge of the law of the Church, a reading of the holy books.'

There was a shuffling from the workmen who feared that anything they said would not be taken into consideration. The gentry raised their heads, adopted looks of knowing and reason. Rhudde continued.

'There is the matter of the background. As some of you have observed, the scenes show our local village, a fine place with a great tradition. They are not the scenes that I should have chosen if I was obliged to choose scenes of our village. They are ordinary; they lack the elements of holiness that are usually seen in such paintings. I could point to the works of… no, that would be invidious. But I have to consider the position of this painting. An altarpiece. I come to the conclusion that the scenes of Our Lord's life should not be belittled by these ordinary scenes that we have before us every day. Would we bring our children to believe that the Birth could have occurred in the Bellframe, surrounded by bells? That would be tantamount to sacrilege; the Birth took place in a holy place now sanctified in the Holy Land. The painting does not show the blessed stable, the sheep and asses.'

'Begging your pardon, Rector,' spoke the florid farmer. 'But isn't that what is most powerful about the scenes, that they bring it all home to us?'

'Bring it all home?' The Rector spoke with scorn.

The farmer was not to be put off.

'Yes, sir. You see Church for many of us is a long series of stories about things that happened a long time ago with people of another land and in a strange place that we have no knowledge of at all, not at all. And then it's all about us, births, christenings, weddings and funerals. And that is more real to us. And we are taught that God is everywhere, sees all.'

'But the Bible tells you all of that; have you not paid heed to your Bible readings?'

The farmer smiled. The Rector frowned; his jaw tightened.

'With respect, Rector, the Bible was writ a long time ago and we cannot see the things that the Apostles saw. Now—'

'Enough, enough. You come close to sacrilege.'

All heads dropped as though in prayer; nobody would meet the Rector's eyes. He continued.

'Secondly, the choice of scenes of Our Lord's life is bizarre if I may be permitted such a word. I acknowledge that triptychs, those of a classical theme as they all are, show a variety of scenes. But here we have, at best, a layman's choice. The Birth, but surely where we should see Our Lord in Majesty? The Annunciation, but not with the Mother of God out on a field? And the Sermon, but not on a Mount?'

He looked around as though to appeal for an argument, or at least some support. But nobody would take up his challenge. Golding felt cold and regretted coming. He should have known that the Rector would reject it, that nothing he might present would satisfy. Poor John. But he was young; he would do other good works.

'Thirdly,' Rhudde droned on. 'I must protest the viewpoint of these supposedly religious scenes. Note that the view of the Annunciation is a bird's eye view; when have we ever seen an Annunciation from the eyes of a bird? How can we be awed by the humility of the Lady and the graciousness of the angel of God? Here we have a woman, a woman of the village out upon her business in the fields no doubt, hardly a lady awaiting the angel of God.'

‘That’s my wife,’ said a young farmer. ‘What’s wrong with that? It’s only a paintin’, he had to choose someone, why not my wife?’

‘And is your wife the Blessed Virgin that Mary was?’ The Rectors voice cut through the air like ice. There was a shuffling in the crowd; one of the squires made to leave the room but was stilled by a look from the Rector.

The florid farmer spoke. ‘Might it not be an angel’s viewpoint?’

‘And how are we to presume the eye of an angel?’ said Rhudde.

A pause.

‘And what of the Sermon? It is a snail’s view, so low that we are hardly permitted to see the great crowd that Our Lord attracted on that holy day. It is a view of clods of clay, of clogs and of the worms and beasts of the ground.

‘Now, is there any person who wishes to dispute these matters with me?’

A cold weariness had pervaded the room. The men standing shook their legs to restore circulation, those sitting pulled their coats around them and dropped their chins into their collars. More silence. Rhudde stood looking around the room; he felt exhausted, drained, wasted on this crowd of villagers… it had been a matter of great regret but he had been obliged to do his duty. Have I said the right things, he wondered… surely, it would not do… the villagers, they will not think well of it… think that I have ignored their words… and the painter is one of them… they cannot understand… I have not taught them well… my next sermon… I have neglected them… let us pray… Oh Lord… He felt removed from everyone there, receding into the darkness of the room. With a few words and a prayer, he brought the meeting to a close, announcing the date of the next meeting.

At once, there was movement. On one side, the farmers stood as one, clutching their caps, shuffling towards release. On the other, the landowners were standing, pulling on capes, exchanging words. A few touched Golding on the arm, a smile, a shake of the head. The gentry strode out, heads high. The room emptied, the last hurrying.

Rhudde had not moved.

'He paints well, your son.'

'He attends the Royal Academy of Arts in London.'

'Can you spare him? Do you not need him to work with you in the business?'

'Young Abram has come along well; he will take my place in time. John must do what he intends.'

'There may be opportunities for him to paint for other churches. Brantham is in my living and other churches would be happy to have a local painter of such skill. But he will have to moderate his ideas; these local scenes will not do, will not do at all.'

'I shall tell him of your advice. And now I must return home.' He closed the triptych, leaving it to be picked up the following morning, and turned to the door. Rhudde watched him, did not lend a hand, but strode to meet him at the door.

'There is one other matter that I wished to mention; it is awkward. My granddaughter, Maria, stays with me occasionally. She is a good girl, I am always pleased to see her. She brightens the life of an old man.

'However, I am told that she has been seen walking with your son John. This is not seemly, it is not right. I hope that you can appreciate that she has her place in society; her father is Solicitor to the Navy and she is intended for some estate.'

'I am sure that my son is always proper; he is a polite young man though not well used to London society.'

'If you could have a word with him? I should be grateful. Well, goodnight, sir.'

Golding stood outside, breathing deeply. The air was cool but fresh with a slight glow of warmth from the brickwork behind him. He sighed. He had done his best; he could do no more. What a crowd he thought. All of his friends, the shopkeepers and farmers, those who he knew so well, all seemed changed within that mausoleum behind him, touched by a heavy hand. He would not judge them harshly; they could have done no more.

The air smelt good, a slight autumnal damp… perhaps there was time for a jug at the Red Lion before he turned in, time for meaningless banter before he had to face his wife. She would have words to say about the matter, he was sure. And John; had he really expected that his painting would be accepted? It seemed clear now. It was not the type of painting that would sit well with this society or be praised for its qualities. And there was Maria.

19

LATER

He sat in a corner, alone. He was a rare visitor to the tavern and did not want to spoil the peace of the village men, embarrass them with the presence of their employer. But tonight he felt one of them, apart from the squires and gentry. Now and then, one of the villagers who had been at the Parish Meeting came over, offered their condolences, praise for the painting, murmurs of doubt about the Rector and the squires. He smiled, accepted their compliments, and replied with a few comments. Careful to not attack the Rector; it was all simply a matter of liturgy or whatever, that simple folk like us could not understand was what he said.

He ordered his thoughts, preparation for wife and son. The first would be the harder. Life was too short for these petty battles. Perhaps he could offer her a journey to London by sea to avoid the discomfort of the roads; she could stay with her family, exchange news, re-acquaint herself with the fashions, dresses and bonnets. He would not accompany her. A daughter or two would be happy of the change in scenery at the cost of supporting their mother.

When he returned home, he entertained the hope that she would have retired for the night.

'Is that you, Golding? I am here in my room.'

He closed the front door behind him, throwing the bolts. Hung his coat in the back hall. Looked into the kitchen; all was quiet, the range damped down, the lamp over the table turned down to a dimness. In the dining room, he poured himself a glass of whisky and faced the stairs, each tread a great weight, fatigue mixed with frustration. Threw himself into a chair in the bedroom that his wife used as a boudoir.

She was sitting at her dressing table, gown, mop cap, looking far from sleepy.

'You do not look well, my dear. Was the meeting very fatiguing?' She spoke with some sharpness; he felt as a toad must feel as the stone is lifted from above it. He wondered if it were possible to delay the discussion. Indefinitely.

'Is that whisky, my dear? You know that it does not agree with you at this hour. You will not sleep well, not well at all. We shall have a restless night, and tomorrow I am busy. There is—'

'A small nightcap, to settle myself.'

'It is not well, is it? The painting, it has not been accepted?'

Her colour had risen; she rose and paced the room.

'Well, my dear, that is the problem, is it not?' An impatient tone.

'Well, whether it is a problem or not—'

'Indeed it is a problem. It is an insult to our family. A substantial gift. Snubbed. And I'm sure that John made a fine painting; why, do they not realise that he is at the Royal Academy Schools, the most superior painting establishment in all of England?'

'It is not quite as simple as that.'

'I believe it is. And we shall not let the matter rest. I shall speak to a few friends, a few ladies. They will agree with me I am sure.'

'Before you do, I should tell you of the Rector's opinion.'

Mrs. Constable snorted. 'The Rector's opinion? Do you think I care a jot for the Rector's opinion? I should have said that it is a matter of the squires; do they not hold weight in this village?'

'Indeed they do, my dear. But they had little to say.'

'Little to say? Little to say? They have enough to say when affairs in the village are not to their liking.'

'True, very true. But in this case—'

'In this case, they could have determined the case. And chose not to.'

'It is not as simple as that.'

'Why is it that men have to complicate matters? Simple? I should have thought it simple enough.'

'It is a matter of the painting, the image… the…'

'How so? Is John not a student at the Royal Academy for these last three years? How can it be a matter of the painting?'

'His painting is good, I thought so myself. The Rector said that he painted well. But…' He faded away, gazing at the floor.

'There; what more can I say? It is a snub to us, not of their background. How dare they? If his painting is good, there can be no sound reason for the refusal. We must pursue the matter.'

'Is it possible? Can we leave the matter for the night? I should like to rest.'

He rose, turning towards the door. Mrs. Constable looked after him. Golding did not like the glint in her eye; it meant trouble. She slapped her hands together, gave a low sigh.

'Tomorrow morning, my dear,' he said. 'We shall speak of it further.'

Golding did not sleep well; his wife was restless, muttering, tossing to and fro. He rose early and lay in a spare room, eyes closed until he heard the maids attending to the fires, and breakfasted early, leaving for the mill before his wife appeared.

Early in the afternoon, he sent his trap for John; he wanted a private discussion. There was some delay. The studio was empty but his clerk had gone on to the Red Lion where he found John in the company of some men, drinking, telling tales, exchanging news, and swapping jokes. It was with difficulty that John had been prised from the tavern, loaded into the trap and driven down to Flatford; he kept standing, hailing the ploughmen and any working labourer, loud halloos, hiccups, laughing and clapping the clerk on the back.

'I finished it, you know. Finished, all finished. Father will be pleased; so good of him to call on me.'

At the mill, John tumbled out of the trap, swaying, leaning on the clerk. He smiled at the miller, the labourers, the dog, the ducks and tripped into the office, apologising to the doorframe. Steadied himself, concealing his grin behind a large spotted handkerchief. His head was in a whirl. There were two of everything, confusing, difficult to choose. It was an entirely unaccustomed state of mind. At first, a wonderful feeling where nothing could trouble him as he floated on a cloud of… but now he was not sure if he liked it. Was that what too much drink did to one? He must remember if he could. Why did others not sway? It was all so unfair. He slumped against the wall.

His father sat at his desk. He was applying himself to some papers, shuffling, re-arranging, silent. Shot his cuffs, gazed at the fire. Waited. Eventually, he pointed to a chair.

John sat. Waited. Hiccupped. An ache inserted itself into his head. His father raised his eyes, looked long and hard into John's face. A brief sigh.

'Are you well, sir? Your colour—'

'Yes, Father. Quite well. I have been cebrelatin'… I mean, I was with men at the alehouse. We were… wass…' John faded into silence. Blinked.

'Can I get you anything, John?'

'No... I think...' John got up quickly, stumbled out of the office and bent over the wall, to vomit into the mill pool. After a while, he stood up; if that was what beer did to you, he wasn't going to drink it ever again. Not ever. He wiped his mouth and went back indoors. The miller's wife, who had come through the garden gate, stared, mouth open.

'Your behaviour, sir. Not becoming of our family nor of an employer. I imagine there will be no reoccurrence.'

John sipped water, humbled, not feeling at all well. Golding cleared his throat, sat up. 'Thank you for the painting, your altarpiece. I presented it last night to—'

'Your altarpiece. I painted for you, Father.'

'Quite.'

'And I did... finish, Father. A commission completed completely....' A silly smile as he slipped sideways on the chair.

Golding clasped his hands, gazed at his blotter.

'It was an interesting painting, not that I am educated in these matters.'

'Father, I worked for a long... ugh... a long long time to get it right. A... a... grand painting for the Church.'

'But the design...'

'Grandest thing I've ever done. Bigger, er... more things, more people, you know... And I painted it for you, Father, for the studio, your support, the years that I served you and failed—'

'Yes, it did take a long time. How many years?' Golding examined his son. John pulled himself upright, sniffed, and blew his nose.

There was a silence, John gazing at the floor, his father looking upon him with resignation.

'The Parish rejected it.' Golding sat back in his chair.

John stared at his father. Open astonishment at first,

followed by a flash of anger, followed by a reckoning, all blurred with drink. He started to speak, clamped his mouth shut. There was a loud quack from the mill pool.

'I did not ask to see the painting while you were preparing it,' said Golding, word by word dropping into the silence. 'I know little of these things, as you know. And therefore, I relied upon your good self to prepare an appropriate image for the village Church.'

'But father—'

'You will let me speak.' He shifted in the chair. 'I was praised, privately by the Rector, for your quality of painting. I believe he said you painted well; I commend you.' Another pause as Golding looked out of the window. 'But I had not realised that there could be a range of suitable themes; did I not suggest a meeting with the Rector, last year?'

'But, Father, I was painting in a common style, that is—'

'That is, the style of the common people. Is that not so?'

'Yes, Father, exactly so. As I paint the land here, the common things of our life, labourers and gates and fields and things.'

'But an altarpiece, it seems, must follow certain rules, certain practices that raise it above the common. Or so I was instructed last night, in the presence of the Council.'

John made no comment. He did not feel comfortable; his drunkenness had evaporated, worn down to an aching fatigue.

'I had assumed, John, that your years at the Royal Academy would have acquainted you with such practices. You must know what is expected of an altarpiece. What is acceptable, what themes and so on.'

'Yes, Father.'

'Yes? I don't understand.'

'I started a conventional painting, a fully prepared sketch, the colours and all selected, a Crucifixion. And it would not do at all.'

'Would not do? And how long ago was this? How long

have you kept me waiting, for what? Really, John, you test my patience now.'

There was a knock on the door. The clerk came in, papers to be approved, signed, discharged. Golding attended to them, ignoring John who stood, went to the door breathing heavily. The clerk left, John returned to his chair.

'It is not a simple matter, Father. The sketch I prepared… well, it was dead, no life.'

'Should it have life, as you call it? A Crucifixion?'

'It must have life to convey the message, to impress, to tell a story. How else can a painting have a life? To construct a dead painting is like brewing a beer without hops.'

'I must take your word for this, John. I shall not say that much hangs upon it; that would be untrue. But you must tell me, did you come under the influence of some advisor, some expert who told you to set aside your conventional proposal?'

John gulped, alarmed. Was it never possible to conceal things from his father? Who sat in front of him, his face closed. Why did that look have so much power?

'It is true, Father. I did discuss it, it was necessary; I have little experience with such paintings, well… no experience. And I sought opinions.'

'At the Schools?'

'Well, actually—'

'Not at the Schools? I should have thought that there would be an abundant source of expertise at that establishment. It is why you study there, is it not?'

'It didn't get that far.'

'Not that far? As far as London, do you mean? But you are there studying, from time to time, are you not? Do you not see your teachers?'

'Yes, Father.'

'Do you wish to tell me with whom you discussed my commission?'

'Dunthorne, Father. He helps me to see, he is a ready ear to my wonderings. There is nobody else here with whom I can talk about my work. But—'

Golding raised his hand; he looked grim. 'Dunthorne is not a skilled artist, is he?'

'No father. But—'

'And you chose to take his advice, rather than consult the Rector?'

'Well,—'

'Is that so, John?'

'If you put it like that, Father, then it is so. But it was my decision to paint the image as you see it.'

'Based upon what? Your inexperience?'

'Based upon Truth and Reality. A painting that would mean something to the common people. Like us.'

A pause. Golding looked down, a slight smile.

'Do not let your mother hear your opinion that we are common people; I fear that it would not sit well with her.

'I must confess, the painting did appeal to the villagers. There were some powerful arguments supporting it. But the Rector over-ruled them; the squires had little opinion except a dislike of meeting their tenants at the Communion Table. I am disappointed, John. I feel that you knew what was expected and chose to set it aside, to follow your own way. And I do not think that was right of you. Do you wish to proceed as an artist? How will you ever gain commissions and sales if you will not conform?'

'I am sorry, Father. I had never intended to embarrass you.'

'And you have. There is no doubting it. Your Mother; she is unhappy. She feels snubbed, put down by the squires. You have seen this before. You do not set her at ease. It is a thorn in her side.'

'Oh, Father. I am sorry, I do apologise. I had not thought to bring so much down upon you. And I am mindful of your goodness and charity, your support through my education, my failing in the family business. If you command, I shall return to the fold; you may employ me as a miller; I doubt I am clever enough for the figures. But I can be useful I believe.'

'And cast away the years at the Schools? I assume that you have learnt something, even if it is not how to paint an altarpiece. Have you earned anything at all from your painting?'

'No, Father. It is too soon.'

'Or you work too slowly on the wrong things.'

John looked away, away over the river to the meadows, to the sky. It would be good, he thought, to go walking, to Dedham or Cattawade and allow all the problems of the day, including his headache, to evaporate in the afternoon breeze. He turned back to his father.

'There are a couple of other matters,' said Golding. 'The Rector spoke well of your method of painting; I have told you already. If you can return to an appropriate style, he may like to have an altar painting for Brantham that is in his living. But it would be necessary to complete it in good time. There will be no commission except from me; it is a gift from me to replace the lost commission. Is this of interest to you?'

'Oh yes, Father. If I can please, please give me the opportunity.'

'You will need to attend on him. He will advise you of the subject of the painting. I suggest you do this before the week is out. Or he may feel that you are too proud to work locally.'

'Thank you, Father. I shall call on him tomorrow.'

Golding shifted in his chair. Looked out of the window. Looked down at his blotter.

‘There is another matter.’ He paused, glancing at John. ‘You are no longer so young, it is not my business to interfere in your private life.’

‘Father? Please, tell me what is concerning you.’

‘It concerns Maria, Rhudde’s granddaughter.’

John looked at the floor, frowning. Raised his head, a direct look at his father.

‘Father, I have done nothing improper. We meet, we walk, that is all.’

‘Sufficient to cause whispering tongues in our village, John. As you must know. The word has reached the Rector. He spoke with me last night.’

‘What would you have me do, Father? We walk, I make no demands on her. We… we get on well. I admire her. Are we to be strangers to each other?’

‘Is it appropriate, John? I assume that she is not chaperoned, no female company. It is not for me to dictate your behaviour, John, but you must know that it is not the same as running around with the village girls; you are no longer a child. Those years are long gone. But if you are speaking with Mr. Rhudde, be warned. I can say no more.’

John stood. He was uncertain what to say, how to act.

‘Father, I am sorry that I have caused you pain. And Mother. I do work, I do try to establish myself. I am grateful for the opportunity. I shall paint for Brantham Church. But I cannot promise to avoid Maria.’

Golding stood.

‘I’m weary. Now I have to face your Mother; perhaps you would do me the favour of facing her with me.’

They rode back up the hill, the pony clip-clopping at a slow walk, both men sunk in their thoughts.

20

FEBRUARY 1803

The door slammed behind him. He jumped. There was a cord running over the top of the door supporting a flint. He smiled at the ingenuity; he had not thought John capable of it. The flint was a large beach flint with a hole through it, hung on waxed sash cord. He stamped the snow off his feet and looked around.

A harsh brightness outside, the inside was sombre, high, space flowing away into darkness at the far end. On the left, three tall windows with shutters open, casting shafts of light over a brick floor to John, working at an easel.

Dust motes floated in the sunlight.

John whipped round; a smear of umber ran over the edge of the canvas.

'I have you to thank for that,' said John, pointing to the paint. 'But, Dunthorne old friend, how good to see you; it has been too long.' He threw down his brush and mahlstick and walked towards him, arms open.

Dunthorne held him off, looking him up and down.

'I have to say, I see it now, you are thriving on the life of an artist. Why, you appear to be growing into the very figure of a gentleman; where is the boy I hauled from the river?'

'By God, it's good to see you. Only the one brief time last year; have you been so busy away from the village?'

'What is this you are working on now?'

'How is Sarah, the boys… they must be growing?'

'Still up and down to London, I dare say.'

'Your workshop here. So quiet, I have not seen you there.'

'And your paintings. Where might I see them?'

They stood, staring at each other. He thought of the happy days sketching, the early afternoons he took off and how they would drift away down the Flatford Lane to that other country, the world of colour and line away from obligations and family. He remembered John's lessons, a quick deliberate pencil cutting up the view as he struggled to see the point of it. He remembered his own watercolours, a tendency to put in too much. He remembered sheltering from rain, running from a bull, drifting in a skiff from Dedham, friction with young Golding, the ghost at Willy Lott's; were those days all past? Had they both moved on, no longer young men, no longer time to spare?

John looked well, thin but healthy, a good country glow to his cheeks. Perhaps a little nervous, quick movements, an impatience in his eyes. Like a terrier who has just been told off and wants to move on to the next thing.

He looked round again. There were paintings and panels around the walls, large sketches of landscape, farmland and scrubland, a few mountains; canvas, stretchers, cans and bottles; the detritus of a well-used studio. The sharp smell of oil and turps. And a biting damp cold.

'You have been travelling, I see. Foreign countries, no doubt.'

'No, no. All England; we have a wonderful country, everything from marshes to dales, city to hamlet, mountain to desert, but I never go for long… But, come, let us go to the tavern.'

He took Dunthorne by the arm, hurrying him away from easel and paint, out of the cold studio into the raw day. Grey crusts of ice and snow on the road, a bleak sun shining low through the bare trees. There was nobody about.

'How I wish winter were gone,' said John. He was shivering.

'It doesn't help my work, that's for sure. But it's only February; can't expect too much. I imagine that you will fly away to London; it must be warmer and more commodious. I came by a couple of times last year. You were away.'

He sighed, loudly. This was the one time of the year that he wished he were a bailiff for the Constable estate, wrapped warm in the counting-house drawing out the examination of accounts and plans until the end of the day. He had no work in his own workshop and no windows in hand. Nor had he for some time.

John laughed, clapped his hands together. 'Would you have me for a city gent?'

He pushed into the Red Lion, ordering drinks and food before Dunthorne could open his mouth. The few men, all off the land for the duration, moved away, murmuring, a few greetings. Behind the bar, Jem smiled, asked after them and their families and stoked the fire into a fresh blaze. Even moved an old boy away into another bench. Expressed pleasure at seeing Dunthorne again, so rarely these days. And how was the family? Dunthorne replied, a few words, pleasure to be sitting here, good beer and company. He ignored the sullen crowd on one side. And don't you be worrying about them, says Jem; they're no trouble.

Dunthorne wondered when bridges might be built to overcome the distrust between his family and the villagers. It was absurd; he had grown up with all of them, gone to school with them, broken the skin on his knees with them, pissed behind the Bell Cage with them, swam in the river with them, spied on the girls stripped for swimming, raced and fought. He couldn't say when things had changed. Was it the education from Miss Hambleton, now sadly passed on, that had set his expectations and abilities above those of his mates who could barely read and write? Was it his wife, a widow with social expectations above those of her neighbours? He suspected that they disliked her behind her back. Perhaps it went back to the occasion at the skating when he had stood in the water holding young Golding looking up into dark closed faces.

'It's been a long time since we have stretched our legs before this fire,' said John. 'I have missed our conversation, our journeys.'

Dunthorne stared into the fire. A grim set to his mouth.

'I go where there is work,' said Dunthorne. 'It is the nature of it.'

'But, old friend, is there not work here in this village or nearabouts? You used to be so busy, much work for my father. Were your repairs so good that there is no return, all made good for an eternity?'

'I go where there is work, John. I must.' Dunthorne sat back, looked away.

'Please tell me. Does my father not place work with you?'

Dunthorne looked at him, looked away. A sip of beer.

'This is good beer, Jem,' he called.

'There was a time, you will recall it, you would tell me all. Your life from the beginning to the present day. Are we to be strangers?'

He looked at John. What would he tell him? That his father had dropped him like a bad penny? It could do no good and yet he could not hold the truth of it from John. They knew each other too well. He wondered if John still had need of his company now that he had his London life.

'You must have good company in London, many young men to discuss the painting business. And professors and the such.'

'And would you believe that I have left all this behind?' John gave a wide gesture that encompassed the men, the room, the village. 'No, I could never leave for long. This place, it is my life. I thought you knew it.' John looked at Dunthorne sadly.

'All right John. All right. I don't get work around here presently. The Squire and your father; I believe they employ Wheelers for all their work. So I travel, plenty of work in Ipswich. The builders are getting to know me. Though sometimes,' he paused, a bitter laugh, 'sometimes, they don't know a lead roof from an earth floor.'

John looked shocked. He stared at the floor, took their tankards to Jem for a refill, and sat upright looking stern.

'It will not do, Dunthorne. I am appalled, shocked.'

'It's not your business, John. Don't you be getting into the muddle of it.'

'It is a muddle. I'm sure, they don't know a thing, don't know the truth of it.'

'Truth is a difficult word when men's minds are made up.'

John was angry, a slight stutter. 'I had not thought it had gone so far. I suppose it is my mother; I fear it is. She will have persuaded Father, spoken with the Squire's wife. And all because of my brother.'

'You stick to your work; that is the most important thing, is it not?'

'The most important thing? More important than old friends? Ah, that is a rare question.'

'Well, I didn't mean—'

'Dunthorne, I apologise for my family, their bad manners; I don't know, it is most unsatisfactory. I don't know.' He dropped his head, muttering, spilling beer on the floor.

'You hear me, John. This is no business of yours. The world goes round and men's business goes round with it.'

'If I knew what you meant, I would agree. I think.' A sigh, shrugged his shoulders. 'Now, tell me, have you been sketching at all?'

And the conversation rambled into fields visited and shepherds and clouds and sunny afternoons and work and wives and women, on into the afternoon.

It was getting dark, a wintry evening chill and still when they stepped outside and retreated to the studio where John built up the fire in the stove, feeding in old sketches, branches, split logs, anything that came to hand. Dunthorne would grab some sketches, looking to see what he could keep. But John was impatient; all rubbish, he said, all to burn. They stood around, hugging themselves against the cold, rubbing hands.

'John, you never did tell me. Was the triptych finished? I did wonder. Was your father satisfied? What did the Council say? I have not seen it yet in the Church; I did go looking a few times.'

John coughed, looking away, and sighed.

'It wasn't the sort of painting they wanted, my father said. The Rector thought my painting was good; he told me so. It was the subject matter; it did not satisfy.'

'A shame. I never saw it. Would you show it to me?'

John looked at him, shrugged and went over to the wall.

'Give me a hand. It's heavy, you will recall.'

The triptych was hauled out, panel by panel. John swept his painting materials to one end of the table, and they erected it, fixing the sections together in the right order.

A panorama of local country, of scenes that Dunthorne knew well, but composed into a single wide view. He felt bathed in sunshine, carried back to summer months, long warm grass.

The centre panel: the Bell Cage opened up, bells hanging dark and pregnant in the background, the Mother and Child resting on straw against the bellframe, a crib with a cohort of supporters, shepherds, serving girls, lambs, a couple of sheep dogs. The left panel: a view from above looking over the valley, wheat growing tall, Dedham Church and the hills of Stratford hazy in the background, with an angel hovering over a woman working in the fields, a ray of divine light touching her. The right panel: a hill outside Old Hall viewed looking uphill low from the ground, Our Lord standing beneath the oak speaking to seated farm workers. Bright and warm summer colours, deep shades, trees all in leaf.

Dunthorne was stunned. He remembered their discussions, his disappointment at the watercolour sketch, the comparison with John's watercolours, his opinions and questions. He pulled up a chair, sank into it, and gasped.

'By God, John, you have it. It is marvellous, a rare thing. And you say that it would not do?'

'No.'

'But the painting of it; I can see the holy scenes, the nature of our land, where we belong, where we worship.'

A pause. 'Yes.'

'And you have our people. I know them, I see them. There's the old shepherd by the crib. And that girl from the shop, your Madonna. And all the farm men, sitting on the ground; why, I could name them all.'

John sighed, looked down, shuffled some papers.

'Father made no comment about it, only that I had done a good workmanlike job.'

'Your father is a good man.'

'He took it to the Parish Council. Was sure they would accept it, a generous gift. My mother was furious, railing against the Rector, squires and all. Couldn't blame the shopkeepers and farmers; no chance their word would be taken.'

'It's the best thing that you have ever done, John. Best thing I've ever seen. Will it go to London?'

'No. It cannot, they will not want it. I have other work in London, even some portraits commissioned.'

'But the triptych… is it all lost?'

'I don't know. It will come to no harm here.'

'It is not right. I don't understand it. It is a marvellous painting. You can't just leave it here, ignore it.'

'Well, maybe, some day… I don't know. It was a lot of work, a lot of time. My father, he was not always patient; I cannot blame him. I didn't know if I would finish it at one time.'

'But it is finished. It's all here.'

'Yes. Help me, let's put it to sleep for the present.'

Dunthorne stood up, helped John replace the triptych, covered face to the wall and looked at the other work in the studio. The painting on the easel was covered with a sheet.

'What are you working on?'

John looked at him, at the sheet, at his feet. Said nothing.

'John, is this one of your life studies you told me about? The naked—'

'No, no, far from it.'

'Are you teasing me now? Would you conceal it from me? I know, I do recall being shocked, the idea of it. Naked women. And men. I don't know. Is this one of those?'

'No, not at all. I've told you. It's just an—'

'May I see it?'

John looked reluctant, but pulled the sheet from the easel, looking away. Went to stoke the stove.

Dunthorne looked at the painting.

'It is far from finished,' said John, from the far end. 'An

altarpiece for Brantham Church; it is in the living of the Rector and he has commissioned it.'

'It doesn't look like your work, John.'

'No, not what you know. But it is a commission and I must do a painting that will fit, will satisfy.'

A figure of Our Lord, welcoming children. Dunthorne felt that it was dead, as dead as the original watercolour. There were some sketches, presumably of characters in the painting; he thought he recognised John's sisters, Mary and Nancy. He made no comment.

21

THE NEXT DAY

The following day, he called again at the studio. John had pressed him.

'You can't work in this cold and I have missed you. Let us spend some time together, even if we cannot be down to Flatford; I can talk drawing to you here until the cows come home, and later. Come about two, won't you?'

It was warmer; John had stoked the stove to a dull red, a coffee pot on one side. The easel was covered, pushed aside, and the table cleared with paper, cups, sugar, pencils, and charcoal.

'What is that outlandish drink you have there?' said Dunthorne.

'I got the habit in London. It makes me think at twice the speed, keeps me awake when cold. Will you have some?'

Dunthorne swirled it around in his cup, sipped and sipped again.

'You'll be giving me expensive habits.'

John laughed, filling his cup again.

For an hour, they drew on paper: patterns, imaginary landscapes, sheep and cattle, lines, marks, drops of ink blown into fantastic hawthorn trees. Dunthorne relaxed into his old mood, watching John, copying, developing marks, challenging, teasing.

There was a knock on the door. Bold looked up and dropped his jaw onto his paws, eyes closing. John rose. Dunthorne saw him frown, twist his hands together, glance at him.

'I'll be away,' said Dunthorne, standing up. 'I wouldn't want to be intruding.'

He started to collect his things, coat and drawings.

'No, stay awhile. I'll see who it is.'

John opened the door. 'Oh Father, you are welcome. Come in. Will you take coffee?'

Golding was silent. He stood, rubbing his hands together, looking at John and Dunthorne. A cold smile. He strode up to Dunthorne, shook his hand.

'How do you do? It's been a while.' And sat down on one of the chairs. 'I came to see how your Brantham painting goes. You would like my opinion?'

'Yes Father. Dunthorne and I have been drawing. I'll pull the easel up.'

'I should be leaving you,' said Dunthorne. He felt incapable of moving, gazing at Golding like a rabbit caught in the glare of a lamp. John was dragging at the easel with much noise and little movement. He stopped and turned.

'Father, I wondered… no, that is not right, what can I say… it's not right at all. And I would wish it were so.'

Golding looked at him; eyebrows raised. Dunthorne felt frozen, wondering what John was about, what was going to be uncovered. He made a move towards the door but John laid a hand on his arm and gestured to the other chair.

'Perhaps, John, you should tell me what is not right.' Golding's voice was quiet, the words dropping clear into the space between them.

'I understand, I have been told… my brother Golding… and then Mother…'

Dunthorne shifted in his chair as though to stand. He felt uncomfortable, wondering whether John had arranged this meeting, a confrontation with Golding. That he could not allow at any cost.

'I believe,' said John with a rush, 'that Dunthorne is not able to find work in the village. That he must travel, leave his family for days, return exhausted. I do not understand it. Is there not work for him in the village? Do Wheelers have the lion share?'

Embarrassed, he stared around at anything except his father and Dunthorne. Dunthorne did not know what to say or do. He looked at John, wishing he could be released.

'It was a matter of comparing contractors,' said Golding. 'Of ensuring that trades are not lost in the village. I wasn't aware that there was no spare work.' He spoke in a level voice, a voice of reason.

'It doesn't make sense, Father. You are losing Dunthorne, and Wheelers, surely they have enough work—'

'There were some issues. This is not the place to speak of them.' Now his voice had an edge.

'Please, Father. Can we not… it is my brother, is it not?'

'John, I told you—'

'But, Father. It is not fair; someone has made accusations, undeserved. You have always taught me to be just, to be honest—'

'Your mother is not happy that Golding has not been respected.'

'As he goes blundering his way around the parish, shooting this an' that, accosting innocent bystanders—'

'What do you speak of, John? Take a care.'

'Father, did you hear how I met Maria?'

'I believe you met her walking around the village. Did you not?'

'No, Father. She was being held by Golding, against her will.'

'Am I to believe it? It sounds nonsense to me, a fabrication. How could Golding hold her? No, I don't believe it.'

'I was there, Father. Saw it all. It was awful; Golding looked as if he might… No, it was too awful.'

'You saw it?'

'I was there, Father, with Dunthorne. We were walking up Flatford Lane, and… there they were.'

'Where?' Golding was cold.

'In the drive to Old Hall, you know, the bottom where it comes down to Flatford Lane. We heard them first; Maria was crying out, a pitiful sound. And Golding laughing, not an amused laugh, cruel—'

'Take a care, John. I will not accept an exaggeration; I am aware of the ill feeling between you.'

'But, Father, it is all true.' John was bleating.

Golding held up a hand to John and turned to Dunthorne. For the first time, he looked at him directly, a cool appraisal.

'Perhaps you could tell me what you saw. I rely upon you. The truth, if you please.'

Dunthorne shifted in his seat.

'It was a while ago, now sir, but I do remember it well.'

'Then proceed.'

'Well, as John was saying, we were walking back to the village and we heard these sounds, people, in the park of Old Hall.'

'Sounds?'

'It was a woman; begging your pardon, sir, it was a lady's voice. She was crying, saying something. "Help", I think. Not happy; I thought she sounded afraid of something.'

'And the other voice?'

'Well, if you'll excuse me, sir, I knew directly who that was. No mistake; I'd heard it a few times around the village.'

'Yes?'

'Why, it were Master Golding, sir.'

'And what was he saying?'

'Well, not much really. But he was laughing and sounded as if he was boasting of something. She was screaming by then.'

John burst in. 'So we—'

'If you please, John. I'll hear it from Mr. Dunthorne. What happened next?'

'I told John to stay out of sight; I didn't want him mixed up with Golding, begging your pardon, sir. I knew they don't always mix—'

'Quite. Thank you. But then?'

'I went up to Golding. He was in the driveway near the bottom. He was holding this lady, an arm round her. Looked as if he was trying to turn her round and she was struggling. Saying "leave me alone, let me go". That sort of thing.'

'Did you know her? Recognise her?'

'No, sir. I didn't think she was anyone who lived in the village. A visitor, I guessed.'

'And next?' Golding was looking weary, his head dropped.

'Well, I… I tricked him. He wouldn't let her go so I sort of suggested there was someone coming down the drive. And he dropped her and she ran behind me. So I called John, told him to take her away home.'

'And that was the end of it?'

'Nearly, sir. Golding, he wanted to fight me. I wouldn't, sir, no, I wouldn't. I started to go home but he kept hitting me. So…' He faded away, looking embarrassed.

'I was there, Father. With Maria at the end of the drive. Golding was shouting, swearing and hitting Dunthorne. I never saw Dunthorne hit him once, not a single blow. He felled him.'

'He… what?'

'He just tripped him up and walked away.'

'Excuse me, Mr. Constable,' said Dunthorne. 'He wished to brawl and I could not let him; it would not have been proper. I pushed him to the ground and left him. No damage, I assure you, sir.'

'The tale my wife and I heard was somewhat different.'

'But,' said John, eager and loud. 'There were no marks on him, were there? No black eyes, no broken limbs. Only a hurt sense of pride. And Mother—'

'Enough, John. It does put a different complexion on things; I must talk to Golding. But there was another occasion in which you were involved, was there not, Mr. Dunthorne? Skating. Golding came home cold, almost at death's door if I am to believe the womenfolk in my house. I have never been able to hear the story; my men profess to know nothing of the matter. Can you enlighten me?'

Golding had a look of mild regret, looking from one to the other.

'You never told me,' said John, looking at Dunthorne with a look of deep affection. 'And everything seemed to change from that date. You were gone; I couldn't find you. Your workshop was empty, cold.'

Dunthorne was silent, gazing at the floor. He raised his head, gave a low chuckle.

'I guess it looked bad, Mr. Constable. Very bad.'

'Nobody would tell me what happened. Golding was in a poor way. His mother feared for his life.'

Dunthorne was quiet, recalling the evening a year before. The dark huddle of men, growling like animals, the cold that cut through his body and made him insensible to everything but warm human touch.

'I can't tell you the whole of it; I was not there.' A pause.

‘If you please, tell me what you know.’

‘It was another matter altogether, sir. A crowd of villagers was over by the bank having a good time. Girls and their fathers, children, families. You know, the usual thing. And your son, he was there too.’ He paused. ‘I was out for a late walk, look at the river, meet a few friends.’

‘You must tell us all, Dunthorne.’ John standing leant towards him.

‘Well, as I said, Master Golding was skating too, fast through the other skaters. I thought at first he was just showing off, if you will excuse me, sir, so fast and close to the other skaters.’ He nodded to Golding.

‘You may tell me all you saw, Mr. Dunthorne.’

Dunthorne fixed his eyes on Golding. He didn’t want to be thought he was spinning a tall tale. ‘But then I realised. He was knocking into them and not gently but to throw them to the ground. To the ice, I mean. It may have started as an accident; I couldn’t say. But he kept doing it, time after time. I was away on the road looking down; there were a few men, fathers or whoever, I don’t know, and they were getting angry. Shouting at him. Standing in his way. And he went faster, avoiding the men, knocking into the girls.’

‘Knocking into them?’ Golding was shocked, his face curled in indignation.

‘There is no other way I can put it, sir. It looked just like a game we used to play in the playground, us boys. But it weren’t no game for the girls; you could see that.’

‘And what happened after that?’

‘Well, sir, things changed; in a moment it seemed. I’d looked away for a minute, a brief word with a friend, and when I looked back the crowd had split. The girls and their families were over by the bank, staying close. Not much skating. And a crowd of men were all around young Golding, moving away towards the other side.'

'You mean, they were threatening him?' said Golding.

'I couldn't say, sir. I couldn't make out who they were, all their backs to me, on the dark side of the field. I could make out Master Golding though, knew his hat, at first skating in circles, and then standing or moving back. I couldn't say; it was dark that side.'

'Go on,' said John. 'Tell us all.'

'Well, I didn't want to make more trouble but I couldn't stand there and watch your son getting into difficulties. Not again if you'll excuse me, sir. I started across the ice; it was mighty slippery I recall. Maybe it wasn't so cold that evening. I was wondering where it was going to crack, like it often does near the trees. Where Jem lost his old dog.'

'That wasn't Jem's; it was Walt's,' said John.

Dunthorne blinked, looked at him. 'Is that right? I always thought—'

'You were saying?' said Golding, a look at his son.

'Yes sir. Well, they had all moved well over that side when I came up to them. Nobody said anything to me but they were muttering, cursing some of them, out for trouble. I heard some comments but I don't know if you want to hear them, Mr. Constable.'

'About what? I would have the full tale, if you can give it.'

'Well, sir,' said Dunthorne, looking at the floor and dragging up memories, one by one. 'There was a word about the Church weathervane, the shaft split... and then many of them had had fences broken as he went a'shootin'... some had shot through their windows... and there were a few had daughters troubled in the Street. They don't like that sort of thing, you know, sir.'

'I hear little of such things, I am sorry to say. I would recompense any man or woman for the damage, you know. I shall speak to my bailiff.'

'Father, you should speak to Golding; it is not right.' John was loud, an outburst that his father greeted with a weary look. Dunthorne wondered whether he knew of the bullying that John had suffered in the past. He did not feel comfortable telling the history of the incident, getting involved in a family problem. He liked to stay out of family problems, even his own; after all, the boys were his wife's, not his own. And village problems always ended with having to take sides. And who was to know which was the right? He stayed out of it, always had. Since he had been in a gang and they had won a battle; the other side had been beaten badly, and so had he when he got home. It was a tough lesson.

'How did he end up in the water?' asked Golding.

Dunthorne sighed. Kept his eyes on Golding. 'Well, sir, young Golding, I beg your pardon, Master Golding raised his fists at the men, calling them dogs and rude names; I won't say. The men just moved forward, always forward, no arms raised against him.

'There was a loud crack. The men all retreated, bumping into each other. But in a circle, watching.

'And Golding disappeared. Like a rat in a trap. One minute raising his fists to the crowd, next gone.

'I thought somebody would go after him but they were backing away from the cracks, silent now staring at Golding. He'd stood up in the water, came up to his chest. He wasn't shouting anymore, but begging for help. Begging and cursing them at the same time. Nobody moved.

'Couldn't see a way to get him out on the ice. And he was beginning to collapse; saw his head go under once. So I went in; held him up and asked for help.

'I don't know what had got into that crowd. They're not all friends of mine, if you see what I mean. And they were silent, just staring at us. Until you arrived, sir.'

Silence. John and Golding were staring at him, mouths open in astonishment.

'You… you saved him,' said John, at last. 'I never knew…' His voice faded.

Golding stood, went to Dunthorne who stood up, a surprised look on his face.

'Thank you. Thank you for the truth and thank you for saving the life of another of my sons. I am forever in your debt.' He shook hands with him.

Dunthorne didn't know what to say, stepped back, still in the clasp of Golding. John stood beside him, smiling.

'Father, may we see more of Dunthorne in the village? Is there not work for him?'

'I am sure that work can be found. Now, would you excuse me? I have to attend to matters at home. John, I shall see you later, no doubt? Perhaps you would escort Dunthorne to the Red Lion; you may refer any expenses to my account.'

A brief bow, and the door slammed behind him.

'Oh Dunthorne, I never knew.' John was sobbing with relief. 'But do you have a hard time of it in the village? That friends would not rush to help you from the water?'

'They did after Golding had gone. But it were an ugly crowd, you know. I don't know what got into them.'

'I believe my father will change his mind. He is generally fair. He was embarrassed, I could see that. The men I worked with at the mill; they all think he is the best employer around, a fair man and considerate when family problems arise. You know, when Walt had that accident—'

'Come John, no more talking. You're making me thirsty.'

'And he never looked at the painting,' said John with a quick laugh. He loaded the stove with more logs and then stopped. 'But we are going to the Red Lion, aren't we?'

Bold was up, strutting circles around them, woken by the mention of the tavern.

Dunthorne sat, staring into the flames.

'Would I be safe in assuming that you invited me under false pretences?'

'But Dunthorne. The drawing.'

'And your father; did you tell him why he was visiting?'

John looked back at him, hands twisting, no comment.

'No matter. It was well done. And thank you; I shall be glad to be working hereabouts more.'

22

MAY 1803

Bold is up, chasing downhill after the white scut of a rabbit, swerving from side to side, tail flying like a flag. He is too slow; the rabbit hesitates, steps sideways and is gone into the ground. He halts, sniffing, thrusting his muzzle into the burrow, a low whine. John calls him back.

They are sitting in a favoured spot, halfway down Fen Lane. It gives enough elevation to look over the valley, either over Dedham to the Stratford hills or down into the haze at Cattawade where the river becomes estuary and occasionally the masts of ships can be seen drying out on the hard at Manningtree. Dunthorne has observed that John often looks upriver, drawn by the majesty of the tower of Dedham Church standing tall against the land beyond. It seems he prefers a view with more definition as though he needs to see where he is going. And the haze downstream is like the future, uncertain, only viewed as one journeys into it.

John is one of his "working" moods. Pointing out the perspective of a gate and the construction of the latch. Drawing quick sketches of the clouds, the difference between them, the height of them. Analysing the state of the crops, observing the way that the green ears of the wheat ripple to a gentle breeze, a quickening of the view, movement leading the eye.

'Do you see, Dunthorne? Are you following me? Oh, ignore Bold for a moment. Do you see how the movement of the wheat leads the eye into the heart of the scene? The clouds too play their part in the composition. The invisible forces, they are as strong as the lines of trees, the curve of the river, the gentle rise of the valley side. Oh Dunthorne, you are slow today.'

'I was setting here remembering a young artist who spoke to me of panoramas, the capturing of the whole scene before us, from the haze below us to the hills above us.' He smiles, tickles Bold's ears and chooses a stem of grass to chew.

John is silent. Dunthorne cannot tell whether he wishes to ignore him, avoid the possibly painful subject of the triptych or whether he is simply buried in his work. Probably concentration. He speaks on.

'The triptych, it were a powerful piece of work. I'm sorry that the Parish choose to set it aside; I'll be betting that their sons or grandsons would feel different, would want to see it. Have it on the altar. But there. Not much we can do about it, I guess. Has it crossed your mind... well, I do understand that you have a great deal on your mind, with Maria and all, but—'

'Dunthorne, you really do wander on this morning; I don't know. It is an excellent day, good clouds, shades, life, and all you want to do is a'blather about things that cannot be.'

Dunthorne sits up. 'Oh but John, you could have a powerful say, your paintings. Has it occurred to you to spread your wings a bit—'

'Spread my wings? What are you on about? Unless you are back on the sea, pressing me to consider the shore and the ships, spreading their sails to the fresh breeze... yes, it would be an interesting subject. I have seen many ships at Harwich as we set off for the London river; it makes a lively scene though not one with which I am well acquainted, in spite of the voyages to London and Holland.

'It is only a few years ago; there was a fleet of warships set off for Holland; I saw them off the Goodwins. And I thought we traded with the Dutch. The papers said that we were the conquerors but I know nothing of it.

'I am not a great sailor, you know. I don't have the constitution for it. The sailors mock me and have me endure all rainstorms, squalls and winds. I prefer to be below in the captain's cabin. Quiet, though heaving. I need a bucket, sometimes.

'But on shore, there's another thing. I might learn the ropes and rigging; my father would be… There, Dunthorne, my palette is quite dry and you will have me a'maundering on.'

'I was thinking of something altogether different. I was thinking that your triptych told a powerful tale and you could do the same where the tale needs to be told.'

John shakes his head, wetting his palette and trying to work again.

'I'm no politick man, Dunthorne. You know that. Nor a storyteller.'

'Not the way I see it. Your pictures, your sketches and drawings, they all tell a powerful story of the life hereabouts. Your Truth and Reality; how often have I heard that?'

'And so it is, the Truth and Reality of all I see around here.'

'But what of London? They tell me it is a great city, grand houses, warehouses, factories, a great many people.'

'Yes, it is so. All, those things and many more.'

'More?'

'Oh, I cannot tell you of all the things I have seen. Beggars, Chinamen, sailors from all parts of the world, sometimes fighting in the docks, long knives—'

'John, you have never told me of such things.'

'I see it all and I feel apart from it. It is not my world; I have no curiosity to join the crew of a ship to the Indies or sign up with the Navy.'

'But tell me of the housing, near the docks. Is there much? Is it cottages like here?'

'Oh Dunthorne, where would I start? The warehouses are huge, as large as the Church, and the houses.' He pauses. 'All sorts, large and small, palaces and sheds, yes rough sheds with two or more families. It is not right, really. But they say there are not enough homes for all the workers. So many people, crowds on the streets all the time as though there is a Fair. The noise, the smells.

'And the things that happen. A British Army officer to be hanged for attempting to assassinate the King; can you imagine such a thing?'

Dunthorne sits, chewing a stem of grass. He is looking down, wondering.

'John, could you not paint it all, the rich and the poor, as you do the village, fields and all here. Could you not paint the poor and the wealthy, the hungry and the fat of the land? It would tell a powerful message.'

'To whom, Dunthorne? To whom? Who would wish to purchase such paintings? What would be the point? I am no proselytising angel, no one would listen to me.'

Dunthorne hangs his head.

'I thought, maybe, with all that you have seen, your painting might help people see. The Truth and Reality.'

John stirs, smiles and leans towards Dunthorne.

'Have I not told you of the new machines? I know you love your new machines though we see little of them here.'

Dunthorne shrugs and lies back.

'Tell me of them. I hear little though they tell me steam engines are becoming common.'

‘Indeed, for cranes at the ports, and hauling on slipways, and… oh, many things. There is a paddle boat, a tug for pulling ships; just the one. Last year, they tested a tug in Scotland on the Caledonian Canal. *The Charlotte Dundas*. Went well, they said. They build a Railway near London to be completed any day. And last year, there was a flight of a balloon over the city.’

‘Thank you, John. I don’t know; these things will come to us one day I suppose. In the meantime, I endure the carrier’s cart to Ipswich; it takes me half a day. Progress.’

He sighs. A lighter passes slowly upriver, a gentle breeze lifting the sail. Dunthorne asks John if he knows the helmsman, whether it is one of his father’s. The horse plods along the far bank with the lad astride. A gull lifts off the river over the willows and sets course for the sea. A ladybird climbs up a stem of grass, hesitates at the top.

‘Panoramas. Maybe one day,’ says John. A pause. ‘Maybe. But I need to concentrate on the form of paintings, the composition. The subject is there before me; I have no need of disputing it or trying to change it. Now, are you with me? The invisible forces.’

‘Yes, John.’ Dunthorne’s eyes are closed.

‘You see the lines of perspective; they draw you in, lead the eye. ’Tis like a grand room, and we are the spectators… oh, Dunthorne, do you sleep?’ John sounds disgusted. But he smiles, pure affection. Dunthorne snores. John sketches, leaning forward as though to draw the landscape into his sketchbook, absorb what he sees, staring forward into the future.

Matador